DEBORAH SHELDON is an award-winning author from Melbourne, Australia. She writes short stories, novellas and novels across the darker spectrum of horror, crime and noir.

Her short stories have appeared in many well-regarded magazines including *Island*, *Quadrant*, *Aurealis*, *Midnight Echo*, *Andromeda Spaceways* and *Dimension6*. Her award-nominated titles include the novels *Body Farm Z*, *Contrition* and *Devil Dragon*; the novella *Thylacines*; and collection *Figments and Fragments: Dark Stories*. She won the Australian Shadows "Best Collected Work" Award for *Perfect Little Stitches and Other Stories*, which was also short-listed for an Aurealis Award and long-listed for a Bram Stoker.

As editor of *Midnight Echo 14*, she won the Australian Shadows "Best Edited Work" Award. Her anthology, *Spawn: Weird Horror Tales About Pregnancy, Birth and Babies* features work by best-selling authors Jack Dann, Kaaron Warren and Sean Williams, as well as fiction by established and upcoming Australian writers.

Deb's fiction has also been nominated for various Australian Shadows and Aurealis Awards, and her stories included in "best of" anthologies.

Other credits include feature articles for national and international magazines, non-fiction books for Reed Books and Random House, TV scripts such as NEIGHBOURS, and award-winning medical writing.

For more information, please visit:
http://deborahsheldon.wordpress.com

Deborah Sheldon's titles published by IFWG Publishing Australia

Dark Waters / Ronnie and Rita (novellas, 2016)
Perfect Little Stitches and Other Stories (collection, 2017)
Contrition (novel, 2018)
Figments and Fragments: Dark Stories (collection, 2019)
Liminal Spaces: Horror Stories (collection, 2022)

IFWG Titles Edited by Deborah Sheldon

Spawn: Weird Horror Tales About Pregnancy, Birth and Babies (short fiction anthology, 2021)

LIMINAL SPACES

Horror Stories

By Deborah Sheldon

Liminal Spaces: Horror Stories

All Rights Reserved

ISBN-13: 978-1-922556-67-7

Copyright ©2022 Deborah Sheldon

V1.0

Stories first publishing history at the end of this book.

Printed in Palatino Linotype and Signo.

IFWG Publishing International
Gold Coast

www.ifwgpublishing.com

For Allen and Harry

Table of Contents

For Weirdless Days and Weary Nights

The six caravans, identical and single-berth, were arranged in a ring as if whispering to each other. Covered in mildew, abandoned bird nests, fallen twigs and branches, their tow bars and wheels settled into grass and desiccated leaves. *Creepy,* Hamilton thought. Not exactly what you'd expect to see in a forest. He consulted the map given out by Mrs Armstrong and read through her handwritten notes on *Points of Interest*. No mention of a shitty caravan park. He put the map back in his pocket. Manna gums, paperbarks and wattle trees surrounded the vans in a larger, looser ring. Everything was still and quiet.

His friends caught up to him.

"Oh cool, an abandoned camp," Kyle said.

"How do you know it's abandoned?" Susie said.

Kyle laughed. "By using my eyes. Nobody's touched those vans in years." He left the track and began making his way over. "They circled their wagons just like in the movies."

"Circled them against what?" Hamilton said.

Click, click, click. Susie had already lifted her camera. "Not *against* anything, Ham. They probably gathered around a communal fire to keep warm and cook their food."

Susie followed Kyle into the clearing. Hamilton adjusted his backpack, tucked his thumbs beneath the straps to ease the chafing on his shoulders, and looked about the forest floor, half-expecting to see evidence of a bitumen road somewhere. Nope. Only the walking track through the tussocks and mat-rushes, the same worn ribbon of dirt they had been trudging all morning. His feet hurt.

What this hike had to do with Chemistry, he couldn't fathom.

"How did they get the vans out here in the first place?" he said.

Susie turned to make a face at him. "By car, dumb-arse."

"Oh, yeah? Show me the road, Einstein."

"By helicopter then," Kyle said. "Who the fuck cares? Come on and check it out."

Every caravan window appeared dark and blank. Sweat gathered on Hamilton's lip. His feet didn't want to move, and he stared down at them. At the edge of the clearing ran a line of mushrooms. Tall, grey fungi with caps the size of bread plates. The mushrooms seemed to hem the entire clearing. He kicked at a few. The broken caps landed on their heads. Their wet, reddened gills reminded him of living, moving things, like hooked fish brought to land, mouths opening and closing as they suffocated.

Kyle stopped peering at a caravan to throw both arms in the air at Hamilton.

"What are you waiting for, mate?" he called. "A written invite?"

Typical. Kyle jumped from roofs into pools at backyard parties, ate the worm from mezcal bottles, would chuck a cricket ball through the gym window on a dare even when there was no stake to win. The guys at school liked Kyle, for sure. But Hamilton had no idea why Susie liked him so much.

Hamilton checked his watch. "Mrs Armstrong wants everyone at the town's information centre by one o'clock, remember?"

"Yeah, let me take some photos first," Susie said. "My folio's due next week."

"We're not here for Visual Design."

"Oh, fuck off, Ham."

"Get over here," Kyle said. "Mate, for Christ's sake!"

Cautiously, Hamilton crossed over the line of mushrooms.

The dry grasses crackled beneath his sneakers. A sensation of static electricity tickled and quivered through the nerves in his skin. Kyle and Susie seemed unaffected. *Don't be such a baby*, Hamilton thought. *Ghosts in the dark, ghosts by the bed...* He'd relinquished his nightlight during Year 7 on his mother's insistence. At eighteen, he still slept with the sheet wound about his head as protection against…what? Spectres he couldn't see, phantasms that didn't exist. *He's a sensitive child,* his mum had said once to his grandfather when Hamilton had been presumably out of earshot. *He* feels *things.*

Hamilton came to a standstill. "Let's get out of here."

"Oh, calm your tits, would you?" Susie said with an exaggerated sigh.

Cheeks burning, he followed her inside the ring of caravans.

There was no central fire pit. Kyle grabbed the nearest door and wrenched it open. The exhaled air smelled like dirt, damp, yeast, decay. Kyle put a foot on the step.

"Hey, what are you doing?" Hamilton said.

"Taking a gander."

Kyle went in. Susie followed. Hamilton remained outside and peeked. Kitchenette, booth with a table, cupboard, single mattress. The whole lot covered in dust. A skylight slicked with black and green slime.

"Okay," Kyle said, bounding out. "Now for the other vans."

Susie trailed him, eyes shining. "Oh my God, Mr De Stefano will *love* these photos."

"Let's go," Hamilton said. "I mean it."

He stood within the ring as Kyle and Susie explored the next four caravans. At the last caravan, the sixth one, Kyle and Susie went inside and stayed there. Hamilton glanced towards the walking track. The opening in the trees was gone. His heart gave a little jump. Perhaps he was disoriented. Perhaps the opening was on the other side of the clearing.

"Ham," Susie said. "Look at this."

"At what?" he said.

Kyle appeared in the doorway. "You're not gonna believe it."

The grimy metal step had cross-hatched treads to prevent slipping. Tentatively, with just the toe of his sneaker, Hamilton touched the step. Kyle grabbed him by the arm and hauled him inside.

Hamilton blinked, gaped. "What the…?"

Pristine was the first word that came to mind. The same arrangement of kitchenette, booth with laminate table, cupboard and single mattress. But clean and tidy. No, *more* than that. Every surface unblemished. As if brand new, rolled off the factory line.

Kyle opened the bar fridge.

Food lay on the shelves. Fresh food. Unwrapped wheels of cheese and cured meats. Oranges and figs. A bunch of baby carrots. Delicate plant stalks, probably herbs. Bottles of some kind of liquid. Six small clay pots with God knows what kept within them.

"Fuck this for a joke," Hamilton said.

"What about my folio?" Susie said. "I want headshots of the owners. They'll be back any minute. Look at the kettle."

Hamilton looked. Steam drifted from the spout.

"But we're trespassing…" he began.

Then he heard the voices.

Distant, overlapping, indistinct, thick with the fizzle that lies between radio stations. Hamilton shivered. Long ago, his grandfather had owned some kind of walkie-talkie or scanner. As a child, Hamilton used to reluctantly listen with Pa to the disembodied words and feel afraid. He could never distinguish the voices. The people always sounded lost, confused, begging, pleading. *You need to tune the station*, Pa would say. *Once you tune the station it starts to make sense.*

"Can you hear what they're saying?" Hamilton said.

Kyle and Susie froze, their faces tensed in concentration.

Susie said, "No, I can't make it out."

"Is there a speaker?" Kyle spun this way and that. "A laptop, maybe? An iPod?"

"We should go," Hamilton said.

None of them moved. The mash of distorted voices went on. He drowsed for a moment. When he opened his eyes, he was standing at the open doorway. The three of them were clustered around it. Hamilton looked at his watch. The hands were missing.

"Come on," Kyle said. "What's the hold up?"

"Who's leaving first?" Susie said. "Hurry."

There was a blur of movement. A middle-aged couple in shorts and t-shirts—the man bald, the woman fat—had stopped at the walking track, both staring into the ring of caravans, staring at

Hamilton, staring right into his eyes.

"Help!" Susie called, waving her arms. "Please help!"

"Hey, you there!" Kyle yelled. "Shit, they must be deaf."

Hamilton glanced at the kettle. Steam wafted from its spout.

The woman stepped over the ring of mushrooms. The man followed. They came towards the hushed circle of vans and opened one door after another. Hamilton knew that this particular caravan would be their final pick.

The couple entered. They smelled like sunscreen lotion and perspiration.

"My goodness," the woman said. "The owner must have just popped out."

"For a piss, most likely," the man said.

"What the fuck?" Kyle said. "Can't they see us? Hear us?"

The woman opened the fridge. "There's food."

"What kind?" the man said.

Susie's fingers ripped at her own hair. "I can't understand *any* of this."

The woman smiled. "All kinds. There's ceramic pots with lids. I wonder what's in them?"

"Pâté, maybe. The home-made kind. Oh wait, better not touch them, love."

"I don't like this," Susie wailed. "Oh God, I don't like this."

The man perked up, turned his head. "Huh? What was that?"

"What was what?" the woman said, closing the fridge door.

Susie screamed. The couple cocked their heads, birdlike. The man cupped one hand around an ear. Hamilton found himself sitting on the mattress, flanked by Susie and Kyle. The hiss of distant radio voices droned on, the voices sounding lost, confused, begging, pleading.

"I want to leave," Susie said, over and over.

"We have to stand up," Kyle said. "Can you stand? Ham, try to stand up."

"Maybe later," Hamilton said. "I'm tired."

Not tired, exactly. *Detached*. Before Christmas last year, he'd had a wisdom tooth removed under twilight sedation and he felt the same kind of lethargy now. He should be panicked but couldn't drum up the energy. Instead, he watched the couple from a distance, from afar, down a long and dreamy tunnel.

"I want to leave," Susie said.

"We have to stand up. Can you stand? Ham, try to stand up."

"Maybe later. I'm tired."

"What's that babbling noise?" the man said. "Is it voices?"

The woman frowned, listening. "Could be. Perhaps the owner left on a radio."

"Can you hear what they're saying?"

"Help us," Kyle said. "Please help us get out of here."

The couple's faces went slack at the same instant. Their eyes turned blank and dark. Together, they sat at the table and instantly fell asleep, chins on chests. The desperate voices still murmured. A few moments later, when the couple woke up, Hamilton's vision began to dim. It gave him the queasy feeling of dropping in slow motion down a well. Colours went first. When everything had turned grey, black or white, ghostly shapes became apparent, hanging in the air.

Dazed, Hamilton looked around.

There were dozens of shadowy people inside this caravan. No, scores, maybe even hundreds, overlapped and overlaid. He reached out an arm. Static electricity lifted the hairs on his skin. The ghosts reached for him in return, their fuzzy mouths open, their muffled voices sounding lost, confused, begging, pleading.

"I'm frightened," the woman said. "I want to go."

"Ladies first," the man said. And then, "Well? What's stopping you?"

Eyesight fading, Hamilton watched the couple. They stood together at the door, bickering, trying to leave, willing themselves to leave, unable to leave. They clutched at each other. Steam rose from the kettle spout.

"Let's get out of here," Susie said.

"We have to leave," Kyle said.

"I don't think we can," Hamilton said.

Caught on flypaper, he and his friends were a page in a preternatural book. And this middle-aged couple was a fresh page, ready to be turned over, ready to cover Hamilton and Susie and Kyle, to dissolve them into phantoms. The pattern would repeat itself. How people were chosen and how often they were taken, and why, Hamilton could not even guess. Was too tired to guess. He looked down at his hand and saw right through it.

Ghosts in the dark, ghosts by the bed…

"Let's get out of here," Susie said.

"We have to leave," Kyle said.

"I don't think we can," Hamilton said.

Carbon Copy Consumables

Look, what you've got to understand about industry—and I'm talking about the food industry in particular—is that the pursuit of money always trumps common sense. It's been this way since Year Dot. For instance, there's only one type of banana for sale across the whole planet, the Cavendish, but here's the kicker: each piece of fruit is a clone. I'm not bullshitting you. They're grown from suckers. So, every banana is genetically identical. If a pathogen comes along that can wipe out just one banana, it'll wipe out the crop worldwide.

And this isn't a theory, mind you. It happened already.

Prior to the Cavendish, the only commercial banana was another cloned variety, the Gros Michel, and that crop got destroyed by a kind of soil fungus in the 1960s. The Cavendish was its replacement. But did the food industry learn anything from putting all its eggs—or Gros Michel bananas—into the one basket? No, except to do it all over again because of economics. Even when the smallest possible risk is complete and utter catastrophe. You see where I'm coming from? Money trumps common sense. Every. Single. Time.

Don't get me wrong, I'm not against food cloning. That's my trade, after all. Cloning is a great idea. Finding a way to computerise, mechanise and standardise the process solved a lot of problems like overfishing, deforestation, famines, and suchlike and et cetera, but hey, I don't need to make a speech. Anybody with half a brain knows that food cloning factories are a boon to mankind. I'm only stating my point of view for the record.

Also, for the record, my name is Charles Pomeroy but everyone calls me Charlie. I'm thirty-four years old, single, no kids, Aussie by birth, and a factory runner for Carbon Copy Consumables. For the past eight years, I've worked at their Antarctica plant servicing the research stations, hotels, resorts, casinos, theme park, restaurants, private homes and what have you. The busiest time of year is summer when the tourist ships come by the dozen and every business is running at full capacity. With about nine thousand mouths to feed, I have to run the factory twenty-four seven. Yeah, all by my lonesome.

The company website explains their setup if you're interested, but in a nutshell, the Antarctica factory is about a kilometre long, three storeys high, covered in gantries and stuffed to the gills with machines. Carbon Copy Consumables is "lights-out" manufacturing with everything controlled by a bunch of computers. Even the trucks that pick up the supplies are automated and self-driven, and each truck is packed by robot arms.

So, the four reasons I'm needed there…

One: feed the machines. Our base material looks like bouillon powder. It's actually a combination of elements including carbon, nitrogen, sulphur—I forget the others—but ninety-seven percent of every living thing on Earth is made up of just six elements. Amazing, right? At full storage capacity, I've got six vats and each one's about the size of a wheat silo.

Two: keep the joint hygienic. The machines have self-cleaning cycles; I top up detergents.

Three: equipment maintenance. Our machines are so smart they're almost self-sufficient, the emphasis on "almost". Nothing beats the human mind. Training to be a factory runner takes four years because you need to learn how to service every part of every machine. Yeah, there's manuals to jog your memory, but it's a specialised field with lifelong job security. Why would Carbon Copy Consumables sack a factory runner after investing four years into them? And you get paid top dollar while you train. Sweet gig. If you ever want a career change, look into it. Just be aware the competition is stiff. For every opening, there's a thousand applications. You've got to be the best of the best.

And four: stock control. The machines can't make informed decisions about which foods need to be cloned. I take orders from all over Antarctica. You've got no idea of the vast amounts of produce I churn out to allow three meals and snacks for nine thousand people in peak season. Hold onto your little cotton socks because I'm about to blow your mind. Ready?

Five tonnes of vegetables. That's metric tonnes, mind you, per day. Two tonnes of beef, every cut from chuck to eye fillet. One tonne of chicken. Ten thousand eggs. All. Per. Day. And so on, and so forth. Can you grasp the scale of this operation? Can you imagine trying to fly this amount of naturally-sourced food into Antarctica? Well, that's how they used to do it in the old days. That's why the population was capped at about one thousand; the logistics of supply were too difficult.

Oh yeah, and another reason: a bunch of Antarctic Treaties about keeping the continent pristine. Those treaties were overturned for the sake of money. Capitalism is great, don't get me wrong—it's dragged most of the world out of poverty—but there's a few drawbacks here. Did you know that one-third of Antarctica is now a giant tip covered in garbage? Anyhow, that's progress. Two steps forward, one step back. Don't worry, a company will come up with a way to turn rubbish into something useful, like gold, if there's money in it.

Sure, I'm on good terms with the freight runners, ship captains, pilots, et cetera. You know what? Cards on the table? I'll come straight out and tell you that my partner in the botany scheme was a pilot named Jenny. I'm guessing you're interrogating her anyway, so there's no point me trying to be discreet. The whole sideline about the plants was her idea, with a forty-sixty split. She promised me bucketloads of cash, and boy, was she right on the money.

There are two flowering plants native to Antarctica: the hair grass and the pearlwort. You find them mainly on the western peninsula and on a couple of islands. One time Jenny told me, while she was waiting on her plane to be refuelled and loaded, that some knob-ends from Sydney's North Shore were scouting for unusual plants for their daughter's bridal bouquet and table arrangements, and would I be interested in some quick dough?

Now, these Antarctic plants look pretty dull, but that's not the point. Rarity symbolises wealth. Even if the plants happened to look like busted arseholes covered in fly-blown crap, it wouldn't matter. Do you know what happened in the seventeenth century when the pineapple was first brought over to Britain from Barbados? Well, the pineapple was such a rare fruit, and so expensive, that super-rich people would bung one in the middle of their ballroom and host a party to flex on their high-society friends. The not-so-rich rented pineapples for the sole purpose of bragging. Even a rotting pineapple had prestige.

And hundreds of years later, rich people are exactly the same.

Long story short, yeah, I cloned the plants, and Jenny sold them to this family. Within months, Jenny and me had an enterprise. Strictly under the table, of course. It's not like we took out ads. Word of mouth only. Just like the trade in stolen art works, right? Inner circle stuff. People want to show off to their mates, not get arrested by Interpol.

Oh, we made money for jam. And we never worried about us double-crossing each other. Jenny couldn't run the plants through the machines herself because cloning is locked down tighter than the diamond industry. I couldn't get plants out of Antarctica without a pilot's licence, and besides that, didn't have any contacts with buyers. Jenny and I were partners in crime. Both of us faced jail. We had reasons to be faithful to our handshake.

But word gets around in the upper echelons of the filthy rich.

And soon, Jenny came to me with another request, this time from Asia. Some billionaire wanted to throw a dinner party with penguin on the menu.

Look, I'm not going to debate which animals are okay to eat and which ones aren't. As far as I'm concerned, once you've eaten meat, you've crossed a line and can't wag the finger at anybody for their choices. Still, I had to think about this offer for a long, long while. Could I really offer up cloned penguins knowing they were destined for someone's cooking pot?

Jenny had convincing arguments, namely... I provided beef,

lamb, pork and chicken as food, didn't I, so what's the difference? The penguin destined for the table wouldn't be the original or "real" penguin, just a clone, while the real penguin would be released back into the wild, unharmed, free to live its life, swim and raise babies. Penguins get eaten by seals and orcas every day, so why not by people? Et cetera. Bottom line: the money was jaw-dropping.

Antarctica has lots of different penguins like king, adélie, chinstrap, gentoo. Penguins are fast in water; on land they're bumbling idiots. My first penguin was a chinstrap, so-called because it has this little banding of black feathers under its beak. It's an aggro species but small and real clumsy on the ice. It took five minutes to stuff one in my backpack. Hey, there's about eight million of the buggers; it wasn't like taking one for a couple of hours would upset the balance of anything important.

Right?

And yet…I'd never put a live animal through the machines. For some reason, I imagined the cloned penguin would be turned inside-out. Crazy, huh? I had to keep reminding myself that fruits and vegetables are alive when they're cloned. Oh yes, of course they are—if they were dead, they'd be withered and black.

Even so, I had a big problem. The machines can't read anything that's moving because they work on similar principles to 3D food printers. I had to find a way to keep the penguin as still as possible. I chose sleeping pills. My working hours are all over the place. Naturally, I've got stashes. I figured the medication would stay in the bird's guts and blood, and not migrate into its muscles. Therefore, anyone who ate its meat wouldn't get dosed.

I cloned the drugged bird.

The process takes seventeen minutes for the first replication. After that, once the sequencing is worked out, the replication rate is lightning fast: pow, pow, pow. The cloned penguins were asleep, which made packaging and transportation much easier. Since we use automated systems to load trucks and planes, only me and Jenny knew what was going on.

Good God, over the next year…

Money, money, money.

So much money…

Occasionally, there were "exposés" on blogs and threads about illegal penguin meat, but the mainstream media figured it was an urban myth. Hah! I supplied every kind of penguin that exists in Antarctica. Yet each specimen I kidnapped was returned, unharmed, to the ice shelf where I found it. I never penned any of them to save time. That would've been cruel. And remember, the clones exported for eating purposes weren't "real" in the same way the original penguins were real. Manufactured clones don't count. That's law, right?

Soon we got other requests. Antarctic seabirds became popular: blue-eyed shag, giant petrel, snowy sheathbill, cape pigeon. But these birds can fly! Trapping them required ingenuity on my part; luckily, I'm very intelligent. The price per kilo had to be higher than for penguins. Astronomically higher. That said, Antarctic seabirds are stringy. You've got to braise them low and slow. Even if you're a pro chef who does everything perfectly, the meat still comes out dry, chaffy, tasteless. Look, it's not about flavour. Remember the pineapple? If dog shit was rare, the one-percenters would serve it at dinner parties with silver spoons.

Did I eat any of these meats? No. Beef, chicken, lamb, pork: that'll do fine. Occasionally I eat fish and seafood but don't come at me with weird shit like eel, oysters or sea urchin. Novelty doesn't interest me. I won't try a food just for the "experience". Not that I'm shaming anyone who's into that kind of thing. Live and let live, I always say.

So, dealing in cloned plants, penguins, seabirds… As you can imagine, I was busy.

Busy enough that I swapped sleeping pills for amphetamines. The factory ran twenty-four seven and I had a side business that was essentially a full-time job in itself—when could I sleep? And the money was another time-sink. Do you know how difficult it is to launder and hide cash? You can't use bank accounts without explaining why, how, when, and the tax department always sticks in its beak. From necessity, I stayed awake for three, sometimes four days at a stretch. Ah, crazy times… But after a few years, I was going to retire and cruise the world on a five-hundred-foot yacht.

It was exhaustion, I guess. Desperation. Amphetamines don't create energy; they stop you from sleeping, and the sleep debt adds up. Then you start making dumb decisions. That's the only way I can explain it. One day, when I was popping another pill and staring in the mirror at the black bags under my eyes, I thought, "Why the hell am I killing myself, burning the candle at both ends—and in the middle too—when there's such an easy solution?"

Sure, the idea gave me pause. Each of us likes to think of ourselves as unique. But I got to pondering about identical twins, triplets, quadruplets, quintuplets. I'm an only child. Would it be so bad to have a "brother"? We could split the chores. Perhaps share some of my money. I was the mastermind, so any divvying of funds would be at my discretion since the clone would be my employee, right? I know how it sounds, but it made perfect sense at the time.

Putting myself into the machine was like taking a seat in an untested rollercoaster. You're doing something that should be perfectly safe, at least in theory, but feels terrifying. The machine clicked, hummed, buzzed, whirred, knocked, whistled, tapped, and each sound scared the absolute shit out of me as I lay on the table, motionless, because I'd never heard those sounds before and I began to panic, wondering if something had gone wrong, if I would die. Get turned inside-out.

Let me tell you, that was an excruciating seventeen-minute wait.

The alarm went off: the sequencing and first replication had finished. I laughed and cried in relief. I'd only keyed in one clone. Just one. I got off the table and ran to the other end of the factory, which took about five minutes. The Other Charlie was standing there in my uniform. You know what surprised me? It turns out I'm bow-legged. I had no idea. The other thing that bothered me was his posture. His shoulders were tilted one way and his hips the other, as if there was a sideways bend in his spine, but subtle, very mild. I guess I was critical because I was seeing myself in the flesh for the first time. I looked old. Maybe that was on account of how tired I was, so empty and rundown.

"Charlie?" I said. "Do you understand what's going on?"

"Perfectly," he said. "Let's get started."

"Sweet," I said. "Run the shift while I get some shut-eye. I'll be back later with a chinstrap penguin."

"No worries," he said, and went about his—*our*—business.

I had the most restful sleep I'd enjoyed in ages. Then I took a snowmobile and headed to an ice shelf. Have you ever visited Antarctica? It's beautiful. Light-blue ice mountains, clear sky, snow in all shades and textures. Anyway, I spotted a crowd of chinstrap penguins—they stick out like dog's balls against the white landscape—and parked my snowmobile about half a kilometre distant so the engine noise wouldn't spook them. I walked the rest of the way. And as I trudged over the last little rise, damned if I didn't find the Other Charlie squatting there, wrestling a penguin into his backpack while a horde of angry penguins shrieked at him.

"What the hell's going on?" I said, pissed off. "Why aren't you at the factory?"

"What are you talking about?" he said. "You're the one supposed to be running the shift."

"Bullshit," I said. "So, who's running the shift?"

"I guess nobody is now," he said, and looked annoyed, pouting, as if I was the one who'd done the wrong thing. "We'd better get back. I've got a penguin already, so let's go."

We rode to town on our respective snowmobiles. I was fuming the whole journey. Clearly, the Other Charlie was throwing his weight around. He wanted to be equal partners, not my employee. But as the original Charlie Pomeroy I had first dibs. As we neared civilisation, I wracked my brains, trying to figure how to rein in this cheeky bastard.

Back at the factory, we both got a surprise.

Some Other Charlie was there and he looked just as shocked to see us.

"How come there's two of you?" he said. "What the hell's going on?"

"You're asking *me* what's going on?" I said. "I'm the one who deserves answers."

"Why do *you* deserve answers?" the Other Charlie said, hands on hips.

The three of us got to arguing. My theory: Other Charlie had the same bright idea and had cloned himself while I'd slept. However, Other Charlie and Some Other Charlie were both now insisting they were the original, which was ludicrous, considering it was me who first went through the replication process. Meanwhile, the penguin thrashed inside the backpack, squawking its head off, and I started to worry the little bugger was going to hurt himself. When the three of us headed to the backpack at the same time, we halted, stunned.

"What the hell's going on?" said a voice, and blow me if there wasn't a fourth Charlie walking over, his face pale and shocked. "How come there's three of you?"

And the four of us yelled at the same time, "What the hell's going on?", which made the hairs stand up on the back of my neck. But it scared my clones in the exact same way and when I saw the identical expressions of fear on their faces, I started to shake. They started shaking too in perfect mimicry. I was caught in a hall of mirrors. My heart banged hard enough to explode. Meanwhile, the trapped penguin screeched over and over. We turned to the backpack as one. And then—

"What the hell's going on?" said a voice.

Christ, it was another Charlie. I can't explain the horror!

Then another Charlie appeared. And another…and another…

God, the way I figure it, each clone must have cloned himself, unaware.

After some fraught arguing, the bunch and I ended up cooperating to scour the kilometre of factory from one end to the other in order to flush out any other Charlies. Meanwhile, more Charlies kept arriving at intervals with kidnapped penguins. Each time, we'd have to stop and have another pow-wow.

God, if it wasn't so terrifying, maybe it'd be funny.

We walked together in a line, shoulder to shoulder. Each of us ignored the distressed penguins without discussion. We found about a dozen more Charlies at various points, who joined our search, while others kept coming in from outside, bearing penguins. The birds wouldn't stop calling to each other, distressed and frantic. The chinstrap sounds a lot like a seagull, did you know that? I kept closing my eyes against their cries, trying to imagine that I was on a beach somewhere and only dreaming this nightmare, until I noticed my clones doing the same thing, and felt a heart-seizing panic attack coming on.

When the alarm sounded, we froze and stared at each other in terror. The alarm meant that yet another Charlie had been created, and would soon be jogging towards us from the far end of the factory, shouting, "What the hell's going on?" I'd forgotten to turn off the machines. We all had. How many clones in total? Oh God, I don't know. I couldn't even guess...

Getting sprung by the authorities was my fault.

Whenever I cloned a plant, penguin or seabird, I deleted the history from the logs. For some reason—probably because I was sleep-deprived—I forgot to do that after making the Other Charlie. And because he's me, he forgot to delete the history when he created his own clone, and so on. That tripped a red flag at Carbon Copy Consumables, and then military police came, and well...you know the rest.

Listen, I understand that clones aren't protected under any laws or Geneva conventions. Fair enough. Unauthorised clones have to be put down. No complaint from me on that score. My only issue is that you destroy the clones and not me by mistake. I'm happy to go to jail if that's my punishment, or pay a fine or whatever. Surely, there's some way to tell us apart? A medical test. Isn't there? There has to be. The clones might be telling you the exact same story, but my statement is the truth, I swear to God, because I'm the real deal. Okay? Hand on heart. I am the original Charlie Pomeroy.

The Sea Will Have

North Sea, calm and green, an English meadow
Lifts the ship on gentle swells, storm long gone.
For cod, sprat and herring, the deck hands throw
The trawling nets on their last bloody dawn.
North Sea, flat and harmless, bath for a child
Voices a note that sings through the marrow.
The men lose their heads, blood-quickened and wild,
Visions of women, sea nymphs Calypso.
The crew cannot swim but leaps overboard,
And each mate is held in unyielding grip.
The women are gilled, and some of the horde
Slice through the nets to free fish from the ship.
Dragged to the seabed, the drowning souls pray;
Unanchored, unmanned, the ship drifts away.

The Littlest Avian

Maude was a goddess disguised as a bird. More specifically, as Winston's budgerigar.

One year ago, to this very day, Winston had put an empty cage in the back of his car and crossed the three suburbs that lay between the caravan park and the breeder's tumbledown weatherboard. In the rear of the breeder's yard sat a long tin shed, its double doors open in the stultifying summer heat. The sunshine reflecting off the tin was blinding, migraine-inducing. From the shed's darkened insides emanated a frantic cacophony of calls and shrieks. The smell of so many budgerigars, something akin to the scent of overheating electrical equipment, lifted the hairs on Winston's arms.

The breeder gestured for Winston to follow. Inside the shed, the clamour was deafening. Winston's eyes adjusted to the gloom. Scores of cages ran in stacks, row after row. Alive, each cage brimmed and shimmered with movement, colour, energy.

"You want a young'un, right?" the breeder said, voice raised above the tumult. "I got a batch of six-week-olds just about ready to quit the nest. Male or female?"

"No preference," Winston said, because he knew the right bird would present itself.

"Males are better behaved. And they talk too, which is a bonus. Females like to bite."

Winston smiled. "Thank you. I've owned birds before."

Many birds, countless birds, birds for every moment of his life and crowding his every memory, cages hanging from the exposed beams in every room of his mother's house, the den kept as a supply closet stocked with seed mix, vitamin drops, lice sprays, cleaning products, cuttlefish, shell grit, perch covers, and swings, ladders, ropes, balls, bells for all the birds, birds, birds that sang and chirped and whistled throughout every moment of his life from his first breath. Every single waking moment that he had ever known.

Except for the moments comprising these last three weeks. At the age of sixty-one, freshly and strangely alone, his mother's house inherited and commandeered by distant relatives, he had been unable to relax in the empty, dead silence of his rented caravan.

The breeder opened the hinged lid of a box.

"Have a gander," he invited, stepping back.

Winston peeked. It was a nesting box crammed with baby budgerigars stumbling and bumbling around on uncertain feet, their stubby wings flush with brand new feathers. But there, trampled at the bottom, something stirred. Something so little. A bird, eyes screwed up tight against the scuttling onslaught of claws.

Winston said, "Give me that mauve one. Hurry. The one getting stepped on."

The breeder looked inside the box. "The runt? Nah, mate. It's weak. Liable to be sickly."

"I don't care."

The breeder shrugged and pulled out the fledgling. Dishevelled, blinking about in momentary confusion, it came to its senses and squawked indignantly. Winston felt a rush of love. The breeder opened his palm and turned the bird over and over beneath the fingers of his other hand. Complaining, the bird thrashed its tiny feet.

"No injuries," the breeder said. "Sometimes a brood attacks and kills the runt."

"I know," Winston said.

The breeder lifted the fledgling to rub its beak against his own fleshy nose. "See that?" he said, chuckling. "See how she's trying to bite me? That's how you tell it's a female."

Winston nodded, and took out his wallet.

"She's used to getting fed regurgitate from her dad," the breeder said. "So, watch her when you get home. If she can't figure out how to eat seed by herself, bring her to me straight away or she'll starve to death. I'm happy to look after her for another week or two. Righto?"

Like all hook-billed birds, a budgerigar must husk a seed before consuming it. As soon as they returned to the caravan, Winston cupped the fledgling and held a saucer of seeds to her face. "Come on, Maude," he whispered, for he had named the little bird after his mother. "Don't make me take you back."

Her black, beady eyes considered him. A silent communion passed between them. And then she bent her neck and delicately selected a sorghum seed. In the quiet, he heard the *crack* of her beak splitting the husk. She ate the sorghum. And then a seed of millet. Confident, she commenced her first solid meal with enthusiasm.

"My clever girl," he whispered, stroking her, since Maude had allowed him to fondle her in those days, back when she had been unable to fly, dependent, not yet matured into her formidable powers.

And today, on their paper anniversary, the goddess Maude decided to grow.

Today, she was the size of an owl.

Winston sipped his instant coffee and contemplated this fact. Meanwhile, Maude sat hunched on her lowest perch, head pulled into the ruffles of her neck so as to avoid the bars on the cage's ceiling.

"You'd best come out of there while you still can," he said, and opened the cage door.

As usual, he offered his forearm as a perch. Rustling her wings, she flew. Landed on his wrist. Good God, she was *heavy*. Winston laughed in surprise. Her feet, scaly and hot, gripped his skin. Her claws brought to mind the curve of scimitars. Now that she was larger, he could more clearly discern her eyelashes. Long. Dark. Straight. *Not many people know that birds have eyelashes*, his mother used to say. *Can't you see how pretty they are, darling? Oh, can't you see?*

Maude trilled her familiar call, an upturned sound that mimicked a question: *Are you there, darling?* Winston whistled his usual, flat response: *Yes, I'm here.*

She angled her head towards the window. Across the path, on the step of the neighbouring caravan, lounged the cat. Its shining yellow eyes glared at them. This black cat, a familiar named Jinx, stared in this threatening manner every day. Winston understood that Maude was growing to fight and defeat Jinx's power.

The cat's owner, a crone named Florence, also happened to be Winston's nemesis.

When he had first moved in with his cardboard suitcase and shopping bags full of belongings, Florence had shuffled out of her caravan and waved.

"Ooh, a fresh face!" she had croaked. "A fresh face in Pauper's Row!"

Because that's what permanent residents called this backstreet of rusting vans and cabins pushed up against the perimeter fence. The more solvent tenants enjoyed abodes nearer the toilet block and barbecues, while the wealthiest lived in proximity to the swimming pool.

"I'm Florence," the crone said. "Come on over for a cuppa. Let's get acquainted."

Her caravan was stuffed with straw dolls and other spell-casting paraphernalia. Winston, confounded by a headache, only pretended to sip the scalding tea in case it was poisoned. Florence enquired: what had brought him to Pauper's Row? Well, the truth was that his mother had died in hospital of a stroke. But Mother would still be alive if they had simply allowed her to sleep on the dove-feather pillow. *No one can die while resting on a dove-feather pillow, darling.* For shame, the nurses had refused, insisting his request would be a contamination risk. Security guards had dragged Winston, screaming, from the ward and ejected him from the hospital, throwing the pillow after him.

Instead, he told Florence, "I wished for a change of scenery."

She lifted her mug in the mockery of a toast. "Well, the forest behind the fence is a pretty sight, I'll give you that much."

Throughout the whole visit, the cat fixed Winston with its

golden eyes, tail flicking, mouth yawning to reveal its rows of pointy teeth waiting within.

Florence's hag-like nature confirmed itself one week later. Winston, installing a bird feeder, had inadvertently attracted pigeons and sparrows instead of rosellas and lorikeets, yes, but birds all the same. Florence had complained to Management while never admitting her treachery. So, the feeder had come down. And Jinx had begun its constant vigil.

Now, moving foot over clawed foot, the weighty bulk of Maude settled on Winston's shoulder. As was her habit, she nibbled his earlobe, plucked his greying stubble, pecked at his lips. Thanks to her new size and strength, these marks of affection hurt.

"If you kill Jinx," he said, "you'll have to kill Florence. Or she'll create another familiar."

Maude unlooped the coils of her long neck to put her face directly in front of his own. They stared at each other. As it transpired, her eyelashes weren't long and curved after all, but stumpy and straight, resembling broom bristles. For the first time, Winston appreciated how truly sphincter-like Maude's eyelids appeared. How the raw, flaky ring of bald skin encircling each black iris resembled the reptilian look of a cold-blooded dinosaur.

"If you intend to keep growing," he said, "you can't return to the cage or you'll get stuck. Where will you sleep, Maude, if not in your cage?"

In reply, she swivelled her head to look out the back window. Towards the eucalypt forest, he realised. Once she was too big to fit inside the caravan, yes, he could hide her within those close-knit trees, their entangled canopies keeping out the light. She would be truly monstrous once she attained her final goddess size.

He said, "After we kill Jinx and Florence, shall we fly away? I'll design and build a saddle. Where should we go? To the hospital first?"

He waited, heart racing. The bird rolled its stygian eye. Winked.

Next morning, Winston's arm could no longer support her weight. Maude was the size of an eagle. The day after, an emu.

Her nipping kisses drew blood. Her claws opened his skin in razor cuts. The strong, musky smell of dander made him dizzy. By week's end, Maude had to repose lengthwise along the floor of his caravan, her butt cramped against the kitchen cupboards, tail feathers fanned over the ceiling.

Giddy with anticipation, Winston could no longer sleep. The crone and her familiar, the nurses, security staff, the distant and commandeering relatives—in fact, the entire convoluted web of co-conspirators—would soon feel Maude's murderous wrath and be laid waste.

"You're a miracle," he whispered.

Maude clicked her beak. The sound was loud enough to squeeze the pain in Winston's head even tighter, bringing spots to his vision. Since it was after breakfast, Jinx appeared on the opposite veranda, lounging, glaring and spell-casting, his usual habit. Where was Florence? Soon to appear.

"Let's go kill them both," Winston said, taking up a cleaver.

The goddess hoisted her bulk from the floor. The sole of her foot felt hot, dry and scabrous about his neck. He smiled when she drew him close. Tears of adoration filled his eyes, heart and head pounding. Maude's beak, as pearlescent and tessellated as an oyster shell, opened wide. In a flash, he saw a rasping tongue, the corrugated pink gullet. Then a terrible agony flared through his head. The worst agony of his life.

Maude got to work, shucking his skull like a seed.

Soon she would rend his brain. And then, abandoning him, she would soar into the sky, her colossal wings blocking out the sun. Bereft, he began to weep at the familiarity of betrayal. Yet through his grief and the halo of intense pain, mind stuttering and shutting down, Winston could see her in full flight, rising, rising, her body lifting into the heavens. His beautiful goddess, his great and terrible dragon.

Mourning Coffee

"While I was hospitalised, my husband needed sleeping pills just to get some rest," she said. "Understand? He couldn't manage by himself."

I shrugged. She reminded me of my grandma. We were alone in the hall. This visit had started off as a welfare check. Now, fellow cops and forensics were here. The house was sparse, clean, but swarming with flies.

"Didn't the smell bother you?" I said.

"Not as much as he did."

I cuffed her. Upon returning home, she'd crushed a handful of sleeping pills into hubby's coffee. Then left his corpse to decompose across the kitchen floor.

Barralang, Pop. 63

1

The two-lane highway ran in a straight line to the horizon, as far as Jody could tell, and on both sides the terrain lay dry and flat, empty save for meagre pockets of scrub and the odd straggly gum tree. Like driving across the moon if it were made of red dust. No, more like driving across *Mars*, she corrected herself, since Mars is actually red. Good observation. And on that observation, she would hang her article's opening line: *Travel to the forgotten town of Barralang in Victoria's north and journey through an arid Martian landscape—* Ugh, no. Such a lede might be okay for a travel brochure, but it wouldn't suit the Walkley Award-winning investigative piece on generational poverty that Jody had in mind. She was being overly anxious again. Trying to write the damn thing in advance. Her editor had always scolded her for pre-empting the story and—just last month, in fact—had sacked her for it.

On the passenger seat was her satchel containing laptop, note-pad, pens, business cards (new ones, now that she was freelance again), phone charger cord, spare thumb drives. Organising this research trip had taken a whole day. A whole day without any writing, pitching or earning. But an in-depth article about a town with one of the lowest median incomes in Australia ought to sell, for a good price too, and surely its publication would sweeten her resumé.

Up ahead, two buildings flanked the highway, reminding her of gate pillars. The outskirts of Barralang, perhaps? She sat tall behind the wheel. As she closed the distance, the buildings revealed themselves to be farmhouses. Derelict, with crumbling barns nearby, rusted iron skeletons of equipment and stripped car bodies hunkering out front. What sort of produce could these farms have possibly grown in their heyday? There didn't seem to be any water out here. Jody drove between the properties. She pictured the farmers rising every morning to slurp coffee on their verandas and glower at each other. Could that vision be her lede? It was colourful enough.

Minutes passed with no further evidence of civilisation. Jody began to fidget. A "welcome to our town" sign hadn't materialised. She flicked her gaze to the GPS screen. Apparently, she had reached Barralang, so where the hell was it? Her lower back ached from nearly five hours on the road. Setting out mid-morning, she had planned to start her interviews upon arrival, but screw that. She would need a hot bath and a long drink, not necessarily in that order, and after dinner and a night's sleep at the hotel, she would start her interviews first thing tomorrow.

The highway doglegged and then split down the middle. The lane that headed back to Melbourne began to veer away at a sharp angle. Barralang materialised suddenly and without fanfare. Between the split lanes appeared a broad median strip, which contained a stand of spindly gum trees and a rotunda listing wearily to one side. Jody slowed to fifty kilometres an hour. *Shit!* She must have missed the speed limit sign. She couldn't afford a ticket. Then again, would there be police radars in a town with only sixty-two residents?

A skinny black dog watched her approach and limped onto the road anyway. She braked hard. While the dog crossed at leisure, Jody noticed a trio seated in the rotunda. Two men, one woman: potential interviewees. She opened the window and waved.

"Hello there!" she called. "Hello!"

They stared but didn't wave back. Awkward. Maybe they weren't used to strangers here. The dog finished crossing the road. Before she pressed the accelerator, Jody had a better look at the trio, now standing up with beer stubbies and lit cigarettes in hand, thin bodies dressed in heavy coats against the early winter chill, their long and sharp faces tracking her car as she drove past. She closed her window. Unsavoury types. Druggies, most likely. Similar to many regional towns, Barralang had problems with drugs—ice in particular. Jody stared firmly out the windscreen and motored onwards. *If you don't want to get mugged, don't make eye contact.* A decades-old snippet of advice from her mother which had obviously worked, since Jody had never been mugged in all her forty-four years, despite inserting herself into countless thorny situations for the sake of journalistic truth.

With no other vehicles on the road, she slowed to a crawl and gazed about at what passed for the main street. A couple of dozen dilapidated stores—some weatherboard, others brick— most of them boarded up with FOR LEASE signs mouldering in the windows. A petite, narrow church in a rubbish-strewn lot, its front doors chained shut. Depressing. Where were the townsfolk? Apart from the druggy trio, the streets were deserted. The sight gave her a strange, hollow feeling in her guts.

Barralang wasn't just "forgotten", it was dead and gone. Had died a long time ago.

So, who the hell would want to purchase such a town in its entirety? Barralang was poor enough—*worthless* enough—that a single person had recently bought the place. Jody's investigations had failed to turn up the mystery buyer's identity. Maybe that should be her opening line: *A northern Victorian town, blighted by unemployment and drug abuse, has attracted an anonymous benefactor who must somehow believe that better times lie ahead.*

There was the hotel, shabby but still grand, incongruously out of place with its sweeping verandas and extravagant cast-iron balustrades. The Royal Hotel. Such a moniker seemed pointedly sarcastic. She pulled into a parking bay out front, switched off the engine, and checked her notes to refresh her memory. The owners were Lorraine and Bruce. Lorraine had taken Jody's reservation over the phone. *No one's stayed at the Royal for years,* she had said. *I suppose I'll have to search the attic and dig out the bed linen.*

Jody alighted from the car and stretched. Her feet felt puffy.

The cold air bit at her nose. She grabbed her satchel and suitcase. With a cautious glance down the road towards the druggies—they were back in the rotunda again, thankfully, as if they had lost interest—she locked the car. The buckled steps required attentive negotiation. She crossed the creaking veranda and entered the hotel.

The place looked ready for a siege. Half the furniture in the dining hall was stacked up against the far wall, with free-standing shelves laden with packaged goods taking up the floor space. Beneath a yellowing, handwritten sign proclaiming TODAY'S SPECIALS sat a basket filled with dented, swollen, dusty cans of sliced beetroot, pumpkin soup, sausage and vegetable stew, baked beans in ham sauce, creamed corn. *What a dump,* Jody thought in despair. And what was that *stink*? Cabbage and sewage?

Oh, there was no story here. Barralang was just a shithole on its last legs. Oh Jesus, she had wasted so much time and money. Tears sprang to her eyes and she blinked them back. Wait: she was tired, that's all. From the long drive. From the strain of losing her job and watching her bank account dwindle at an alarming rate, and dear God, her rent was due in a fortnight and what was she doing paying for a two-night stay in this godforsaken ruin? She felt dizzy for a moment. Sick and dizzy.

"Jody Jones?"

She turned. The old woman coming towards her from the shadows was tall and pot-bellied, grey-haired, with a bony head drooping on a thin, bowed neck. Her slacks and buttoned cardigan looked as if they would smell of mothballs.

"Lorraine, isn't it?" Jody said. "Hi. Pleasure to meet you."

"You're early. The room isn't ready."

"That's okay, I'm in no rush. To be honest, I'd like to have a drink anyway."

Lorraine frowned. "Here? At the bar?"

"Well, yes. If that's okay. Unless... Is there anywhere else I could go?"

The old woman narrowed her straw-coloured eyes. They were small and close together, frosty over a beaked nose. A striking face. Jody would have to photograph it: a dramatic portrait with split lighting to draw attention to the severe, vulturine features. Perhaps this Barralang article might be better as a photo-essay.

"Come on," Lorraine said and headed to the bar, weaving between tables. "We've not much in the way of alcohol. If you're expecting the same range as the big smoke, you'll be disappointed."

"That's fine. Can you explain these groceries?" Jody said, pointing at the shelves.

"There's no supermarket here. We're not just the hotel, but the corner store too."

The bartop was cluttered with empty beer stubbies and food wrappers, giving the impression that patrons had left unexpectedly. Jody decided on a cheap moselle. Lorraine ended up joining her. As it turned out, the old woman liked to talk.

"Barralang started out as a gold rush town," Lorraine was saying, "but it was fool's gold. We grew barley for a while. If you drank beer anytime during last century, you've tasted Barralang. Then in the 1970s, a bunch of religious folks arrived and set up headquarters."

"They built that church up the road?"

"No, but they commandeered it. Didn't last. God ran out on us too."

"You've got nowhere to worship?"

"And nowhere to work, educate kids, go shopping. For that stuff, people catch the bus to Kanninvale. Or beg a lift off me. I've got one of the only cars in town, don't you know."

"But if there isn't any God, employment, schools or stores in Barralang, what does everybody do all day?"

Lorraine threw back her head and laughed. The noise was a hacking bray. After a few seconds, Jody started to laugh too, although she wasn't sure why.

"Residents are retired, on the dole, on the run, or crazy," Lorraine said. "What do you *think* they do?"

Self-medicate, Jody mused, and gulped at her wine. "Tell me, what's your background? You sound quite educated."

"Do I?" the old woman said.

Jody waited and then offered a placating smile. "Next question: who bought the town?"

"So, you've heard. It's why you're here. All right. Our benefactor is Mr Blank."

"What kind of name is that? Swiss?"

Lorraine poured herself another drink despite the colour already blazing in her sharp cheeks. "No, that's what the townsfolk call him. 'Blank' because they don't know."

"But do *you* know?"

"Let me tell you my take on Mr Blank: he's a collector."

"Of towns? Or of people?"

Lorraine gazed into her wine glass and shrugged. "Same difference."

The Royal Hotel offered meals only on Thursdays, or "pension day" as Lorraine called it. This being a Monday, Jody had to make do with whatever Lorraine happened to be cooking for dinner, which turned out to be bangers and mash. They sat together at one of the dining tables. The husband, Bruce, was absent. Perhaps he ate his dinner in the privately-owned section of the hotel. Lorraine didn't mention her husband and Jody didn't ask.

Upstairs, the guest facilities had no bathtub, worse luck.

At least the buzz from the alcohol had eased the kinks in her back. Jody's room was small and sparsely furnished. The dresser drawers were stuck, so she put her unpacked suitcase beneath the double bed. A chill draught blew. She pulled aside the curtains. The sash window was slightly open. She tried to push it closed but it refused to budge. Damn. Was *everything* out of plumb in Barralang? From the threadbare set of towels on the dresser, she took a hand towel and wedged it into the window crack. Good enough. Fatigued, she fell into bed.

Sleep wouldn't come easy.

Jody was used to the night-time sounds of traffic and barking dogs, the trundle of faraway trains, murmurs of disembodied voices on the street. Here, there were no sounds. Not a single one. The silence cupped her ears. She found herself worrying at the bedsheet with anxious fingers, the crinkling of the linen a reassurance that she had not been struck deaf.

When sleep came, it was full of uneasy dreams.

She dreamt of howling winds that plucked at the roof and

poked at the window, of torrential rains that hammered and pounded as if hurled from the sky by an angry hand. She dreamt of frogs, numbering in the millions, slick from the downpour, mute and crawling over one another aimlessly, pointlessly, desperately, crushing each other beneath their combined weight, cannibalising out of hunger.

The next morning, Jody looked out the window and saw water.

"It happens every winter like clockwork," Lorraine said, pushing a box of cornflakes across the bar. "We lose the power every time too. I'm surprised you didn't learn about the seasonal flooding from your research."

"I'm surprised you didn't tell me over the phone," Jody said.

"Why should I think to tell you? Winter floods are nothing out of the ordinary in Barralang. We're used to getting cut off."

Jody, reaching for the cereal, froze. "Cut *off*?"

"Naturally. We're on a small hill in the middle of a flood plain. Water circles us like a moat."

"For how long?"

"Hmm… About two weeks, give or take."

A tingling, skittering sensation started up in Jody's chest. *Two weeks?* Her rent would be due by then. She hadn't even *made* the rent money yet. And how could she afford two weeks in a goddamned hotel? Let alone the cost of food. No, no, no, she had to get out of here. This whole trip was a mistake, a ridiculous extravagance, the delusion of a Walkley Award, the lie she had told herself to keep panic at bay. She scrambled to her feet. Lorraine waved a dismissive hand and began to laugh.

"Ah, sweetie," the old woman said, "it's too late."

Panting, Jody retrieved her suitcase and satchel. Hurried to the threshold. Pushed open the warped front door which juddered in its frame, and stumbled onto the creaking veranda.

Water, brown still water everywhere, but not so much of it, not really. Her car tyres were submerged only a couple of centimetres. Nothing she couldn't drive through if she were slow and careful. She splashed to the car boot and pitched in her belongings. The water, shockingly chill, seeped into her shoes.

"You're wasting your time."

She looked up. Lorraine stood on the veranda, hands in pockets, a sly smile revealing her pointy teeth.

"Come on back inside," she continued, "before you catch your death."

"No, I'm leaving before the flood waters rise too high," Jody said, slamming the boot.

"The flood waters are too high already."

"I'll be back in a month or so, okay? To finish the story."

"You'll be back in ten minutes."

2

Jody jumped behind the wheel, twisted the key in the ignition and backed out in a wide arc. The sky gleamed, cloudless and blue. She drove at a reasonable clip towards Melbourne, water hissing under her tyres. Shadows moved within the lopsided rotunda. She slowed down for a better look. The druggy trio stood up, beer stubbies and smokes in hand, to stare blankly at her, heads tracking. Alarmed, she stamped the accelerator.

Maybe she wouldn't come back. Maybe she'd treat this "generational poverty" piece as a bust. She could hustle up horoscope articles, right? They were quick sales. Low-paying, but still... With a cute angle, they might be worth more money. What about perfumes to suit each zodiac sign? Or horoscopes for pets? Oh, she'd slap something together—

She braked.

At the dogleg, the road dipped into a brown lake. In the distance, the two farmhouses that marked the outskirts of town were submerged to their rooflines. She switched on the GPS with trembling fingers. Kanninvale was north-west. From there, she could jump on a different highway. She executed a clumsy U-turn. When she drove back past the rotunda and the Royal Hotel, she kept her gaze straight ahead.

Beyond the shuttered shops of Main Street, the houses began. Despite herself, she slowed down to gape. Decaying cottages with blistered, rotting boards and drooping verandas. Roofs patched with plywood. Collapsed picket fences. More often than not, garbage bags and broken furniture in the yards as if the occupants considered the outside world a tip. *Barralang is a place where hope comes to die.* Yes. This would be her opening sentence. A creep of prescience tapped along her spine and lifted the hairs on her nape. *Oh God...* But if she could win that Walkley Award, if she could just do that... Tears filmed her vision. She drove on.

The calm voice of the GPS kept giving her directions. *Turn left* it said when she reached the other side of Barralang. Yet she couldn't obey. At the foot of the road ahead lay another shore of the same wide, brown lake. Half-heartedly, she attempted other escape routes, knowing that she was trapped. When she walked into the Royal Hotel, suitcase and satchel in hand, Lorraine consulted her watch.

"A little over twenty minutes," she said. "You're the persistent type."

"Look," Jody said. "If I'm forced to stay here, will you still charge me full rates?"

"Sweetie, I'm not a charity."

Jody sighed, took a seat at the bar. "It's early but give me a drink anyway."

"When in Rome," Lorraine chuckled. "Aw, don't feel too bad. Day drinking is the national sport around here."

She poured a glass and left the bottle on the bar, retreating through a door that presumably led to the private quarters where the husband, Bruce, remained hidden.

The wine hit Jody's empty stomach like a fist. She necked the first glass. Tried to take it easy on the second. By the third, felt the warmth of liquid courage. All right, she would pitch and compose articles right here in Barralang. There was no electricity, but she could charge her phone and laptop in the car. She had the cords, didn't she? Enough petrol to keep the engine idling? And there must be 4G access. *See?* she told herself, lips quivering as she swigged at the wine. *Everything will be okay.*

"Are you crying?"

Jody looked up. Lorraine was lugging a heavy laundry basket.

"Of course not," Jody said, brushing at her eyes. "What have you got there?"

"Supplies. The whole town will be wanting groceries in the next day or so."

"You've got quite the monopoly."

"Hey, I don't make much profit, you know. A few cents here and there."

For a time, Jody watched the old woman stack cans on the shelves. Finally, she said, "You don't rotate the stock? Put the new stuff towards the back?"

"No need. Canned stuff lasts forever."

"I'm not sure if that's right." Jody stood up and wandered over, took a condensed mushroom soup off the rack and inspected its label. "Wow. Nearly seven years out of date."

"Doesn't matter."

"Okay." Jody went to the bar. "I'm off to interview people."

"That's nice. How do you intend to find them?"

Jody hesitated, remembering the empty streets, the empty front yards. "Well, there's always the group in the rotunda."

"Yeah, if you want to get mugged."

"They're druggies?"

"Stay here and wait," Lorraine said. "Let Barralang come to you."

"I don't have time. Maybe I'll knock on some doors."

"Suit yourself."

Jody grabbed her satchel and went outside. Her car wasn't there. Which didn't make sense. She blinked and looked again. No, her car definitely wasn't there. Where the hell was it? Dazed, she scanned up and down the street. She felt fuzzy, a little buzzed from the wine.

"Joyriders," came Lorraine's voice.

The old woman was standing next to her on the veranda, nodding sagely, her beaked nose even larger in profile.

"I'm sorry, what?" Jody said.

"Joyriders. The devil finds work for idle hands."

"Somebody stole my car?" Panic rose in a flutter. "Shit. What do I do? Call the police?"

"No point. The nearest police station is in Kanninvale. Without helicopters or boats, they won't be able to attend even if they wanted to. Ah, don't worry. Your car will get dumped in a side street soon enough. And if not, there's always insurance."

"But...but how will I charge my phone and laptop?"

"You can't, sweetie."

"Don't you own a generator?"

"No. My advice? Consider this trip an unscheduled holiday."

Jody allowed Lorraine to lead her back inside the hotel. She felt lightheaded. The half-empty bottle of moselle was waiting for her at the bar and she finished it off, which was a dumb decision, yes, but she could never *think* straight during an anxiety attack; the white noise always blasted her mind with static. She had to drown out the noise *somehow*.

"You've got a car, haven't you?" she said at last.

Lorraine swallowed a mouthful of wine—since she had joined Jody at the bar—and licked her dry, narrow lips. "What if I have?"

"Can you drive me around town? To help me look for my car?"

"I'm not your chauffeur."

Jody grappled with her satchel, pulled out her wallet and rummaged through it. Only fifteen dollars in cash. Shit. Like everyone else, she used credit cards. Buy now, worry later.

"I'll pay you," she said, holding out the notes.

"I'm not a taxi driver either."

"Oh, please," Jody begged, ready to go mad. "*Please.*"

They found her hatchback in the car park behind the church. At first glance, Jody didn't recognise the smudged and sooty wreck sitting on bare rims, every window smashed. Lorraine waited patiently for the truth to dawn. And when it did, Jody got out of Lorraine's ancient, rusty, square-edged station wagon and shuffled towards the hatchback in stupefaction. Icy water soaked her shoes. She put her hands on the driver's side windowsill and leaned down. The burnt-out cabin stank of plastic, carbon, sulphur. Wisps of smoke rose from the seats. How had her car been destroyed so quickly?

"Well, that's that," came Lorraine's voice.

The old woman was standing nearby, crossed arms resting on her belly.

"I don't understand," Jody whispered. "Why would anybody want to do this?"

"Come on, sweetie," Lorraine said, steering Jody away. "Let's go."

They climbed into the station wagon. Lorraine drove quickly, confidently, the floodwaters hissing and susurrating and singing beneath the tyres. Jody felt numb.

"I should contact my insurance company," she muttered.

"All in good time."

Good time? There was no such thing in Barralang.

Jody contemplated this fact next morning while lying para-lysed in bed. Yesterday, while her laptop still held charge, she should have written a horoscope feature, but didn't. When locals failed to arrive at the Royal Hotel as Lorraine had predicted, she should have traipsed around the neighbourhood on foot, but didn't. Lunch had been a sandwich. Dinner chicken and chips. How much would this end up costing? Dessert another bottle of wine she had consumed upstairs in this room. Sleep a hotchpotch of fever dreams that kept waking her in a shivering sweat, over and over. One nightmare in particular about a dark, seething mountain that turned out to be made of spiders: millions of huntsmen embroiled in a dying tangle of interlocked and thrashing legs.

She ought to take a shower… But the thought of it exhausted her. Brush her teeth then. Get rid of the sour taste of booze furring her tongue—

What was that noise?

She held her breath. The sounds from outside were certainly not birds, since there didn't seem to be any in the skies or trees of Barralang which, upon reflection, struck her as odd. No, it was a puddling, paddling, slapping, slipping and sliding series of overlapping noises and her mind conjured a knot of a thousand snakes twisting through the mud of Main Street.

Jody leapt out of bed, ripped aside the curtain, and saw a crowd of locals.

Singly, in pairs, in groups, shambling through the shallow waters from every direction, most of them holding various kinds of shopping bags, all of them homing in on the Royal Hotel. There must be fifty or more people out there, Jody thought. Most of the town's population. Gathering in a coordinated effort like ants following a pheromone trail back to the nest. How had they known? It was as if the hotel were sounding a siren but no, there was no sound, none, apart from the wet and slippery glissade of feet.

Jody got dressed and hurried downstairs. At the threshold of the dining room, however, she hung back in the shadows.

People thronged the grocery shelves, solemnly inspecting each can. More people kept coming inside. She didn't dare count them. What if it were the whole population? She just wouldn't know what to think about that. The dining room felt chilly after so long without central heating. Breaths plumed. Built into one wall was an unused hearth; empty, clean and cold, with firewood stacked next to it. Silently, the townsfolk nodded their heads over the cans. Jody pulled her jacket tighter about herself and took a few steps backwards.

"I told you," came Lorraine's voice.

Jody turned towards the staircase. Standing in the hallway was the old woman, arms akimbo, looking smug.

"I told you they'd visit," she continued. "Now you can hold interviews in comfort."

"Why is everybody here at the same time?" Jody said. "Did you send a mass text?"

"That's the couple right there if you want intelligent comment. Retired scientists. Never short of an opinion, those two."

"But I record interviews. And my phone is dead. I don't know if I'll be—"

"Angelo and Layla. Go on, before they leave. Here's your chance. Take it. Hurry."

She approached with hands outstretched as if she meant to give Jody a shove. Alarmed, Jody scooted into the dining room. Paused. *Don't be an idiot.* And went over to the couple.

They were elderly, short and frail with matching helmets of snowy hair, their startled eyes deeply set in faces as wrinkled as raisins. They wore the same long, creased, off-white raincoat, resembling doves with their wings folded. And both wore a petite cross on a shining gold chain. Odd. Jody had always assumed that scientists—with their insistence on proof—would be agnostic.

"Good morning. My name is Jody Jones. I'm a journalist."

They took a lengthy second or two to respond. First, they swivelled their heads and then their eyes, until they finally had her in their sights. Their irises were the same shade of violet.

"A journalist? Out here?" Angelo's voice was a reedy whistle. "Are you lost?"

"No. I'm actually writing a story about Barralang. Would you care to be interviewed?"

"Interviewed? About what?"

"Different things. Yourselves. Everyday life. The mystery buyer of the town."

The man's face closed up tight. "Oh, you mean our esteemed Mr Blank."

"Who told *you* about this private sale?" Layla said. "How did you find out?"

The couple stared, violet eyes wide, mouths pinched.

Jody blushed. "Sorry, I didn't realise it was confidential information. When I heard about the sale…uh, read about it, actually, on the Internet somewhere I think, on some site or another, a newspaper… I figured—"

"He brought you here," Layla whispered. "Leave us alone."

"What? Look, I'm sorry, I only wanted—"

"Get out of Barralang."

Jody touched her forehead and found that she was perspiring. "Well, okay, here's the thing. Even if I wanted to leave, there's the flood, and my car got stolen and so I'm—"

"Don't take any of these cans!" Layla yelled, lifting her face to the ceiling so that her voice would carry throughout the dining room.

"They've come from the devil himself!" Angelo shouted.

The townsfolk froze, gaping at the couple with alarmed faces. Jody froze too.

"Piss off," Lorraine said, and even though she stood at the other end of the dining room behind the bar, her voice carried loud and clear.

Layla tottered away, dragging her husband in tow. They left the pub. The townsfolk resumed shuffling about and choosing cans. Already, the shelves were almost bare. There was not enough food to last two weeks. Barralang would starve. Perhaps helicopters might airlift everyone to safety and take Jody home. She retreated to the bar.

"Don't worry," Lorraine said. "Angelo and Layla are difficult at the best of times."

"And hardly rational. Why did you tell me to talk to them?"

"I thought you might find them interesting."

Jody thought this over. Then she said, "Are they twins?"

"Husband and wife."

Jody frowned. "But they look alike."

"It happens with married couples after a few decades. Like dogs and their owners."

"I think that's a myth."

"No, it isn't."

Lorraine had already poured a glass of wine and pushed it across the counter before Jody realised or had time to demur. Unexpectedly, the wine tasted cold even though the fridges shouldn't be working.

"Why is everyone so quiet?" she said.

Lorraine laughed and shrugged. "Oh, I don't know, sweetie. Maybe floods and food shortages make people feel a little down in the dumps, but that's just my theory."

"If Barralang is cut off every winter like this, how come no one's prepared?"

"Oh dear. For a journalist, you're not very observant. Look at these people. *Look* at them."

She did. Cheap shoes or bare, dirty feet. Dishevelled clothes. Unwashed hair. Missing teeth. Rounded shoulders and bowed heads, haunted faces, wet and empty eyes. *Barralang is a place where hope comes to die.* Jody rubbed at the headache squeezing her temples.

"I'm going upstairs," she said.

She slept through lunch, a welcome savings. The dining room was empty when she surfaced later for a few more drinks;

Barralang had reabsorbed its townsfolk. Dinner was chops, carrots, peas. Jody sat with Lorraine at one of the dining tables. Bruce was absent. Again. Lorraine didn't mention the husband and Jody didn't ask. Dessert two bottles of moselle. Sleep held fever dreams and sweat. At one point in the night, she heard the farting of air bubbles in the floodwater—*blerp blerp blerp*—as if alien creatures, rehydrated, were rising from the mud and taking breath for the first time.

The next morning, Jody looked out the window and saw fish.

3

Hundreds of little fish carpeted the street. No, *thousands*. Silvery, shimmering darts, flapping and wriggling and struggling in the mud, tails winking in the watery sunlight. *Huh,* Jody thought obliquely, her mind coming to a stubborn stop. *Huh.* She went to the bathroom. The walls and floor of the shower recess were made of plastic. It felt like standing in a bucket. The hot and cold taps were reversed, which made perfect sense for this town. She got dressed. Perhaps, if she chose to look out the window again, the massive shoal of beached fish would be gone. She avoided the window. Instead, she hummed to herself. The room was very cold. Cold enough to make her joints ache.

Lorraine was waiting at the bar with cornflakes and wine. Jody went onto the veranda.

The street glimmered with scales. Yet the shoal extended only fifteen metres or so in either direction, as if disgorged from a dump truck parked directly outside the Royal Hotel. The pulse flittered in Jody's ears. She descended to the last step, squatted to her haunches and picked out a fish, half-expecting her fingers to pass through nothing but silt and icy water. But the fish was real. It had a forked tail and a dour, disapproving mouth. When she noticed the peg-like teeth, the fish twisted in her palm and tried to bite her even while its gills heaved torturously from suffocation.

"The Southern black bream," came Lorraine's voice.

Jody sighed, not bothering to turn around. "Someone ought to put a bell on you."

"Being a city slicker, I bet you've never seen black bream in the flesh before."

"Jesus, that's your takeaway from this?" Jody said, standing up. "The road is chock-a-block with goddamned fish, and that's all you've got to say?"

The old woman's yellow eyes became flat and narrow. Jody threw the fish into the street with all her might. It arced through the air and landed back in the shoal with a wet kiss. She rubbed her hand against her jeans, over and over and over, until she forced herself to stop.

"How did they get here?" she said. "Smack-dab in front of this hotel?"

"Waterspout."

The sky was a bright and crystalline blue.

Jody's laugh cracked into a high register. "Oh, I find that pretty bloody hard to believe. For a start, where's the storm? And even if it *was* a waterspout, what about the other creatures that live in rivers and lakes? The crabs, yabbies? Or different types of fish? Trout, redfin, perch? Seems to me there's only black bream. How could a waterspout be so selective? How? You don't find any of this strange? There's *bream* in the goddamn *street*."

Lorraine took the steps and stood next to Jody. The breeze ruffled the old woman's hair. The dull, meagre tufts resembled the down of a baby bird, and her scalp shone pink.

"I'm not freaking out," Lorraine said, "because this kind of phenomenon has happened before. Lots of times, actually. I thought you'd researched Barralang."

"I did."

"Not very well. Listen up. Over the past, oh, hundred and fifty years or more, we've had lots of funny rainfalls. The first recorded one consisted of earthworms, a great lump of them, oozing around right here at our feet. The townsfolk thought it was Armageddon. Many killed themselves, apparently."

"Killed themselves—?"

"Tadpoles are common. In fact, I remember when I was a girl and saw my first fall of them. I can still remember my surprise. Some tadpoles were in transition and had grown tiny back legs. Kind of like half-frogs, I suppose. Us kids ran up and down the street with sharpened sticks, bursting them like balloons. What a lark!"

Frogs? Jody tried to understand her sudden, vertiginous sensation of déjà vu, but the image flitted too quickly across her mind's eye and was lost.

Lorraine pointed up the street. "See that church?"

The modest spire rose above the roofline of single-storey shops. Jody squinted at it, the intense blue of the sky hurting her eyes.

"The religious leaders that moved here in the 1970s brought a lot of people with them," Lorraine went on. "Worshippers of their oddball faith. I guess you could call them a cult. But we didn't mind. The population boost was good for the town. Oh, we had a school back then, a post office too. Even a cricket club. Then one day it rained spiders."

Spiders? Jody held her breath, tried to grab hold of a distant remnant as if from a dream.

"Hah," Lorraine continued, "the big knobs of the church didn't like that, did they? It was a *sign* in their view, so they pulled up stumps and pissed off."

"A sign of what?"

"Once they left, Barralang started to perish, one establishment at a time. Now here we are: a ghost town with funny little rainfalls, and nobody gives a rat's arse."

The journalist in Jody roused. "Have you ever witnessed animals dropping out of the sky? Has anyone seen it rain like that? Maybe taken photos or footage?"

"No. It always happens when we're asleep."

"Why do you think that is?"

Lorraine crinkled her beaky nose and winked. "Because God, the contrary bastard, likes to move in mysterious ways."

"So, you believe these fish are some kind of divine miracle?"

"Bottom line, sweetie, I'm not about to look a gift horse in the mouth. Tell you what: help me prep them and I'll discount your bill for room and board."

"Prep them?"

The old woman nodded. "I'm thinking stew."

"Stew? You're kidding. Oh, come off it. You actually expect people to eat these fish?"

"Good timing, actually. I was wondering what to cook for service tomorrow."

"Wait, tomorrow is Thursday?" Jody rubbed at the back of her neck. "Already?"

She gazed across the glistening backs of countless bream. Their fidgeting had quelled. They were dying. Suffocation wouldn't take long, after all. Bewildered, she shook her head. Just a few weeks ago, she had been touch-typing in the magazine's city office, working up her story about synthetic marijuana and psychosis, saving for a washing machine and dryer so that she'd never have to return to the laundromat with its depressing clientele. Now these seemed like the details of someone else's life, someone she didn't know or recognise.

"Well?" Lorraine said. "You want to be my sous chef or not?"

Surely, eating dead and dying fish plucked out of mud couldn't be sanitary. But Jody thought of her bank account and said, "Okay. It's a deal."

Lorraine smiled.

The two of them gathered the fish in plastic buckets. They never ran out of buckets. How did Lorraine have so many? Why would anyone *need* so many? From the tail of her eye, Jody kept noticing townsfolk watching from a distance, peeking from around the corners of buildings. Whenever she straightened up to take a better look, they ducked away.

She hauled buckets of fish into the kitchen over and over, for hours and hours, until her back ached and spots flashed in her vision. Lorraine didn't seem affected. The spry old woman kept up with her and then some. The monotony lulled Jody into an empty, hypnagogic state. She had the vague idea that she would gather these fish for ever and ever.

"Let's break for lunch," the old woman said.

Lunch turned out to be wine. Jody didn't mind. Somehow, the wine was *still* cold.

The pub's kitchen belonged in a farmhouse rather than a commercial establishment: long wooden benches, a central wooden table big enough to seat twelve, an ancient stovetop and oven, no extractor fans, not a scrap of stainless steel anywhere. The one exception to the farmhouse design was the sink: a long, deep trough the size of a bath.

They washed and descaled the fish in giant colanders under running water. Gutted them with knives. Snipped out the spines with scissors. Chopped off the heads and tails. More hours passed. Jody's back screamed. Her hands turned red and sore. By the time the light faded from the window, the kitchen benches seemed to bow beneath the weight of so many buckets of cleaned fish.

"Wash your hands with cut lemon," the old woman said. "To get rid of the smell."

The acid stung. Jody closed her eyes and kept rubbing the fruit across her raw skin, the water from the tap icy-cold and biting. She felt like weeping but didn't have the strength.

The evening meal was rissoles, carrots, peas. Jody sat with Lorraine at one of the dining tables. Bruce was absent. Again. Jody finished another glass of wine.

"Where's your husband?" she asked, despite herself.

Lorraine said, "Where's yours?"

"I don't have one. I never married."

"Listen, it's always a full house on pension day so we've got an early start tomorrow. Five-thirty. Lunch service at twelve, dinner service at six, with a lot of cooking to be done."

That night, Jody slept like the dead. She swam soundlessly and dreamlessly through a darkness so complete that she felt frightened when she opened her eyes. If there was a strange sight out the window, she wouldn't be able to take it. The knocking at the door stopped.

"You awake?" came Lorraine's voice from the other side of the door.

"Yes."

"Five-thirty. Get a move on."

"I'll be down in a minute."

The water heater was electric, and Jody couldn't face a cold shower. Instead, she got dressed and went downstairs. The kitchen table was covered in cans, jars, bottles and packets. Tomatoes. Kalamata olives. Garlic. Dijon mustard. Sugar. Chilli flakes. Vinegar. Brandy. More white wine. Giant steel pots sat on the stovetops. Lorraine wore an apron.

"We're in luck," the old woman said, hauling three enormous mesh bags of onions from a cupboard. "The last of my fresh vegetables just happens to be what we need for this recipe."

A folded apron sat at the end of the table. Jody put it on.

"What are we cooking?" she said.

"*Bream alla diavola.*"

"What's that? Italian?"

"Yeah. Bugger we don't have any bread to serve with it."

For her entire adult life Jody had only cooked for one, so the quantities for this recipe were staggering. Tin after tin emptied into the pots until she lost count. Her fingers throbbed from cranking the can opener. The sauce had to cook for hours, needing to be stirred, stirred, stirred with giant wooden paddles. Jody panted and sweated. Lorraine didn't seem affected.

"Okay, get the fish from the pantry," the old woman said at last. "Here's a torch."

The pantry was at the rear of the kitchen. Jody didn't remember it. She opened the door. Pitch-black. The room smelled of ammonia and brine, an odour unpleasantly reminiscent of piss. She crossed the threshold and switched on the torch. Buckets of dead bream covered the floor. Yet she couldn't remember putting the buckets in here. Briefly, she felt afraid but she had consumed a lot of wine yesterday; memory blanks weren't so unusual. *Take courage.* She stepped into the room. The air felt expansive, cavernous. When the torch couldn't find the back wall, Jody decided to focus her attention on the nearest bucket.

She called out, "Don't you need to store fish below a certain temperature?"

"In an ideal world, sure. But sweetie, we're living in this one."

The buckets pulled at Jody's shoulders. The metal handles cut into her fingers. She poured one bucket after the other into the steel pots. Lorraine turned up the gas beneath the stove burners until it sounded like the hissing of a thousand snakes. The red sauce farted and blerped. At last, the kitchen warmed up and began to smell savoury, spicy, spirited.

49

"These fingerlings take no time at all," Lorraine said, churning a paddle. "Okay, I'm nearly ready to serve. Get the bowls from the shelves back there."

Jody didn't remember seeing the shelves yesterday, but obeyed.

Lorraine used a ladle to transfer the stew. "Chop chop. Don't keep customers waiting."

Jody picked up two bowls and left the kitchen. The sight in the dining room surprised her. She stalled for a moment, unable to move. Dozens of people were huddled silently by the pub's entrance as if they had come through the door together and collectively lost their nerve.

"Pull your bloody finger out, sweetie," came Lorraine's voice. "Get a move on."

And, so it went: Jody putting bowls of stew on the tables, customers seating themselves and eating without uttering a word, Lorraine ladling more stew into a never-ending supply of bowls that Jody kept fetching from the shelves. The monotony lulled Jody into an empty, hypnagogic state. She had the vague idea that she would ferry these bowls for ever and ever.

The arrival of Angelo and Layla startled her from her stupor.

"Stop!" Layla commanded.

Everybody did. A frozen tableau.

"Stop eating the food!" Layla continued.

"It's come from the devil himself!" Angelo added.

"Hang on a goddamned minute," Jody said. "I helped cook this stew—non-stop over the last couple of days, in fact—and the devil had nothing to do with it."

The kitchen door banged open. Lorraine ran into the dining room brandishing a paddle that dripped blood-red sauce, her yellow eyes flashing and wild. Customers gasped and quailed.

"You two can piss right off!" the old woman shrieked as she swung the paddle. "Get out!"

Layla and Angelo clutched at each other's gnarled hands and scuttled from the Royal Hotel. Lorraine sniffed imperiously, ran the back of her wrist beneath her nose, then cast her stern gaze around the dining room. The customers bent their heads and began eating again.

"What the hell was that about?" Jody said.

"Nothing. Forget it. Just a couple of crackpots. Plain and simple. When our religious cult left town, those two stayed behind. Didn't I tell you that?"

"No. You told me they were scientists."

"Did I? Well, in any case, scientists can be crazy too. Angelo and Layla: perfect case in point. All right, let's get on with it."

4

When lunch service ended, they spent hours washing up, followed by hours cooking the next batch of *bream alla diavola* for the dinner service, and then hours serving the same customers who had dutifully, silently, returned for more. Lorraine stayed in the kitchen while Jody ferried the bowls to the tables. Someone had illuminated the dining room with scores of candles but Jody decided not to be surprised or even curious about that. Hidden draughts tugged at the yellow flames. The shadows of the townsfolk bobbed, twisted and writhed against the walls and ceiling. It felt as if Jody were underwater amidst the swaying arms of seaweed. She had to close her eyes occasionally to keep balance.

After dinner service, only three steaming bowls remained in the kitchen. Amazing. How Lorraine had portioned that vast quantity of stew so precisely, down to the last gram, Jody had no idea. And there was wine, of course. Always plenty of wine.

"Grab a spoon," Lorraine said.

But the quantities didn't make sense. The number of fish out there on the street, why, there had been *thousands*, enough to feed an army, and yet—

"Sweetie? Now. While it's hot."

The old woman was eating the stew with gusto. Jody took a cautious taste. Delicious; unctuous and spicy. Around a mouthful, she said, "I'm guessing the other bowl is for your husband. Will I ever meet Bruce?"

Lorraine cocked her bony head and rolled her yellow eyes as if considering. "Why yes, I'd say so. Not tomorrow, not the next day, but the day after that."

"Which would make it…Sunday?"

"Sunday. Yes, that sounds about right."

"Did Bruce light all those candles?" Jody said, despite herself.

"Have a pat on the back. You did a terrific job today. You're the perfect employee."

"Wow, really? Thank you," Jody said, and felt the unfamiliar warmth of pride. She went to take another mouthful of stew and stopped. "Uh oh. Nobody paid."

"Don't worry about it."

"I'm telling you, nobody paid for lunch or dinner, no cash or credit."

"Relax. Balancing the books isn't your concern."

They spent hours washing up. Didn't Lorraine ever tire? At least, it felt like hours, but—exhausted, hands bleeding—Jody couldn't be sure.

That night, sleep wouldn't come.

She got up and opened the curtains to a glimmering dawn. The night had somehow passed her by. Out the bedroom window, she saw birds.

Hundreds of little birds carpeted the street. No, thousands. With black plumage and a white band of feathers at the rump, flapping and wriggling and struggling in the mud. *Huh,* Jody thought. *Huh.* She dressed, went out on the veranda. The street glimmered with feathers. Yet the flock extended only fifteen metres or so in either direction, as if disgorged from a dump truck parked directly outside the Royal Hotel. Déjà vu. Wait, was it?

Motion in the tail of her eye.

Jody spun about, expecting the cat-footed Lorraine, but it was the druggy trio from the rotunda, peering at her from around the corner of the Royal Hotel. They ducked out of sight. Jody took after them. As soon as they saw her approaching, the trio fled. Their coats fanned out behind them like black, glossy wings and their breaths plumed in the frigid air like clouds, and Jody was soaring through the sky pursuing giant crows.

She caught up with them in the rotunda. For half a minute, she had to lean over, gasping, for she hadn't sprinted in a long time. The druggies watched her casually, beer stubbies and lit cigarettes in hand, giving the impression that they had been sitting here all along, which would mean Jody had been chasing phantoms.

"I'm Jody Jones," she said. "I'm a journalist staying at the hotel."

"We know," the woman said. "We've met."

Had they? Jody couldn't recall. She said, "Why did you run from me just now?"

One of the men, the taller one, said, "We've been sitting here all along."

The trio smiled kindly, gently, as if Jody were a child to be coddled.

"Did you steal and burn my car?"

The other man, the shorter one, said, "Why would we do that?"

Jody couldn't think of an answer. While she thought it over, a lump formed in her throat.

"Have a beer," the woman said.

The stubby pressed into Jody's hand was ice-cold, the glass bottle sweating. She drank. Hot tears slipped down her cheeks.

"Get out of Barralang," the tall man said.

"Now, while you still can," the short man said.

"*If* you still can," the woman said.

"Don't get stuck like us," the tall man said.

"What about the flood?"

"What flood?" the short man said.

Jody decided to stay calm. *These druggies wouldn't know about the flood,* she thought, *because this rotunda is the extent of their world.* But they would know about Barralang.

"Tell me about Lorraine's husband: Bruce," she said.

The trio exchanged quick, furtive glances.

"He's a blank slate," the woman said.

"Blank? Are you talking in code?"

The druggies looked at each other again, lips compressed. *Aha,* Jody thought. *A lead.* Her Walkley Award-winning story with its opening line — *Barralang is a place where hope comes to die* — came floating to the surface in sharp focus.

"Because," she continued, "it sounds like you're trying to tell me that Bruce is Mr Blank, the town's mystery buyer. Am I right? Look, if you want to remain anonymous, I won't mention you in my article. Just give me some insight."

They kept regarding each other in a taut, silent communion that made Jody uneasy.

A car engine sounded. Jody turned. The station wagon pulled up and the driver's side window rolled down. Lorraine's nose looked sharp in the dawn's milky light.

"Hop in, sweetie," Lorraine said. "Now, while you still can."

Jody's glance to the druggies was apologetic but they were angling their faces the other way and didn't see. Chastened, she left the stubby on a railing and climbed into the car.

"What did they tell you?" Lorraine said, driving towards the hotel.

"Nothing that made much sense."

"Good girl. Don't listen to the ravings of druggies."

"Or religious crackpots."

"Yeah? Like who?"

Jody bit her lip. "Angelo and Layla. You told me they belonged to the cult, remember?"

Lorraine took one hand off the steering wheel and pointed up the road at the sea of black feathers. "On the menu tomorrow: *fowl alla diavola*."

Oh, shit no. More gathering, prepping, cooking, serving, cleaning…

"For God's sake," Jody groaned. "I thought the hotel served food only on Thursdays."

"Desperate times." Lorraine's vigorous nodding wobbled the wattle of loose skin on her neck. "And these are desperate times."

The fallen birds were of one breed: the fork-tailed swift. Jody thought about the fork-tailed bream and decided against making a connection.

The day went on and on: buckets, buckets, buckets.

The night went on and on: sweat, dreams, sweat.

The next morning: plucking, gutting, deboning, chopping. Tomatoes. Kalamata olives. Garlic. Dijon mustard. Sugar. Chilli flakes. Vinegar. Brandy. Wine. Somehow, more onions.

Lunch service.

Angelo and Layla: *Stop eating the food! It's come from the devil*

himself! Jody: *Hang on a goddamned minute. I helped cook this stew —
non-stop over the last couple of days, in fact — and the devil had nothing
to do with it.* Lorraine: *You two can piss right off! Get out!*

Washing up. Cooking and dinner service. Candles.

Over their bowls of bird stew in the kitchen, Lorraine said,
"How do you like the meal?"

"Help me. I'm stuck in a loop. The same things keep happening
over and over."

Lorraine sighed, put down her spoon, propped her head on
one set of bony knuckles and stared at Jody for a long time. The
gaze seemed maternal at first, concerned and sympathetic, and
Jody felt like crying. And then the vulturine face hardened and
the eyelids began to slit. The yellow irises shone. Jody no longer
felt like crying.

"Don't you know where you are?" the old woman said, the
hint of an amused, mocking smile touching her mouth. "Don't
you know what's happened to you?"

"No. I'm going crazy. Or have I gone crazy already? I can't
make sense of it. Is any of this real? Oh, God. Am I dead somehow?
In purgatory?"

Tut-tutting, Lorraine waved a dismissive hand and picked up
the spoon. "Quit your melodrama. I can't abide histrionics."

After washing up, Jody went upstairs and drank wine from the
bottle until the room spun. Then she fell into bed. The firmament
rolled above, grinding and grating, stars shining brittle. If she
dreamed, she couldn't recall.

The next morning, her heart pounded as she reached for the
curtains. Please, she thought. *Oh, please.* She opened the curtains.
Out the bedroom window, she saw blobs.

Red blobs.

Hundreds of little red blobs carpeting the street.

Mechanically, Jody dressed. Her shoes were mouldy. She went
out onto the veranda. The lame dog, the same that had walked in
front of her car on day one, was wolfing down the blobs at speed,
gulping and retching, gulping and retching. Jody squatted on the
last step and leaned in close to the mud, scrutinising. The blobs
appeared to be meat.

Chunks of red meat.

Feeling Lorraine's presence, Jody said, "Don't tell me this was caused by a waterspout."

"No, by a flock of pelicans." The old woman descended the steps. "When pelicans get a fright, they drop the fish from their beaks. To lighten the load and facilitate their escape."

Jody said, "This isn't fish."

"All right then. It's rabbit. A flock of eagles dropped its kill of rabbit."

"Eagles? Wow. A *flock* of wedge-tailed eagles? Are you serious?"

"I don't appreciate your tone," Lorraine said.

"And the eagles skinned, gutted, deboned and diced the rabbits? Is that what you're trying to tell me? *Is* it?"

The dog kept eating. The meat slapped, smacked and slopped inside its wet mouth, the only sound in the street. Jody looked up. The intensity of the bright blue sky lanced her eyes and pounded through her head. She looked down again, put a shaking hand to her brow.

"I suppose you want me to bring the buckets," she said.

"Waste not, want not."

"How do you know what kind of meat this is? If it's even edible?"

Lorraine crossed her arms. "Meat is meat."

"You can't serve this up to people. You just can't."

"For a city slicker, you've got a lot of attitude about slaughtered animals all of a sudden."

"How do you know it's from slaughtered animals? We ought to call the police."

"About what? Piffle. Go on back to the kitchen. Get the buckets." Lorraine spat into the mud. "Just last night, you told me you'd gone nuts. Remember?"

The lame dog kept lapping and chewing.

Jody's head spun and ached. "Where am I?" she whispered. "In hell? Please tell me."

"In Barralang. Where hope comes to die."

Jody stiffened. "How did you...? Did I—?"

"Get the buckets," Lorraine said, stomping up the steps. "Or I'll charge room and board."

"But wait—"

"Room and board!" the old woman snarled, and went inside.

Jody crumpled, put her head in her hands and wept fiercely, wholeheartedly, hysterically, sobbing and howling and keening. The ravenous dog paid no attention. After a while, Jody ran out of tears. She opened her eyes. The sunshine spangled on her wet lashes, blinding her with points of light. At her feet, in the mud amidst the spatter of meat, something gleamed. A flare of burnished gold. She leaned over. Blinked.

Felt her heart stop.

A cross.

It was a cross on a chain.

She jumped up and broke into a sprint—Layla had warned her to get out of Barralang—running down the dead centre of the road, heading back from whence she had come, towards Melbourne and the life she had left behind and thrown away. Past the hollow-eyed shops. Past the petite, narrow church in its rubbish-strewn lot, its front doors chained shut. Gasping. The air was cold. Each breath drew needles into her lungs.

Movement at the rotunda. The trio stood up to look at her, beer stubbies and lit cigarettes in hand. As Jody raced by, they shook their heads with abject pity in their eyes.

If she wasn't dead, there was still a chance to get out of here.

Perhaps the floodwaters had receded by now. Yes, perhaps. And if not, Jody would swim for it until she reached solid ground. Then she would trudge the highway and thumb for a lift.

She reached the dogleg where the road dipped into a brown lake. In the distance, the two farmhouses that marked the outskirts of town were submerged to their rooflines, just as she remembered. She stopped, catching her breath, trying to assess how far she would have to freestyle, rolling her shoulders to warm them. Had she ever swum so far? No, not ever.

As she watched, the brown lake rose. The two roofs disappeared underwater.

Blerp.

Her chin trembled, hands shook, and her mind dropped away and went blank.

"Return to the hotel," said Lorraine's voice at her ear.

Pell-mell, Jody took off running again. The edge of the brown lake didn't get any closer.

"It's Sunday," Lorraine continued. "I thought you wanted to meet Bruce."

"No," Jody gasped. "I want to go home."

"Here he comes. You'd better get off the road, sweetie. You'd better look out."

The car's radiator grill loomed, high and wide. Jody squeezed her eyes shut.

When nothing happened, she opened her eyes again.

She was sitting on the steps of the Royal Hotel. Meat-filled buckets lined the footpath. She looked near her feet, expecting a shine of gold, but it wasn't there. What had she expected to see? Déjà vu… The image flitted too quickly across her mind's eye and was lost.

Lorraine, standing on the veranda, pointed. "Here he comes."

The car sailing into town was big, sleek, dark grey with a long bonnet. A lame dog stood indifferently in the car's way. The dog began to hunch and work its jaws as if choking.

"You'd better get off the road, sweetie," Lorraine called to it. "You'd better look out."

There was an ornament on the car bonnet: a pair of disembodied wings. Jody imagined birds—their wings flapping and wriggling and struggling in mud—and knew that she was remembering a dream. She looked about. Every resident of Barralang waited on the street. Silent. Respectful. Or was it voiceless? Cowed? The car stopped outside the hotel. The dog had disappeared somewhere. Jody felt afraid.

Lorraine said, "Stand up, sweetie. Time to greet Mr Blank."

Jody stood.

The car door swung open.

Sunshine fell upon the door handle and window frame, both made of chrome polished to a high sheen. The reflected light dazzled Jody so that she couldn't see.

Molly, Dearest Molly

The hospital room features half-hearted attempts at cosiness—a vase of jonquils, wool flatweave rug, throw cushions—but the antiseptic smell is strong, and the drop ceiling has fluorescent batten lights. Katrina lies back on the couch. Dr Wolfe drapes her with a blanket. The other doctor, someone who is there purely to record what will happen, sits against the far wall with a smile plastered across her old, wrinkled face. She seems apprehensive. This other doctor is called Smythe or Smith if Katrina remembers correctly. Perhaps Brown? Whatever.

Katrina, Jack, Molly.

"Are you comfortable?" Dr Wolfe says. His ruddy face blooms with either rosacea or the broken capillaries of long-term alcoholism. "We're ready to start. Is that all right with you?"

Katrina nods. Her doffed slippers are on the floor beneath the couch. As per the clinic guidelines, she's wearing tracksuit pants, t-shirt, windcheater, bed socks. Ordinarily, she would be wearing a two-piece skirt suit and heels. She is a real estate agent. Part-time, these days. And no longer good at her job. Her boss keeps her on out of pity. In Katrina's other life, the life before the accident, she had worn business apparel whenever she left the house, even to visit the supermarket. However, she is a different person now. Unrecognisable to herself. Lying here in this hospital room, wearing tracksuit pants and bed socks in front of virtual strangers…well, it's almost enough to bring her to tears.

Almost.

Because ultimately, whether this experimental treatment works or not doesn't matter. Five years' worth of nightmares, flashbacks, panic attacks, grief, fear, guilt, agoraphobia and insomnia have at last pushed her into a kind of shell-shocked state of mind. In fact, it was Katrina's apathy that had fast-tracked her into this clinical trial. Her psychiatrist made calls, pulled strings, filled out paperwork. His desperation to save her made Katrina feel amused, interested, curious. After his herculean efforts, it would have seemed ungrateful to refuse.

"There might be adverse reactions," her psychiatrist warned. "Fatigue, memory loss, depression, verbal deficits, cognitive problems. Nobody can predict how an individual patient will respond. Even the best psychotherapist in the world is unable to cherry-pick which memories or emotions will surface, or dictate how the patient will react to them."

"What's the worst that could happen?"

"A psychotic break."

Katrina chuckled. "You're not a very good salesman, are you?"

"On the other hand, you might be cured. The efficacy rate is quite good; somewhere between fifty to seventy percent, depending on the study."

"Knowing my luck, I'll be in the thirty to fifty percent who doesn't get better."

"Okay, sure. That's a possibility. Treating PTSD with MDMA-assisted psychotherapy is a new field and there's not a lot of data. But I'm sorry to say we've hit a dead end. I'm afraid we don't have many options left." He looked young for a shrink—in his late-thirties, like Katrina—and she pondered if his failure to help her in any meaningful way had contributed to those worry lines about his eyes, those deep grooves alongside his mouth. He continued, "You should take part in this trial. Of course, the decision is totally yours."

"I don't much care either way," Katrina said kindly, patting her psychiatrist's hand.

Katrina, Jack, Molly.

Dr Wolfe adjusts the blanket, tucks it around her chin. The blanket is cashmere and the earthy, lemon-fresh scent reminds

Katrina of her grandmother.

Grandma Molly liked to knit using cashmere. Scarves, cardigans, wraps.

Nothing beats goat's wool for softness, Kat.

Before Grandma Molly stepped in to do her best, Katrina's mother—a heroin addict—had repeatedly tried to dump baby Katrina into foster care. According to the psychiatrist, this trauma of motherly indifference had caused a "primal wound", which is why Katrina can't get past the deaths of her husband and daughter. Loss hits Katrina *too heavily*. If she'd had a loving mother, according to psychological theory, Katrina would have bounced back by now.

Right?

Consider that Katrina had named her daughter after Grandma Molly. According to both the psychiatrist and Dr Wolfe the psychotherapist, this was proof enough of Katrina's emotional hobbling. Katrina has PTSD not because her husband and daughter drowned, no, but because she has a "primal wound". Sure, the primal wound might be a *factor* in her inability to recover, but…whatever. Katrina is tired of arguing the point. So what?

And suddenly, she wonders—it's a dark, troubling, anxious thought—if Dr Wolfe has chosen a cashmere blanket on purpose. To trigger childhood memories. Katrina feels tricked. Unsafe. But it's too late. She's taken the medication. It would be in her bloodstream already; must be creeping and spreading throughout her brain like a low-lying fog. Like mustard gas.

"How are you feeling?" Dr Wolfe says. His eyes are full of thread veins. Just looking at them makes her own eyes water.

"No different," she says.

"That's to be expected. It needs an hour or so to take effect."

Katrina's chest feels tight. Good Lord, she has taken *ecstasy*. After a lifetime of nothing harder than coffee. (Well, she *was* the unloved, abandoned child of a drug addict—would anyone be surprised at her temperance?) As per the trial guidelines, Katrina received 120 milligrams of MDMA, produced in a laboratory, which meant it was *nothing* like the ecstasy tabs for sale at clubs or raves. The dose she swallowed with a glass of water happened to be pure, not cut with adulterants like methamphetamine, para-methoxyamphetamine, synthetic cathinones, ketamines or dextromethorphan. Katrina had done her homework. Or rather, her psychiatrist had; sitting next to her with print-outs, explaining, warning, cajoling, while Katrina watched his animated face with what felt like a bored sense of detachment. To use a favourite saying of Jack's: she didn't have a dog in this fight.

Katrina, Jack, Molly.

"It's pretty ironic," she says.

"Meaning?" Dr Wolfe is distracted, reading a file. *Her* file, presumably. What else?

"My daughter's name was Molly," she says.

"Oh, yes?"

"And I've taken MDMA."

Frowning as if puzzled, Dr Wolfe closes the file. "I don't understand the irony."

"Because 'molly' is the drug's street name."

Dr Wolfe works his jaw, raises his furry eyebrows, tries to smile and tamps it down as if he doesn't know whether a smile would be appropriate. "I see. Aha. Yes."

"What a coincidence!" pipes up the other doctor, the old woman perhaps named Brown.

Dr Wolfe shoots Brown a look. The old woman bows her head, focuses on her clipboard.

How odd that both of them aren't familiar with the slang terms for MDMA. You would assume that such doctors must know everything about the trial drug, inside and out. That they would be *experts*. Perhaps Katrina's participation is a mistake. If only her psychiatrist were here. He's never been of much benefit, true, yet he'd be a comforting presence.

"The coincidence is actually why I signed up for this trial," Katrina says, smacking her lips, her mouth drying out. "Concurrence."

"What?" Dr Wolfe says, checking his watch, leaning over her, looming.

"Fortuity."

"And how are you feeling now?"

"Fine. Is it even working?" Katrina wipes at her clammy forehead. "I'm getting a bit hot. Can we lose the blanket? I need to take off my socks."

"Of course. What else would you like to do? Would you like to talk to me?"

Katrina feels gracious. "Sure. I can talk to you. About what?"

"Let's start with the day Jack picked up Molly from childcare and didn't come home."

"Oh, yes," Katrina says. "What would you like to know?"

"Tell me what happened once you realised Jack and Molly were late."

Katrina takes off her socks, drops them to the floor, wriggles her toes. Her skin feels sheened in a light film of sweat, which is relaxing rather than unpleasant, as if she were lounging by a hearth and listening to the crackling hiss of roasting applewood and oak. However, beneath her skin, she feels cold. It is a disconcerting dichotomy.

"My body temperature feels weird," she mutters.

"Back to Jack and Molly. Can you remember what time you started to worry about them?"

She blinks. There's the kitchen in technicolour. "As soon as I got home. Five-eighteen on the microwave clock. The real estate agency where I work isn't far from our house. Jack is a schoolteacher and usually gets home with Molly by four-thirty. I blame the rain. It's been raining non-stop for a couple of days, and today, it's been absolutely *pelting*. And you know how people drive in the rain! As if they've never driven a car before in their lives. Also, you've got people who normally travel to work on public transport or a bicycle waking up and saying, 'Oh stuff it, I'll *drive* in this rotten weather', and all the roads get really *busy—*"

Surprised, Katrina stops, realising that she's running at the mouth. These days, she doesn't talk much. Her chattiness must be the MDMA. For a moment, she feels anxious. Then she recalls her words, goes over them, assesses them, decides that she is not speaking out of character and is still in control of herself. She simply feels more at ease. More gregarious.

Dr Wolfe says, "You decided they were stuck in traffic?"

"Yes."

"Until when?"

She closes her eyes. Checks the microwave clock. "Five-forty-one."

"What do you do at five-forty-one?"

"Get my phone, call him. It keeps going to voicemail. The panic hits me at about six. Then I ring *everybody*. Jack's school, the childcare centre, family, friends, hospitals. Nobody knows where they are. He picked her up at normal time and nobody knows where they are."

Katrina looks around the kitchen at her best friends, Louis and Tracy. Despite their words of reassurance, she can see the fear and uncertainty in their eyes. The rain hammers so hard on the roof they have to shout to be heard. It's a tumult out there, a maelstrom. Katrina imagines Jack and Molly subsumed by this maelstrom. As it turns out, she's right.

She is right.

Behind the desk, the uniformed police officer looking up is a woman with long, wild and curly blonde hair, reminding Katrina of a sheep, and eyebrows that appear drawn with a pencil. Katrina's clothes are wet from the run through the police station's car park. The rain is too heavy. It's like the whole of Melbourne is underwater.

Underwater, underwater...

"And then what happened?"

Katrina's gaze keeps returning to the policewoman's woolly hair.

"What happened after the filing of the Missing Persons report?"

A night of crying. Sobbing. Screaming. Begging. Stabs of adrenaline and terror so intense that Katrina shakes as if electrified. Fitful scraps of exhausted sleep. Louis has stayed overnight. Dear Louis. Curled next to her on the bed, holding and stroking her, shushing her. Tears puff her eyelids. Snot clots her nostrils. Her face is waterlogged. Rain pummels the rooftiles and thunder booms all night, all morning. The rain is to blame.

Katrina, Jack, Molly.

"Katrina? Open your eyes."

She obeys. Sees a balding man with ruddy cheeks that suggest either rosacea or alcoholism... Oh, it's Dr Wolfe. Katrina gazes around the hospital room. Everything is bright and clear, vivid in brilliant 4K, with a depth that is *more* than three-dimensional. But isn't *time* the fourth dimension? Yes. Katrina understands that she must be off her face. Which feels pretty good, actually. Maybe her delinquent bitch of a mother was onto something. Swapping a cold, black-and-white reality for a warm version that's gloriously resplendent is a fine trade indeed. But at what cost?

The cost of abandoning your baby.

But Katrina doesn't *want* to abandon her baby. Therein lies yet another irony. Hang on... Would grammatical pedants consider the comparison as irony or something else? Perhaps coincidence? She anxiously ponders this critical quandary for hours—

Wait!

The jonquils in the vase are the truest meaning of the colour yellow that she has ever seen. Oh God. The scales drop from her eyes. She experiences the world as it truly exists. A buzz of fizzing energy surges along her every nerve and effervesces throughout her brain. For the first time in a long time—for the first time *ever*, in fact—she feels utterly and spectacularly *alive*. It takes her breath. Nothing has come close to this lucidity of perfect *livingness*.

"Tell me about Jack and Molly. When you found out what happened to them."

A swoon as her eyes close. A swooping sensation of tilting and sliding and spinning.

The police officers are young and brawny, square-jawed, similar as if kin. They each grab an elbow and lift her from the floor, transport her to the nearest couch. *No, not this one*, she wants to say, because this couch is Jack's. He likes to face the TV and prop his feet on the coffee table. Katrina's couch is the one on the right-angle, parallel to the windows, so that she can lie full-length. They have put her on Jack's couch. She smells him in the fabric.

The first officer says, "We pulled the car out of the river. There was lots of water on the bridge yesterday and the tyres must have lost traction. Is there someone we can call for you?"

The second officer says, "The bodies need identifying. Perhaps there's a relative or friend who might be willing on your behalf?"

Katrina rallies. "Why can't I see them?"

The twin cops exchange glances. One or the other says, "That wouldn't be a good idea."

Rain is still coming down, smashing at the roof, bending the trees. The rain is to blame. Waterlogged. After so much time underwater, Jack and Molly are waterlogged. Swollen up and blue-grey. Her father-in-law tells her so. The father-in-law who has never warmed to her, a builder who considers that real estate agents are crooks, volunteered to identify the bodies at the Coroner's Court. Katrina wanted to be grateful but why would he tell her *swollen up* and *blue-grey*? Ever since, her thoughts are forever and ever filled with *swollen up* and *blue-grey*. She can be eating lunch, running a load of laundry, driving, showering, taking a phone call at work, and then it's *swollen up* and *blue-grey*—

"Katrina?"

She opens her eyes. The drop ceiling has fluorescent batten lights. The antiseptic odour reminds her she's at the hospital, going through her first session in the MDMA trial.

Embarrassed, trying to laugh, she says, "Sorry, Dr Wolfe. Am I blathering? I don't mean to be. Somehow, I can't stop talking. I keep dreaming, I think. It's like I'm back there."

"That's good, Katrina. Now let's try to experience those memories a little differently."

"Okay."

"Can you feel the blanket?"

She strokes the soft cashmere. "Yes."

"Do you feel better?"

"Yes," she murmurs.

Her hands conjure Grandma Molly. Katrina is sitting on a chair in front of the cathode-ray TV. Grandma stands behind her to comb Katrina's hair, which is still wet from the bath. It's after dinner. They are watching Grandma's favourite game show.

Grandma likes to shout answers before the contestants hit their buzzers, even when her answers are wrong. The ancient space heater puffs. Katrina is relaxed and receptive, warm and loved.

"Can you hear me?"

Katrina looks from the fluorescent light in the ceiling to Dr Wolfe's face. "Yes," she says.

"I want you to imagine something. The scenario we talked about earlier."

"Okay."

"That instead of imagining your husband and daughter bloated and discoloured in the river, you see them as swimming."

"Swimming?"

"Like fish. Beautiful, tropical fish. Colourful. Composed. Tranquil. Can you see them, Katrina? They're swimming together and feeling happy. Slipping through the water."

She closes her eyes. Gasps. *What is happening here?* The windcheater, t-shirt, tracksuit pants, underwear... She experiences the texture of the materials so clearly that the clothes feel almost sensual—no, *sexual*—against her skin. Her vulva becomes engorged and sensitive, twitching in repeated tics as if she might be ready to come. She considers putting a hand down her pants to rub herself since she's alone in bed. Jack is clattering about in the kitchen, most likely frying a couple of eggs. Molly is still asleep. The kettle is heating.

"Can you see Jack and Molly swimming happily?"

Startled, Katrina opens her eyes.

There is Dr Wolfe and the other doctor called Smith or Brown, the vase of jonquils, fluorescent lights, stink of antiseptic, all of it amplified and too much, painful, like gazing into the sun. She doesn't like this drug. Doesn't like slipping in and out of the past. A moment of clarity tells her this session will take *hours*. Oh God. Maybe if she focuses, concentrates, steels herself, she can overcome the effects of MDMA and stoically *resist*.

"They're swimming, Katrina. Two beautiful, tropical fish. Swimming away. Very calm."

She remembers agreeing to this ridiculous imagery at the interview, agreeing to let go of her husband and daughter. But privately?

No. She wants them back. It's been five long, awful, terrible years and if she can't have them back, she doesn't want to live anymore. It's that simple, really. So obvious and simple, she has kept the plan to herself.

"Fish," Dr Wolfe murmurs. "Happy little fish."

Katrina squeezes her eyes shut. Her heart pounds. She wants to be reunited with Jack and Molly. She understands that she's blitzed on MDMA, that what will happen next can only be a dream. Good enough, though, if that's all she can get. Dreams often feel real, don't they? She focuses. Looks through the river water. Locates the car. Swims towards it. The driver's window is open. There's Jack. He's smiling at her, ruefully, with the "I screwed up" expression that he uses for burnt toast or a forgotten grocery item. In the back seat, Molly is waving and giggling.

I want both of you back with me.

Katrina reaches into the open window. The river water is cold and murky, full of disturbed sediment. She grabs Jack. Then Molly. Pulls them out. They're moving towards her embrace but slowly, ever so narrowly, becoming distorted and far away, breaking up through the turning wheel of a kaleidoscope. The reunion stutters and weaves down this weird pipe and as much as Katrina concentrates, the pipe—delicate as spun sugar—breaks.

It feels like falling.

She lands.

Katrina is alone on a couch in this hospital room beneath a cashmere blanket. She clenches her fists. For a moment, she feels like crying. Until she gets distracted by her erection. It feels bothersome. A weight along the midline of her abdomen. She must have a full bladder. But why is her penis so *heavy*? It's like a sandbag. Reaching under the blanket, Katrina is alarmed by her cock's girth, chunky as a pork tenderloin.

God, her cock is abnormally *swollen up*.

She opens her eyes into the darkness of her bedroom. The curtains block out the first light of dawn. Next to her, Jack is snoring on the mattress, oblivious to her distress. Frightened, she explores the head of her giant penis. There are soft little nubs growing out of it.

Warts? Worms? She feels breathless. What the hell are these cold, rubbery protuberances? She turns on the bedside light. Jack, a hump under bedclothes, keeps snoring like a braying donkey. In dread, Katrina pushes down the sheet. On her belly lies the monstrous, swollen-up cock. The head has five blue-grey nubs growing out of it like mushrooms.

Horrified, she touches the nubs. They look like boneless fingers. Boneless little baby fingers. She bends them over and sees the blackened nails. *Oh God.* The fingers wiggle and reach for her. Galvanised, the cock bobs frantically against her stomach as if coming alive. She starts screaming, trying to pull away, but how can she pull away from her own penis?

"Katrina!"

Her body shakes and bucks.

"Katrina!" Dr Wolfe shouts.

She sees the doctor's face, closes her mouth to stop shrieking. Takes a deep, shuddering gasp. And panting, looks about the room to orientate herself and pin herself down. The room appears normal. Cathedral ceiling, bay windows, the dense pine forest beyond. The chandelier has a few broken bulbs, probably from the storm. A torrent streams down the window frames to flood the carpet. Rooftiles must be broken. She remembers being on the third floor of a ten-floor hospital, but the rain comes through anyway in cataracts. What an absolute pummelling of rain, muddy river water, tears. Meanwhile, Jack and Molly pulse blue and grey in time with Katrina's heartbeat.

"Katrina," Dr Wolfe says. "Can you hear me?"

"Yes, I can hear you."

"Then please sit up."

She sits up. A vase of jonquils, wool flatweave rug, a few throw cushions.

Is she finally awake? Christ. Katrina pushes off the cashmere blanket. Her face runs with sweat. She wriggles her slick toes. The light from the window burns orange as if sunset is approaching. This session must have lasted all day and be at its end. Which means the MDMA has worn off. Tentatively, she takes stock of herself. Yes, she feels exhausted, wrenched, *husked*, but that's to be expected after such an intense experience. At least she feels like herself again. She smells antiseptic. Registers a drop ceiling. Pulls up the legs of her tracksuit pants to cool her steaming legs.

"Holy Jesus," weeps the old doctor named Smythe, Smith or Brown, while her teeth—most likely dentures—click and clack. "Oh, holy Jesus."

"Do you hear me?" Dr Wolfe says. "Katrina. Are you all right?"

There are a great many people gazing down, dressed in scrubs like doctors and nurses. Their serious faces are strange to her. Under a starched white sheet, Katrina lies in a bed with side rails. The door is closed. Machines beep. She must be safe in a recovery room.

"Yes, I'm all right." Katrina laughs weakly. "Damn, that was a rough trip."

The old doctor wails and moans. "What now? What are we going to do with her?"

Dr Wolfe says, "Katrina, can you understand me?"

"Yes. Why wouldn't I?"

"I'm sorry this wasn't...easier on you."

"Easier? Oh no, I'd have gone through *anything*, you name it." Katrina clutches at her bloated cock, thumbs the cool and pliable baby fingers that reach and grasp. "I'm just glad I've got my family back."

Entombed

Oh God, they had buried him alive.

Within the first moment of coming awake, Emil knew he was in the ground. The blackness, the silence, the fecund, ripe and familiar smell of turned earth could mean nothing else. A jolt of panic thrashed him. His limbs struck the wooden sides of the coffin and his forehead banged against the lid. For a time, Emil did nothing but scream, filling his lungs and emptying them, again and again, until he stripped his throat raw and tasted blood.

Panting, he lay back, thinking. Trying to think.

He had been ill. Desperately ill. He could remember that much. The pain and fever still raged in him. Perspiration soaked his tunic and trousers. What had happened in his final hours of consciousness? He must have been abed, surely, yet his memory failed him, flitting in nonsensical remnants as if from a dream: sitting at the table with his wife, Agnes; a strident kind of chaos like a thunderstorm; dogs scampering and scattering from the village…

So, he had been ill. What then?

The women must have tried, and failed, to cure him with their leeks and healing herbs.

He had fallen into a deep sleep, the kind that didn't show his breath against a mirror.

The villagers had performed the rituals and buried him.

The rituals.

Emil scrabbled his callused hands about the floor of the coffin, groping for his axe, his scythe. They weren't there. The villagers had buried him without belongings. His illness, whatever it was, must have mimicked leprosy; the villagers would have wasted no time. But how would be escape without axe or scythe?

By God, he would use his hands.

They were work-toughened, weren't they? Gnarled and knotted like the bark and boughs of red tingle trees from years of working the earth, steering oxen. The coffin lid sat close. No room to swing fists. He placed his palms against the lid and pushed, pushed, while the veins popped in his face. Pushed while his molars cracked.

The iron nails squeaked and gave.

Emil took a breath of fetid air and pushed again, his joints creaking, popping, breaking.

The lid snapped in two. A shower of dirt collapsed onto him.

Could he dig through six or more feet before suffocation?

Twisting around, coughing and choking, Emil got his hands and knees onto the floor. He pressed his upper back against oak and earth. The weight of the world lay upon his old shoulders, yes, but his shoulders were broad and used to hard labour. Pushing, pushing, Emil got his toes under him, doubling himself into an awkward squat. Putting his hands atop his head, squeezing his palms together as if in prayer, he began to stand up, inch by inch. Muscles burning and shuddering, he parted the soil, his clasped hands forming the pointed share of a plough. His lungs needed air.

Craved air.

His every breath sucked in dirt.

No, he would not make it. *Could* not make it.

A breeze wafted over his fingertips. Emil strained to reach his full height. Desperate, cleaving up and up, his arms burst free. Lungs exploding, he struggled, kicked, shoved until air broke over his face at last. He sucked in breath after breath. Sweet, so sweet, even sweeter than the first crop of baby peas. And he wept.

Nearby, a woman shrieked.

And who could blame her? He had appeared like a corpse, a *draugr*, rising from the grave. Emil wiped dirt from his stinging eyes.

It was evening, the autumn sky painted orange and yellow. The fenced grounds of the church lay some yards distant. God, they had buried him in unhallowed ground. Why? He had been a good Christian, hadn't he? An even-tempered husband, a disciplinarian to his children, a doter on his grandchildren. A steadfast provider and protector. One evening, when someone— something?—had broken in, he had defended his wife against teeth and clawing hands, had defended her with his very life.

He hesitated, frightened.

Could he actually be dead?

A ghost?

No. He still breathed. Ghosts don't breathe.

Emil hauled his body from the earth and stood up, unsteady. He squinted about. The woman's shrieks had brought a crowd. Many villagers surrounded him. He looked for Agnes but couldn't see her. His sons, nephews and cousins, friends, acquaintances, customers who bought his produce at market were all staring at him, holding aloft their knives, chisels, clubs, hammers. Indignant, he tried to explain—*You bastards buried me alive*—but his ruined throat could only groan.

A few people gasped, recoiled, but the crowd stayed fast.

Their dozens of white and plump faces reminded him of freshly plucked geese ready for the roasting. His empty stomach growled. He clutched at his abdomen, glanced down. The sweat on his tunic was not sweat after all, but blood. His own blood. His bare arms were covered in wounds, the skin bruised and tattered.

Memories of his last hours came back.

A madman had broken into the house during a storm. Emil fought and killed the man, yet sustained dozens of bites. Delirious, he staggered outside. Dogs howled and fled from him, cowering. Villagers soon converged to stab and bludgeon him. For a moment, he couldn't remember why. And now, they were converging on him again.

Emil's mouth watered.

Those faces.

All those pale, soft, warm, fatty, meaty faces.

Emil licked his chops and bared his teeth. Ah, he knew what he must be: a *draugr*, a living corpse. And he liked it. Liked this long-forgotten sensation of vigour and youthful energy surging through his weary old body. Who would have believed that rising from the dead could feel so marvellous, so intoxicating?

The villagers came at him with their feeble weapons.

Hungry—hungrier than he had ever felt in all his long life— Emil decided he would slaughter and consume each and every last one of them until he was sated. Until he was done.

The Sand

Joel stalked towards the rental car, loosening his tie. Stupid councillors. Wouldn't recognise a gift horse if it bit them on the arse. He popped the boot, flung his briefcase inside and glared up and down Main Street.

The place was a shithole anyway.

Little Corella Bay, a beachside town named after a parrot that looked like a crappy, low-res version of the cockatoo. Little Corella Bay, an upcoming boom town according to management. *Let's build a hotel while prices are cheap,* they said. *The local council will be a pushover,* they said. *Let's send Joel, he has to make his bones sooner or later,* they said. Had management set him up for failure? Maybe. He wasn't a "people" person. Everyone in the office knew it. For his birthday last month, they had given him a coffee mug that read SHUT UP AND GO AWAY.

He threw his tie into the boot, then his suit jacket. Sweat plastered his shirt to his back. Not even ten in the morning and already hot as hell. The car park overlooked the beach. People were sunbathing, walking dogs, splashing around in the water. Right: he would head for the sand. No point calling his boss yet. He had to calm down, think of a way to massage the facts so he didn't sound like a complete and utter dickhead.

The sand turned out to be the kind he liked best: firm enough so that his shoes didn't bog, yet fine and white, soft as caster sugar. The water reflected the deep blue summer sky. He could imagine the postcard. The waves came in gently, shyly, in coy little ripples. No surf beach, sure, but perfect for swimmers, paddle boarders, families… Just the sort of tourists who would want a good hotel.

Aw, *shit*.

The meeting with the council washed over him in all its various shades of humiliation, and he winced. What could he say to his boss? That he'd rubbed the councillors the wrong way from the start? Before the introductions had even finished?

Closer to the water, the breeze coming off Bass Strait riffled through Joel's hair. He stopped walking, sighed at the cool relief, let his shoulders drop. This is what he needed. A bit of nature to stop his adrenal glands firing. He picked a relatively empty spot, sat down and hugged his knees. A young man in boardshorts was throwing a stick into the ocean for his dog to retrieve, an excitable black Labrador that wouldn't stop barking.

Joel glanced around the beach, frowning.

Why weren't these people at work? It was a Thursday. *Bludgers*. Then he remembered it was school holidays.

The squealing of young kids caught his attention. Next to him, some two or three metres away, a couple of girls in frilly, one-piece bathing suits were burying a man, presumably their father, in the sand. They each had a plastic shovel. Joel didn't know much about kids, but they looked pre-school, perhaps three and four years old. The dad caught Joel's eye and smiled. Joel lifted a corner of his mouth in response.

"It's like they want to get rid of me!" the dad called.

"Yeah, sure," Joel said and looked back at the water.

The dad said, "Charlotte, put my hat over my eyes, would you?" After a beat, he continued, "Sienna? Be a sweetheart. Put the hat over Daddy's face. The sun's in my eyes."

Then don't lie on your back and let your rug-rats cover you in sand, Joel thought.

Christ, if only he had shaken that woman's hand. He had shaken with everyone else, hadn't he? The old biddy must have been in charge. Come to think of it, she had been the first one to veto the hotel idea. *We don't want to spoil the country feel of Little Corella Bay*, she had said. As if this shithole had anything to spoil. Except for the beach, Joel conceded. Yes, fair point, this beach was pretty damn good.

The girls' squeals turned into full-throated screams.

What the hell…? The grave-mound hump of sand that encased Daddy's prone body was sinking. Flattening as if the man was somehow disappearing. The girls dropped their spades and bawled. Joel scrambled over to the denim hat and lifted it.

Nothing but sand.

"Where's Daddy?" shrilled one of the girls.

Joel gaped, stunned.

The older girl, shrieking, began digging frantically with one of the plastic shovels. People sat up on their towels and looked over, curious, heads craning. Joel shoved his arm into the sand, pushing hard, trying to reach deeper and deeper, trying to find the dad's face. And when he was elbow deep into the soft and sugary sand, his fingers got caught.

In a cold, metallic nip.

First his little finger, then his ring finger. Quick as a wink. *One, two*. Like he had reached into the cogs of a whirring machine. Yelping in pain, Joel wrenched out his arm.

His little finger and ring finger were missing.

Sheared away clean as if pruned with bolt cutters.

The pulsing of blood from the stumps made him swoon. Only the screams of the girls brought him back. He clamped his ruined hand beneath his armpit, hyperventilating.

"Sweet Mary and Joseph!" shouted a querulous, high-pitched voice.

An elderly woman in a bikini and bathing cap was staring past Joel with frightened eyes. Screams came from behind him. He looked over his shoulder.

People were dropping straight down into the sand.

Plip. Plip. Plip.

As fast as if they had stepped from land into deep water. Except for the *spin* just before they disappeared. Somewhere around shoulder height, right before the sand engulfed their heads, they pirouetted at speed, whizzed by an invisible electric drill.

Joel leapt to his feet and staggered backwards to the water, squeezing his mutilated hand tighter under his armpit.

"What's going on?" the elderly woman demanded, as if Joel had the answer.

The girls cried and stamped their feet and dug for their father.

Joel could see the bonnet of his rental car overlooking the beach. *Plip.* A teenage girl sank. *Plip.* Followed by a distraught teenage boy. *Whizz, whizz.* Both gone.

Cries sounded from everywhere. Stumbling, Joel backed further away. Cold water swilled around his ankles, soaked into his brogues. The young man ran past him up the beach, the Labrador following and barking. People were snatching up children, scattering in panic.

But the strange phenomenon had ceased.

After about half a minute where nobody disappeared, some of the beachgoers stopped rushing about, slowed down to quiz each other, to cross-check, questioning their own eyes and sanity, as Joel was questioning his. The shrugs, the helpless gesturing: *is it over?*

Apparently so.

A few people were still wailing, weeping, digging. The girls hadn't given up on their dad. Faces bright red and contorted with hysterical sobbing, they hacked away at the sand with their plastic shovels, tossing a few teaspoons' worth of grains with every thrust.

Dazed, Joel blinked, surveying the beach, heart knocking in his throat.

What the hell had just happened?

Quicksand.

But wasn't that a myth? Quicksand, the devouring slurry in old Hollywood movies, didn't exist. Right? And even if it did exist, this beach wasn't sodden. This sand was dry, *dry*. And for Christ's sake, what had taken his fingers? The pain made his eyes water.

Some people fled to the car park. Those of the do-gooder persuasion hurried back to comfort the distraught or help them to dig. Joel stood immobilised, like so many others.

He felt the sound before he heard it.

A slow, subsonic rumble that vibrated his bone marrow. Everyone else must have felt it too. Like frightened meerkats, they stopped whatever they were doing and straightened up, heads swivelling this way and that, eyes bugged, mouths agape.

Oh shit, Joel thought, as his heart clamoured harder in fresh alarm.

Oh shit oh shit oh shit…

"Can you hear that?" the elderly woman said to him. "What is it? A truck?"

The thundering bass-note seemed to be coming from every direction now, rising in volume like an oncoming freight train. The ground began to shiver.

Earthquake.

A catastrophic shifting of tectonic plates. A force strong enough to flatten cities. That would explain everything; people had fallen through cracks opening in the earth.

But his fingers…

The noise ground on and on, getting louder.

No, wait, not an earthquake. Other sounds emerged from the rumble. Great drawn-out creaks and groans, as if a giant mechanical clockwork were meshing its rusted gears together for the first time in eons. The ground rocked beneath his feet. The entire beach rose and fell like a wave, from car park to water line. People started screaming again and sprinting for Main Street.

Plip. Whizz. Gone.

Another person.

Then another.

Plummeting as if through trapdoors in the sand.

A few good Samaritans came rushing from Main Street, attracted by the commotion.

"Go back!" Joel yelled, hard enough to strip his throat raw. "Go back!"

They blundered onto the beach anyway. How could they hear him over the deafening shudder of interlocking and grinding cogs?

Plip. Whizz. Gone.

Plip. Whizz. Gone.

"Help me," the elderly woman gasped, clutching at Joel's arm. "Get me out of here."

He shook her off. There was a pattern now. Oh shit, a pattern mimicking the initial wave in the sand. People were disappearing in neat rows from the car park towards the water. The trapdoors ran in one direction and then doubled back to run in the other, people dropping like dominoes, vanishing in a puff of white and sugary sand. The screech of the underground cogs hurt his eardrums.

There was a sudden odour of blood, shit, vomit. Rotting fish, burnt hair, vinegar.

The elderly woman wrenched at his arm. He shook her off again.

"You bastard!" she howled. "You selfish, vile bastard!"

Tottering and staggering, she headed for the car park.

The two girls were desperately flailing at the sand for their long-gone father. A few metres past them, the elderly woman plunged straight down into the beach. *Plip. Whizz.*

Gone.

Joel had to escape. Had to get into the water.

"Girls," he cried, trying to remember their names and failing. "Come with me right now, right now! Hurry. We have to swim for it. Let's go!"

"What about Daddy?" hiccupped the older one. "We have to find Daddy."

The puffs of sand tufted closer.

"For Christ's sake, get in the goddamned water!" he shouted, reaching out both arms.

The girls recoiled and shrieked as blood dripped from his finger stumps. *Oh, shit.* In his terror he had forgotten about that, forgotten that the teeth under the sand had maimed him.

"Hurry!" he implored, but the girls shrank against each other and redoubled their screams.

Plip. Whizz.

Gone.

Both of them swallowed. In one gulp.

The last thing he saw: the whirling, swirling whip of their long blonde hair.

Loping in clumsy strides, gasping and whimpering, Joel waded into the ocean. Behind him, the beach rasped and shuddered. Cool water pulled at his trousers, stung his wounds, closed over his head. Thrashing, he lifted his face to the air and furiously dog-paddled.

The last time he'd been in water deeper than a bathtub, god-damn it, was primary school. Forced to participate in swimming lessons. Mum had insisted. Oh, how he had *loathed* those lessons; hated the sensation of nothing beneath his feet, the feeling that the pool bottom wasn't there at all, that he was struggling on the surface while a yawning chasm lay beneath, waiting to snap him up. It's like a fear of heights, he had tried to explain to Mum. A fear of dying, of falling through the void.

Mum's voice: *See, it's okay. You're floating, sweetie. Just relax. Relax into the water.*

Relax? No, never. How? The bottom was too far away.

He kicked off his brogues. How heavy were wet clothes? His trousers might drown him. Panting, puffing, he stopped dog-paddling long enough to undo his belt, let it go, discard his wallet, phone, keys. He slogged through the water. The swells kept lapping into his mouth.

Where am I going? he thought. *Where the hell do I think I'm going?*

About 500 kilometres of rough seas lay between the Bass Coast and the island of Tasmania. Bass Strait was capricious, full of tidal waves and storms that overturned and ate ships. All right, so he would swim parallel to the beach, find someplace else to make landing.

And if the whole coastline had become a giant, mechanical lathe?

Well, he would just keep on swimming until he came across a boat. There must be fishermen. Or snorkellers, divers, sightseers. Jesus, there must be a boat out here. At least one. Where were all the boats?

He coughed, spluttered, his face sitting lower and lower in the water.

God, he was tiring already. The waves, deceptively small, were so hard to fight.

Warm blood trailed from his hand. Sharks. His blood would attract sharks. He tried to hold his ruined hand above his head but couldn't swim with only one arm. Now what? The options seemed limited: get eaten by sharks, drown, bleed to death, return to shore and be killed by a meat-grinder. He treaded water, looked back. The beach was empty.

Empty.

Really?

Nobody.

Not a living soul.

Was it the same stretch of beach? Yes, there was his rental car, a violent shade of orange.

Holy Christ, was it over? Was the carnage done?

Spitting, burping, panting, he contemplated swimming back. He certainly couldn't stay out here forever, waiting for non-existent boats. The rumbling sounded again. So, it wasn't over. The breeze must be carrying the noise from the beach. No going back.

He struck out, dog-paddling parallel to the coast. The breeze fell away but, somehow, the rumbling got louder. It didn't make sense. Around him, waves began to stipple and shiver, concussed by rising decibels. Panic tasted sour.

The machinery was coming for him.

Clockwork gears meshing along the seabed in pursuit.

Joel turned and swam towards Bass Strait. Was he making any headway? The grinding noises roared in his ears. Beneath him, the water began to draw like an unplugged bath, gently at first, then as a persistent suction that held his feet and tried to pull them down.

Trapdoors were opening, stretching wider.

He paddled as fast as he could.

The noise became unbearable. Putting his face in the water, screwing his eyes shut, he commenced a clumsy freestyle crawl. His primary school swim-coach came to mind: *Use your hands like oars, Joel, and row, row, row.* But one oar was broken. Broken, maimed and bleeding, pumping blood into the deep water, luring sharks. *One day, Joel, you might have to swim for your life.*

Practise, boy, try your best.

The suction got stronger. Joel worked his arms and legs in desperation. His head came up and he glanced around. The beach was lost from sight. Nothing but sky and waves. He stopped, waited for his life to flash before his eyes. It didn't happen. Instead, he remembered the banality of the coffee mug: SHUT UP AND GO AWAY.

Seawater formed a whirlpool around him, the concentric ripples starting to turn faster and faster. Soon, the vacuum beneath would be strong enough to pull him under. He would be dragged to the seabed and sucked through a trapdoor. Any moment now, the giant clockwork gears would grind him up, starting with his toes.

How much would it hurt? How quickly would he die?

The suction increased. He struggled to keep his head above water. Struggled and failed.

Any moment now.

He kicked hard. The water slurped and wrapped tight as a wet caul around his body. He couldn't move his limbs. He glimpsed the sky and then it was gone.

The House Across the Road

The rental property across the road is haunted but not by anything as banal as ghosts. No, I mean the house itself must exert some kind of weird force over the people who live under its roof. I swear to God, every tenant family ends up behaving in the exact same way, and there's been a *lot* of families over the years. The lease never runs longer than six months.

Firstly, no one ever parks a vehicle in the single-car garage. Strictly speaking, it's a carport, but the original owners (the Bakers...the Baileys?) installed a roller door before they sold up about eleven years ago. Tenants use the garage for storage, packing it to the gills with furniture and boxes. Why move into a rental that's too small for your household effects? I could understand if the occasional family did it, but *all* of them?

Instead, tenants park their vehicles on the kerb directly opposite our house. So annoying! We get very little space to manoeuvre our own cars in and out. How come they never use the property's driveway? It's easily long enough. The last nine sets of tenants have parked on the road. Nine! Maybe *all* of them have done so since the place was turned into a rental. I wish I'd been more observant when the Bakers/Baileys moved out, but I was a newlywed and preoccupied with Chris and setting up our first home. (Which also turned out to be our last.)

And for some reason, tenants turn the one square metre of porch into a patio. They might put out a little table and a couple of chairs. Madness! Posties and delivery people struggle just to access the doorbell. Why doesn't anybody put their patio furniture in the back yard? I've looked at the house on Google Maps and the back yard is *huge*. While there's no covered area, plenty of trees along the fence-line offer shade. Otherwise, you could put up a portable gazebo or one of those big outdoor umbrellas, yet tenants prefer to clutter the porch.

Then there's the front yard. The real estate agent mustn't kick up about damage to the grass, so tenants routinely keep a mini-camper, trailer, motorbike or quadbike on the lawn; stuff that ought to be stored in the garage if it weren't already piled high with sofas and desks. Oh, here's a revolutionary thought: instead of wrecking the garden, *why not put the camper, trailer or bike in the empty driveway?*

Chris used to say I was obsessed. Hah! That's not fair. "Curious" is a more accurate description. We used to argue about the rental property—among other things—before he left.

And what to make of this? The council offers two hard rubbish collections per year and, without fail, tenants dump on the nature strip enough discarded goods to stock a house. Big ticket items like bedroom suites, armchairs, entertainment units. A *massive* pile. It's a wonder they have a stick of furniture left inside. Yet the garage stays filled to the rafters.

Which brings me, at last, to the children.

I've got two girls myself, both in primary school: nine-year-old Olivia and seven-year-old Isabelle. They're gentle, reserved, thoughtful, more interested in reading than playing sport. That said, I understand how other people's kids need to cut loose and burn off some energy before dinner. But oh my God, the *squealing* from across the road. As if the kids are in fear of their lives or in the throes of being gutted. (No pets allowed, so they aren't playing with, for example, an over-exuberant dog.) The pitch is piercing enough to hurt my ears. I'll look out my lounge room windows and—no sign of them. The kids squeal in their back yard. Squeal non-stop. For *hours* every day until sundown. What would make them do that? And the squealing happens with each and every family. One family after the other after the other…

Go over there, Kim, and just ask them, Chris used to shout. *If it bothers you that much, go on over there.*

I never did. It isn't wise to involve yourself in the lives of neighbours. Before you know it, they're asking for favours, insinuating themselves, making a nuisance, a scene, trying to get too close and frightening you. One can choose friends but not neighbours.

The children graffiti as well. On the brick column that's adjacent to the porch cluttered with patio furniture. They use chalk. When the FOR RENT sign goes up and a family moves out, the chalk drawings are soon gone—presumably hosed off by the real estate agent—but within a few months of the next tenancy, the drawings are back again, scribbled anew. Green, blue and yellow chalk. Are the children tracing over the old patterns? I don't know. The patterns are small and I can't make them out. My lounge room windows—and letterbox—are too far away and I wouldn't dream of venturing across the road.

One last point: the tenants comprise parents with pre-teen children. Never a bunch of twenty-something-year-olds who flat-share and party. Never elderly people. Never childless couples or couples with adult children. Race doesn't seem to matter, however. There's been Asian, Indian, Islander, white, mixed, all of them average, ordinary, unremarkable. I can remember just one family in any detail: the second-last lot, who were tall, lanky, red-haired and *stooped*—even the children. How odd that only young families ever live there. Maybe this is the easiest quirk to explain as the landlord has power of veto over prospective tenants. Nevertheless, the "cookie-cutter" pattern of occupants leaves me uneasy.

Not uneasy enough, obviously. Because last week, the FOR RENT sign was hammered into the front yard, and I'm thinking about it. Out of necessity. Chris reckons he lost his job and is now labouring at a building site and can't pay the same maintenance, which I don't believe for a moment, yet a lawyer is beyond my budget. I work part-time in admin at the girls' primary school. My wage covers food, utilities, petrol, a few necessities like clothes, haircuts, dental bills. With the reduction in maintenance, I won't be able to make rent. We can't stay here. Our lease is up for renewal anyway, so I won't be breaking the contract, but still… It's painful. This is the only home that Olivia and Isabelle have ever known. The only real home I've ever known too. (Chris doesn't feel any attachment or nostalgia about this place. He's too busy living it up with Bitchface.)

The rent across the road is *cheap as chips*. God, how I'd love that extra money in my pocket. The girls wouldn't have to change school either. And yes, I might even get to satisfy my curiosity. I'm not afraid of living there because we don't fit the mould. There's not been a single-parent family that I can recall. Whatever haunts that rental house wouldn't haunt us.

I've made my application—along with scores of others, no doubt. We probably don't stand a chance. Without a husband and father, we fail the landlord's profile. I've also applied for another couple of dozen properties. For the same rent as across the road, I had to look four or five suburbs further out, so what I'll save in rent, I'll lose in after-school-care fees and petrol.

How I *hate* Chris for doing this to us.

I'm on the shortlist! Clearly, I was wrong about the landlord. (Unless my family is a token?)

The real estate agent took me through the house today. First impressions…Well, it's certainly *very* cramped. Three tiny bedrooms, no study, only one living area. Another con is that the Baker/Bailey installation of a carport roller-door was their only attempt to modernise. Ugh, the kitchen! No dishwasher, storage space is negligible, the drawers fall out if you pull them too far. But the burnt-orange laminate and brown tile backsplash are reminiscent of a fruit orchard. You can almost *smell* the zest. (I'm guessing the real estate agent hides a can of citrus-scented air freshener in a cupboard somewhere.)

Yet there's something…*charming* about the place. Cosy. I liked the flow of rooms off the hallway, the amount of sunlight that shone through the windows, the retro charm of a giant enamelled bath and pedestal sink. When you can picture where you'll place your furniture, you know a house is a good fit.

And I've solved the mystery of why tenants never use the back yard. Hooray! It turns out the drainage is *terrible*. While the lawn appears green and inviting, the ground is a mushy bog all year round, especially now at the tail-end of a stormy Melbourne spring.

At least I made a good impression on the real estate agent. She shook my hand at the end of the inspection and her warm, encouraging smile seemed genuine. Didn't it? Back home, I've taken to staring out my lounge room windows at the place. We could have a good life over there. Me, Olivia, Isabelle. I'll know in a few days.

The wait feels torturous.

I've already given notice to the current landlord. My savings account is running low. Work can't give me extra hours. Last week, I visited every shop in the neighbourhood with my resumé. Most rebuffed me at the door. The electricity bill came and the power company has once more put up the charges. We had tomato soup and cheese on toast for dinner again. I couldn't look at Olivia and Isabelle for fear of crying. What am I to do?

It's hard to sleep. I keep thinking about the house across the road; my one hope, my only possible chance of salvation. I'm owed a bit of luck. Aren't I? Surely, even a loser has to win occasionally. Not from a distant god's benevolence, no, I mean from the roll of the dice. You can't throw snake eyes forever. It's not statistically possible.

We got it! At the end of the call from the real estate agent, I wept and shook with relief. When I told Chris, he laughed. *Aren't you scared of getting haunted by the house?* No, because I don't have a husband and our girls don't have a father, so we don't fit the profile. Bitchface was hissing in the background for Chris to hang up. He soon did.

Friends helped us move. It took an afternoon. Just one single afternoon. Once the main breadwinner leaves, you get to appreciate how poor you really are. Chris had taken what he termed *his stuff*:

the big TV, coffee machine, clothes dryer, PC, exercise bike, yet at the time of purchase I'd picked out each item myself because Chris hadn't cared either way. Now Bitchface has them. I hope she enjoys the PC knowing that my daughters have to borrow iPads from school, but let's face it, a woman who can blithely steal a man from his family wouldn't bat an eye over stealing a computer.

Never mind. Our first night in the new house feels comforting. The atmosphere is calm.

I cook one of the girls' favourite meals, a tartiflette, and we sit around the kitchen table as the buttery soft and westering light slants through the windows. Magpies warble. Little fairy wrens chirp and sing, preparing for sleep as they flit about the tea tree and waggle their tails.

"I like it here, Mummy," Olivia sighs.

Isabelle says, "I like it here too."

That night in bed, I lie awake for a while, listening; the noise of traffic from the main road seems further away somehow. My sleep is the best I've enjoyed in months. When I wake up, sunshine lies across me like a blessing. Now I can afford the electricity bill. Start replacing the items that Chris took with him. Put a bit of money aside.

After I drop the girls at school, I'll go to the old house and clean it from top to bottom, thoroughly, to make sure I get back our—*my*—security deposit.

This bloody driveway! Never again! It's the old-fashioned type from the 1970s: two parallel strips of ridiculously narrow concrete you're expected to navigate in a dead straight line. As I reversed out of the carport today, I veered slightly off course and slid into the recessed dirt, gouging *both* wheel rims on the right-hand side. Damn it! Another few hundred wiped off the car's already pathetic value. And when I phoned the real estate agent to request compensation, she actually *chuckled*. "Go for it, Kim," she said. "Engage a lawyer and get back to me." Who am I kidding? If I can't afford to sue Chris for child maintenance, I certainly can't afford to sue for a couple of ruined wheel rims.

Now I know why tenants park on the kerb.

All right.

Take a breath.

Bit by bit, the haunted house turns out not to be haunted. You know what? I'm fine with that. As a rational rather than superstitious person, I'm glad to have discovered yet another simple explanation. (Not that I'd ever share these insights with Chris. To hell with him.) I just feel stupid, that's all. To have spent *years* watching and wondering and speculating such nonsense; to have spun my mystical, magical, fiendish theories when the answers are so mundane and straightforward. It's embarrassing.

The house lies south-east to north-west, which means the morning sun flatters the porch. Here's my next confession. Since I can't use the back yard—too marshy, the band of concrete hugging the rear of the house too slim for patio furniture—I've put a kitchen chair on the porch. Amazing, isn't it? I'm behaving like the preceding tenants! Another mystery solved.

I get up before Olivia and Isabelle, sit outside at dawn, and savour my first cup of coffee. As the sun rises, the light touches my closed eyelids, my lips, feels warm against my chest. Now I need someplace to rest my coffee mug. Perhaps I could go to the Salvos or Vinnie's and buy a patio chair and wee little table? If bunched together, they shouldn't get in the way.

More news. A few days ago, a family moved into the house across the road. By that, I mean *my* old house. There's a man and a woman—both middle-aged, like me—and at least two if not three pre-pubescent children. These last few mornings as I've been out here, enjoying my sunbath, the lounge room curtains have twitched aside. The wife is observing me. I should go over there, tell her why I'm parking on the road opposite her driveway and why I'm setting furniture on the porch and not in the back yard, yet I feel some kind of perverse pleasure in her confusion. At least, I imagine she's confused. I imagine she's thinking: *What on earth is going on over there?*

Am I awful? Perhaps. It feels good to be awful for once.

The Salvos stores are treasure troves. I had no idea! Most of the furniture and homewares are as good as new—and sometimes *are* new, still in their original packaging—and very affordable. For the porch, I bought a latticed metal bistro set, consisting of a round three-legged table and two chairs. Gorgeous! It takes up more space than I'd intended, but I don't care. Sitting outside in the morning and sipping coffee feels glorious. *Luxurious.*

Over the last couple of months, I've replaced everything that Chris stripped from our family home. *Everything.* And I've decided to redecorate, too. Because when you break up with the man you love, the father of your children, his presence stays in the furniture he leaves behind. For instance, he had "his" side of the couch, and I can still picture him sitting there in the flattened cushions. Here he is again every morning, a ghost at the kitchen table with his invisible breakfast (bowl of cereal, coffee, orange juice), and I'm reminded by the scratches on the glass tabletop how he would habitually toss his keys on it despite my objections. He's in the girls' furniture too. I remember him painting Isabelle's chest of drawers, bolting Olivia's bookcase to the wall, assembling their beds.

I don't want him spooking my new home. Contaminating our new start.

We need fresh, fresh, *fresh*.

And besides, the rooms cry out for wooden furniture. Oak and pine. Natural materials to bask in the sunshine from the windows. Is there a special tinted film on the panes? There must be. What else could explain the effect? At the old house, I never paid attention to the natural light. But here? I notice the change of colour throughout the day, from ivory to blond to bisque to tangerine, and love the different moods. Savour them, in fact. The workers at the three Salvos stores I frequent know me by name, lead me to arrivals I might like, keep stock in the back for me. Oak and pine. Oak and pine. I'm purging Chris, one stick of furniture at a time. Exorcising him from this place.

"I like our new things, Mummy," Olivia sighs.

Isabelle says, "I like them too."

Workers at the Salvos stores keep encouraging me to donate my unwanted furniture, but I'm not an idiot. I come from a poor family. I'm poor now. When my daughters grow up and move out, do I want them to start with *nothing*? With *zero possessions* like I did? No. By the time they are women, my girls won't remember their father's ghost in our former belongings. Olivia and Isabelle will have lounge suites, lamps, coffee tables, all thanks to *my* foresight, *my* squirrelling away for their future.

As I replace items, the old stuff goes in the garage.

Our first Christmas without Chris. He spent the day with Bitchface. He watched her son open gifts, made pancakes for breakfast, celebrated the importance of family by attending a barbecue at her parents' place. Scores of people were there, apparently, even distant cousins. Bitchface comes from a large, close and loving clan, and each of her relatives is simply marvellous and funny and fascinating. Chris dropped over on Boxing Day with presents for Olivia and Isabelle. He didn't stay long. Bitchface and her son were waiting in the car. They're spending the summer holidays down at Apollo Bay. Her parents have a beach house.

God, how I hate him.

As he was urging our girls to hurry up and unwrap their gifts, I had a vision of scratching both eyes right out of his goddamned head.

I can't stop buying furniture. Not from the Salvos stores—their stuff is too expensive to support a weekly habit—but from op shops and garage sales. You know there are websites that offer items *for free*? Some vendors even deliver. I'm running out of space. Oh, I've wasted money on such *crap*. Vinyl armchairs stripped by use and time, stuff that's broken, mildewed or smells like cat piss. I don't know what's wrong with me. I suspect I'm becoming a hoarder. People hoard to fill an empty space in their hearts. Is that what I'm doing? Even the girls are starting to complain.

"You need a different hobby," Olivia sighs.

Isabelle says, "Yes, I agree."

My mind is made up. *The garbage has to go.* There's a hard rubbish collection in a few weeks. I'll start piling the garbage on the nature strip. Let "bin scabs" take what they want before the council carries away the rest to the tip. Yet somehow, the thought of losing this stuff—this *garbage*—makes me unbearably sad.

You know what else I should put on the nature strip? Chris's tinny. He and Bitchface have moved to a city apartment and there isn't space for his dumb little boat. How many times did he go fishing anyway? Half a dozen? *Sell the bloody thing,* I said. He refused. I told him to hire a storage unit, but he dumped the tinny on me instead. He tried to back the little trailer up the driveway. Kept slipping the wheels off the concrete strips. Now the tinny sits on the lawn, the trailer tyres sinking into the earth, the grass beneath turning brown.

"The real estate agent will kick up!" I argued, but honestly? I haven't heard from that woman since I wrecked my wheel rims. I pay my rent online, get my receipts online. Aren't real estate agents supposed to do regular checks on rental properties? For all she knows, I'm ripping out and selling the fixtures, building fires in the rooms, covering every wall in faeces. There's never been an inspection. I've been here for months. Doesn't the landlord care? Occasionally, I think I should call the real estate agent, if only to "touch base", but then I remember her chuckling—*Go for it, Kim. Engage a lawyer and get back to me*—and I decide no, no. Absolutely not.

January is bearing down. Baking the roof tiles. Heating the house. Suffocating us. I open windows, but the air never blows inside. The girls can't stand it. My temper is short. February will be worse. To augment my holiday pay from the school, I do other people's ironing—cash-in-hand jobs—and I'm constantly dripping in sweat. My daughters keep whining.

"Go outside," I ordered them today. "Play in the shade."

"There's nothing to do," they wailed.

"Well, just take a ball and bloody well throw it to each other." Thinking of passing cars, I added, "Go out the back. Wear your gumboots." Because the ground doesn't seem to dry up. Is there a burst underground pipe? I want to call the real estate agent but can't make myself.

Grumbling, they trooped outside. I ironed and pressed and steamed and sweated.

Then the squealing began.

My own daughters, squealing as if in fear of their lives or in the throes of being gutted. I ran outside, panicked. Stopped at the rear steps. Put fists on my hips. Olivia and Isabelle were skipping along the narrow band of concrete that skirts the house, down at the far end by my bedroom, holding hands and squealing full bore into each other's faces like a pair of lunatics.

"What on *earth* are you doing?" I yelled, furious.

They stopped to grin brightly at me.

"It tickles!" they shrieked, laughing, ecstatic.

They recommenced squealing and whirling about in a tight circle, right up against the brickwork, so close I feared they'd scrape their bare arms and legs. I charged down the steps. Their squealing made my ears ring, set my teeth on edge.

"Stop that!" I demanded. "You stop that noise right now!"

Barrelling towards them, I had the maddening urge to slap both their faces. Until I felt it. I stopped dead. *Yes, it tickled.* When I was a child in primary school, there was an area of the playground near the main building that used to create willy-willies: miniature tornadoes of dirt and leaves. Something to do with the architecture, the aerodynamic trapping of winds inside a right-angle, even on a breathless day. I used to frolic there myself every lunchtime. *And squeal.* I'd forgotten. For all these many years, I'd forgotten.

Now, the air at the back of my house behaved the same way: countless wiggly fingers plucking and stroking, tugging at hair and hems, whisking at ankles, cheekily fluttering about. And like the willy-willies from childhood, this one didn't throw grit in our eyes either. *It was fun.* My God, how long since they'd had fun? Since my girls were *happy*? Because they miss their father. They cry for him sometimes. He sees them every second weekend and they come home dejected and refuse to talk about it.

"Mummy, you're in the way!" Olivia giggled.

"Look out, Mummy!" Isabelle added. "We have to spin!"

I retreated. Left them to their game. Watched for a time from the back step, tearful, smiling. I hope this willy-willy stays around as the one at my primary school did.

They're squealing still. It's nearly dinner-time. I've made salad, cooked a few sausages. The sunlight through the panes is burnished, tawny. A cooling breeze has started to drift throughout the house. I feel better now. Better than I've felt in months. It's like we've turned a corner, my girls and I. This house and us. Together.

I bought a box of coloured chalk. Yes, we've been acting the same as the other tenant families, but our behaviour has so far made sense. The chalk will be the deciding factor.

"Doodle on the driveway," I suggest so as not to lead my daughters. "Or on the concrete walkway along the back of the house. It's fine. Chalk washes off."

Hah, no surprise. They graffiti the brick column that's adjacent to the porch cluttered with my patio furniture. Using green, blue and yellow chalk.

There wasn't a *trace* of previous drawings. Olivia and Isabelle acted upon their own impulses, apparently. Or upon the impulses of this house? It makes me wonder if every choice I've made since moving here has been made for me. I ought to feel afraid. Somehow, I don't. Shouldn't *that* worry me? God, I'd like to ask my doctor, but I can't risk the ramifications. Along with my hoarding tendencies, a confession that I believe our rental property to be haunted would suggest I've lost my mind. Wouldn't it? Any doctor would deem me an unfit parent and spirit away my girls.

Their chalk drawings look like hieroglyphics. Along with

squiggles and geometric shapes, I recognise something that resembles the sun.

"What do these pictures mean?" I ask.

"They spell out a name," Olivia says.

"A special one," Isabelle adds.

"Whose name?" I say. "I don't understand."

The girls cock their heads towards the brickwork, as if listening.

"Can't you hear that, Mummy?" Olivia says.

"The whispering voices?" Isabelle adds.

No, I can't hear anything. Because I'm too old to hear it. Only pre-pubescent children can hear it. The landlord's predilections make sense now. I should be terrified. Instead, I'm intrigued. A reverse-image search gave me the answer. No digging through libraries for ancient texts, no consultations with theologians or professors. Just a few seconds online.

Kindred of Aubade.

They have a comprehensive website. *Aubade* is a French word, pronounced *oh-bad*, which means "dawn serenade". Kindred of Aubade is a "communal village", but I'm not an idiot. It's a cult. Hundreds of people live there. A thriving community, not filled with hippies or dropouts or addicts or dole bludgers, but blue- and white-collar professionals like carpenters, builders, plumbers, doctors, dentists, accountants. They have farms, businesses, a retail precinct.

And schools.

Their primary school teaches French, which is more than I can say for Paperbark Primary. The year before Olivia started prep, the Spanish teacher quit and despite the headmistress's strenuous assurances about finding a replacement, there's never been another language teacher and it's been *years*. That's always bothered me. Education is the way out of poverty. I want my girls to be well educated. Reading takes you far, yes, but only bilingualism can take you anywhere in the world. How many Australians with English as a first language can fluently speak a second? Or third? Forget about a fourth.

The website has plenty of photographs. The commune is set

in the rolling, green hills of the Bass Coast right next to the sea. Everyone looks happy. Much happier than me.

One question keeps me awake: how did this rental house communicate the Kindred of Aubade hieroglyphics to my daughters? By telepathy? Possession? There can be only one rational explanation, which is that Olivia and Isabelle saw the faint drawings and traced over them. (Yet I had scrubbed the brickwork beforehand. Not thoroughly enough? Perhaps.)

I've confiscated the chalk. Every day I plan to wash off the symbols. Every day I don't. I keep logging onto that website. I'd like my girls to speak French. And people in the photographs look so happy. I want us to be happy too. Do you know there's a job board?

Olivia and Isabelle are wretched this term at Paperbark Primary. The other students shun them. How come? The women in the office are giving me the cold shoulder too. I've tried everything including homemade cakes—eyes remain flinty, attitudes frosty. What have I done? Today, the office manager intimated that my hours might be cut back. Suddenly, the school has budgetary problems yet only *my* part-time job is at risk.

Our six-month lease is coming to a close. I want to extend, but the real estate agent won't return my messages. Not coincidentally, the primary school at Kindred of Aubade is looking for an administration assistant. The job listing requires someone of my exact experience.

This cult wants us.

Who knows why? The girls and I are ordinary with nothing special to offer. I cry instead of sleep. What am I to do? I sit outside in the morning sun, skolling my coffee and watching the twitch of the lounge room curtains across the road, and I want to run to my old house and scream at the wife *Help me, help me.* But you can't trust neighbours, can't risk letting strangers into your life. When you supplicate yourself, people either recoil in disgust or take advantage, over and over, until you find the strength to cut them off.

I get the letter of termination from Paperback Primary. One month's notice.

The eviction letter from the real estate agent. One month's notice.

Desperate, I check the job board on the Kindred of Aubade website. Apply for the position of admin assistant, which is somehow still open. Anticipate what will happen next. And yes, an immediate email offers an interview. The job is mine; I know it. I only have to turn up.

Will I turn up?

No, no...

Then I sort through the latest round of bills for gas, water, electricity, car registration, and realise I'm caught inside the right-angle, pinned by the aerodynamics of an impossible wind. Meanwhile, Olivia and Isabelle are outside in the back yard, squealing within the willy-willy, spinning and whirling, spinning and whirling, screeching into each other's faces like lunatics.

The management of Kindred of Aubade Primary School presses to interview me on a weekend so I can stay overnight and bring the girls. The council will put us up in the motel and provide meal vouchers. The closer we get to the commune, the better the scenery. Olivia and Isabelle are enchanted by the green hills, the paddocks dotted with sheep, goats, alpacas, cows or horses, grape vines and fruit trees. Beautiful sights around every bend of the road.

At the close of the interview, I'm granted the job. Of course, I accept. Guess what? The house they've allocated us is *rent-free* — what an unexpected perk! I'll be paid for work, my daughters will attend a school with French lessons, our bank account can finally grow.

After the interview, we stroll about. Buy ice creams. It's like a village here. A clean, modern village. People smile at us in the street, actually say things like, "Hello there!" or "How are you doing this fine afternoon?", their faces warm and kind and happy.

And we made friends! We have a barbecue invitation for dinner this very evening.

As soon as I saw that family, I remembered. Their height, skinniness, red hair, posture—the second-last tenants. They remembered me too, even though I'd never introduced myself or ventured out from behind my property line. Olivia and Isabelle addressed their four stooped children by name. Had they ever met? Part of me thinks I should be concerned, but I've been through so much this year that, frankly, I'm grateful for the respite. The *breather*.

"You'll love it here," Mabel said, the wife and mother, blue eyes twinkling. "Let me show you the ropes. Help you fit in. Shall we start your induction right away?"

"Thank you," I said, "but we're still living at our current house."

Mabel took my hand. "Oh, sweetie. I'll show you the ropes about that silly business too."

I can't believe our luck. You see? It'll be okay. Life doesn't always throw snake eyes. Most of the time, yes, but not always.

Talisman

He arranged the wooden sticks into an x-shape, securing them with twine. Bound the armature with cloth and glue, fashioning his beloved's legs, arms and head. Affixed beads for the eyes and mouth. Now the wax. Lighting a candle, turning it into the flame, he dripped the hot melt onto each nipple, along the midline of the abdomen, between the splayed thighs. She strained at the ropes, begging for release, but he wouldn't satisfy her. Not yet. Not until he had anointed her voodoo doll with the same pattern of wax would he fall upon her and finish them both.

All the Stars in Her Eyes

Janet and her daughter sing nursery rhymes at bath time. The last nursery rhyme must always be *Twinkle, Twinkle, Little Star* because that is Aurora's favourite. Aurora is three years old. As she sings, she waggles her fingers to imitate her mother, unknowingly mimicking the shimmer of distant suns. Janet feels both a rush of love and the anxious sensation that time is fleeting. She grabs her phone from the pocket of her dress and takes a photograph. Aurora, used to posing, widens her eyes and purses her lips.

The flash goes off.

Janet inspects the photograph. It is a good one. She will email it to her sister, Megan, who lives in Perth on the other side of Australia. Megan has not yet met Aurora. Neither sister can afford the airfare. They are both young, in their twenties. Megan is a waitress. Since becoming a single mother, Janet—the promising and talented graphic designer—has worked from home, freelance, designing book covers and selling them via her website because she can't afford childcare. She makes enough to pay the mortgage, put food on the table, clothes on their backs, petrol in the car. But not much else. She tries not to think about the future.

Janet is about to email the photograph when she notices something odd about it. She zooms in on Aurora's face. The child has brilliant blue eyes, like those of her father, which is unsettling because Janet's eyes are brown, and Janet remembers from high-school biology that blue is a recessive trait and brown is dominant. She reminds herself, frequently, that she must be mistaken, and while the truth is only a Google-search away, she will not investigate. Janet studies the picture. Aurora's pupils are sparkling as if filled with glitter. This must be a photographic glitch, similar to red-eye. Janet knows that red-eye is the flash reflecting on the retina. She puts the phone back in her pocket.

"Look at Mummy," she says.

"I am," Aurora says, and splashes the bath water. The rubber ducks toss in the surf.

"No," Janet says, and holds her daughter's chin. "Make your eyes big and look at me."

Aurora does so, giggling, as if they are playing. Janet's stomach tightens and falls.

There are tiny specks in Aurora's pupils. Hundreds of them. Thousands of them.

Each pupil resembles a snow globe, but the specks are suspended, unmoving. Fixed. Janet tries to remember if Aurora's eyes seemed unusual in any way prior to bath time. She thinks back to dinner, just an hour ago. Wouldn't she have noticed? It doesn't seem possible that something so catastrophic could have happened to her daughter's eyes in so brief a time. Because this must be catastrophic. Aurora is going blind. Her retinas have come loose and are floating, disintegrating, shedding their light-sensitive cells.

"Let's go," Janet says, and hoists Aurora from the bath.

"Where?"

"Into town."

"No, Mummy, it's time for sleeps," Aurora says, with reproach. Janet recognises the tone as the same she uses herself when the occasion calls for discipline. Now she must keep the panic out of her voice or else frighten her daughter.

"It's a game," she says. "A bit of fun. Come on, let's get you dressed."

Janet's poky two-bedroom cottage is twenty minutes from the town centre, including long stretches of highway with a posted speed limit of 110 kilometres an hour. At first, the roads are gravel and there are no street lights. It is a cloudless night in Melbourne's spring. The air smells of wild daisies; pungent and sickly sour.

From her car seat in the back of the sedan, Aurora chats about the dark. Janet has never driven her daughter anywhere at night before. The unmade roads, lined with ditches and eucalyptus trees, are too treacherous. Aurora seems happy. Whatever is happening to her eyes must not hurt. Janet has to keep lifting her foot off the accelerator and reminding herself to breathe. The town hospital feels so far away.

She ignores the parking restrictions and cuts the engine directly out front of the casualty department. Running inside, the walls and floors beaming with harsh fluorescent lights, Aurora joggles against her chest. Janet holds the toddler against her instead of propped, as usual, on one hip. The urge to scream is powerful. Janet gulps it down.

Two nurses rush over. Their urgency spikes Janet's fear. Yet they must be reacting to Janet's demeanour, her body language. She must look pale. All the blood has left her skin and is pulsing red-hot in the core of her body.

"Help us," she says, as one of the nurses takes Aurora. "Her eyes. My daughter's eyes."

Aurora is crying. Howling. Panic is contagious.

They get home sometime after 3:00am. Both sleep until mid-morning, deaf to the raucous squawks of wattlebirds, the mewling demands of baby magpies trailing after their mothers in the long grass. Aurora, cranky, eats toast while Janet talks on the phone to Megan.

"What's it called again?" Megan says. "Hang on, I'm writing it down."

"Asteroid hyalosis. No one knows why it happens." Janet consults the print-out sheet they gave her at the hospital on discharge. The consultants dragged the town's resident ophthalmologist out of bed to confirm Aurora's diagnosis. "It's caused by globules of calcium and fats in the vitreous humor."

"And what's the vitreous humor again?"

Janet scans the sheet. "The clear liquid that fills the eyeball."

"So, you're sure it's not serious?"

"Asteroid hyalosis doesn't affect eyesight, so they reckon. If it does, they can do an operation called a vitrectomy. They use a needle to drain off the vitreous humor—"

"Jesus, what the hell—?"

"—and replace it with salty water. Over time, the body replaces the water with fresh vitreous humor. Apparently, there's no damage from the condition or the treatment."

Megan remains silent. Janet suspects that she knows what her sister is thinking. Waiting, Janet listens to the line's hum and crackle. Her raw nerves move in concert with the random tide of noise. Through the open doorway, Aurora crumples a piece of toast in her hand and mashes it against her mouth. Aurora seems okay. After the initial fright, she drowsed through most of the examinations at the hospital, through the poking and prodding, the tests.

Asteroid hyalosis afflicts not just humans but dogs, cats, horses and some type of animal called a chinchilla. The condition affects one in 200 people, but Janet finds this hard to believe. She has never seen it before. Except for once. And, with help, she had long convinced herself that she either imagined or dreamed it.

"Are you still there?" Janet says.

"Yeah, I'm still here. I'm… Oh shit, I dunno, I'm just… Do you need me to come over?"

Janet slumps against the kitchen bench. "Thanks, but it's too much money."

"I could borrow some. Pull some extra shifts. I can do it. Be there tomorrow."

Janet's eyes fill with tears. "No. Just having you to talk to is enough."

"Really?"

"Really." Janet bites at a thumbnail. Hesitates. If Megan won't bring it up, then she will. She says, "Look, I asked them if this asteroid hyalosis is hereditary."

She feels rather than hears the frosty silence.

"Oh, come on," Megan says. "Are you kidding me?"

"Please—"

"If you start this again," Megan says emphatically, "I'm hanging up."

Janet hangs up instead. She puts the phone in her pocket, hands shaking.

Later, she takes Aurora into the cottage's back yard. Aurora knows not to venture beyond the patio. Besides, the girl prefers to fossick in the blue shell sandpit. The day is warm. Janet spreads a towel on the weeds and couch grass, and lies down. Crooking an arm beneath her head, she closes her eyes.

When she opens them again, a dog has its muzzle near Aurora's face.

Janet sits up, heart seizing. She imagines toothy jaws clamping around her daughter's plump, perfect cheeks. Fear makes her freeze. The strange dog is sniffing, panting, tongue lolling, tail wagging. The dog is a black Labrador. Full-grown male. No collar. Aurora is smiling and patting the dog, crooning at it. The dog seems to like the attention.

After a few seconds, Janet finds her legs. The dog is a bomb with a mercury switch. Janet's every movement has to be careful, non-threatening, or else the dog is sure to bite. Gently, slowly, she picks up Aurora and takes her inside, sagging with relief when the screen door clicks shut. The dog stays put. Aurora remains by the screen door and babbles. The stray wags its tail, lips arranged as if smiling.

Hours later, at dinner-time, the stray has still not left. Janet considers calling the council, asking them to send a dog-catcher.

Aurora says, "Please feed him, Mummy. He's hungry."

"Good. If he's hungry, he'll go home."

"No! Give him something to eat!" Aurora's crystalline eyes film with tears. "Feed him, Mummy. Feed him!"

Aurora won't stop crying and begging. Exhausted, Janet defrosts some beef mince and puts it on a plate. She turns on the outside lamp. The patio leaps into brightness and shadows. The dog, grinning, cocks its head. It seems friendly enough, but you can't be too sure.

"Hey there, mate," Janet says, wary of teeth. "You want something to eat? Here you go."

She puts the plate onto the ground.

The dog sits up straight. The illumination from the outdoor lamp catches the gleam in the dog's eyes. Catches the multiple gleams. Janet holds her breath and forgets her fear. She approaches the dog. It watches her. Janet's legs tremble. She squats down. The animal's eyes are filled with glitter. Each pupil brims with a thousand, glittering stars.

Janet falls back, gasping. The dog hurries over to her, licks her face.

"Let's keep him!" Aurora shouts through the screen door. "He's our dog, Mummy. Ours."

The coincidence is too great. Janet realises that Aurora's father has sent this dog.

She calls the dog "Comet". Comet settles into the household routine as if he has always lived there. He is a quiet, placid dog who doesn't bark. Janet likes having a dog. It makes her feel safer at night. Their neighbours are few and distant.

Aurora likes having a dog too. She and Comet are constant companions. Devoted to each other, in fact. Sometimes, Janet feels disquieted by the connection between them. Sometimes, they stare into each other's eyes, solemnly, silently, as if communicating telepathically, and it makes the sweat break out on Janet's palms.

Aurora's father had asteroid hyalosis.

The party was at a townhouse in a grotty inner-city suburb. Someone at work had invited Janet. She was twenty-two, slim and fit, and fresh from a break-up. She had worn a short skirt and thigh-high boots. "On the prowl," as she and her friends at the time had called it.

The townhouse was packed, stuffy with grass and cigarette smoke, the stink of countless perfumes and colognes. The old plaster walls vibrated from the thumping music. All the men were young, brash, cocky, loud, overly familiar with a hand on her shoulder, elbow or hip while they leaned in close and talked bullshit into her ear over the blare of music and the general cacophony of conversation, laughter, whooping. They bored her.

She met him in the laundry. Alone, he was leaning against a cabinet, drinking a beer.

The sight of him hooked her somewhere deep in the solar plexus.

Tall, tanned, lean to the point of skinny but with giant, callused hands that looked used to hard, physical labour. Boots, old denim jeans, faded t-shirt. Collar-length, curly brown hair. Square jaw with a dimple in his chin, three-day growth of beard. And big eyes. Big, sad, soulful eyes with long lashes, the irises a startling and brilliant blue. When he smiled at her, she felt it between her legs.

They talked. What about?

He told her his name. Or did he?

They soon tired of raising their voices over the hubbub, and went out the back door. The yard was a scrubby square of grass with a few dead plants and a rusting barbecue. And overhead, through a clear sky, the turning wheel of the Milky Way. They talked some more. She could never recall their conversation. Yet she hadn't been drunk. Only three wines all night. Only three.

He kissed her and she kissed him back. His embrace jolted her nervous system, his fingertips leaving a tingle of electrical traces on her skin. When he pulled up her skirt to peel down her soaked underwear, she was already close to orgasm. He entered her. As she came, she kept her eyes open and they stared into each other. She realised that his pupils held a whirl of galaxies, contained myriad suns and orbiting planets, a slew of asteroids. The earth tipped away. She felt herself travelling through the heavens at the speed of light. And when he gripped her tightly and cried out, she saw the burst of a supernova and understood that her whole life hinged on this moment: forever bisected into *before* and *after*.

She never saw him again.

Didn't know his name. Couldn't recall what happened after their lovemaking.

Megan's take on the experience: the man had roofied Janet, and the drugs in her system had caused hallucinations and amnesia.

Megan had urged Janet to have an abortion, but no, no. Janet knew in the deep, superstitious dark of her mind that she carried a star baby. *You're having another breakdown,* Megan had said. But no, no. Janet was clearheaded about the pregnancy. As the stranger's baby grew inside of her, Janet welcomed being part of the Bigger Plan. She only had to wait. Keep faith, and wait.

For months after the party, Janet tried to track down the stranger. No one knew him. No one remembered him. It got so that Janet doubted her own memory of the event, but then all she had to do was run her hands over her belly. Privately, she called him Archer, the half-man and half-horse symbol for Sagittarius. One day, she would meet him again. He would return and they would be a family.

Megan grew to hate talking about Archer. *He took advantage of you,* she would say at first, back in the days when she would discuss him. *You were drunk and he took advantage.* Megan will no longer talk about him, even though he is Aurora's father. *Stop this bullshit about having a star baby,* she had said in the lead-up to the birth. *Give your daughter a regular name.* But Janet had known better.

And the arrival of the dog, just a few days ago, proved it. She has not told Megan about Comet. Megan wouldn't understand that Larger Forces are at play.

Janet is working on a series of inter-related book covers when she notices that the house is unusually quiet. On tiptoe, she moves throughout the rooms. She finds them in the lounge. Aurora and Comet are sitting opposite each other, motionless, staring, communing with their galaxy-filled eyes. Janet doesn't know what their behaviour means.

Hopefully, it means Archer is coming back.

Cognisance strikes Janet in the night, jolting her from sleep, as if the truth came to her in a dream. She lies awake until dawn, watching the clock. When she pads into Aurora's bedroom, the child is already sitting up in bed, smiling. Together, holding hands, they walk to the kitchen. Visible through the glass of the back door, Comet is standing on the patio, ears cocked. So, Aurora and Comet had the same prophetic dream and were waiting for her.

Nothing surprises Janet now.

Everything is in flow.

Aurora and Comet are patient, unblinking, while she photographs their eyes on her phone. Close ups. They follow her to the study. Watch as she switches on the computer. Neither of them fusses or hassles for breakfast. While the hard drive boots, Janet inspects the photographs. She compares the glittering pattern of Aurora's pupils to Comet's. Their pupils look the same.

Simultaneously, she feels shocked and thrilled. She wonders why she is not hyperventilating, freaking out, as any normal person might. Instead, she taps at the keyboard, clicks the mouse, searching through star maps until she finds proof. And there it is. She sits back in her chair. The confirmation takes her breath. Causes the earth beneath her to stutter momentarily, tilt a little sideways.

Their eyes show the same patch of southern hemisphere sky.

It is unmistakeable. Irrefutable. Here is the Southern Cross constellation with the blackest of black nebulae, the Coalsack, dropped within the scrim. There, the galaxies of Small and Large Magellanic Clouds, the globular cluster named 47 Tucanae, the blip of Omega Centauri. The pearly backdrop of opalescent stars. All of these spheres represented, dot for dot in their eyes, a snapshot of the firmament.

Vindication brings tears. *He's given me a star baby*, she had told Megan, yet Megan had scoffed, cajoled, bullied and gaslighted her.

Now, Aurora and Comet watch Janet weep. They do nothing else. Janet stops crying, wipes her face, studies further the photographs and map. Wait. Each photograph of the pupils has something extra, something that doesn't feature in the star map. A white streak. Perhaps a shooting star? Piece of space junk? A satellite? Janet searches again.

And finds the answer.

Janet's heart thuds in the back of her throat.

She scans the newspaper article, stops, forces herself to read it again, slower this time. Her blood seems to cool and still. She has found what Archer was trying to tell her years ago at the party. Found his forewarning, his promise.

The headline proclaims: *SPACE ROCK ON COLLISION COURSE WITH EARTH.*

Janet leans closer to the monitor. The fast-moving asteroid called 327369 3117XI2, about the size of a skyscraper, is due to hurtle perilously close to Earth in about nine months. Unlike most asteroids, this one has a tail, probably of dust or gas. The hive-mind of the Internet has already dubbed the rock "Dino Killer". Memes abound. While NASA and most astronomers predict nothing more than an interesting night-time spectacle as the asteroid passes, flaring its tail across the sky, a few other experts, including mathematicians, claim that the giant rock just…might… hit.

End of the World cults have jumped on board.

Repent or burn, some say. Or, gather for the arrival of spaceships. For the return of Christ. Or, let's kill ourselves before Armageddon and reach the afterlife together. Each cult has a different message. It is all nonsense. The blather of ignorant people who can only guess, panic, clutch at each other and pray, gibber. Only Janet knows. The only person in seven billion, which sounds impossible, except that it is the truth.

She dials her sister's mobile to explain, trying her best to sound reasonable.

"This is insane," Megan says.

Janet holds the phone tight and bites her lip. "I can send you the photos of their eyes."

"When was the last time you saw the doctor?"

"A couple of months ago. For my Pap smear."

Megan says, "I mean the psychiatrist."

"Oh, him." Janet sits at the kitchen table while Aurora and Comet watch her, unblinking. They are both unnaturally quiet. "I haven't seen him in a while."

"You ought to call. Today. Now. Make an appointment."

"God, Megan. Really? Look, I'll send you the photos—"

"Can't you see what's going on here? It's happening again.

Can't you see the signs?"

"Stop it, Megan—"

"Your Messiah bullshit again? This is crazy—"

"Come on, I want to protect you. Save you. How could you even—?"

"—raped you wasn't a goddamned alien, he was a—"

"—never even tried to believe what I—"

"—for Christ's sake, Janet, listen—"

"—can't you just—"

"No, you *listen to me*!" Megan screams. "You've got a child, and in your state of mind—"

"Oh, fuck off, take my side for—"

"You might hurt her! You might hallucinate some awful, terrible stuff—"

Janet hangs up, breathless, shaking.

Despite its moniker, "Dino Killer" is not big enough to wipe out life on earth. Estimates suggest its impact would be similar to the Tunguska Event, which was when an asteroid hit Siberia in 1908. The Tunguska Event flattened 2000 square kilometres. Registered 5.0 on the Richter magnitude scale. Exploded with the power of 1000 atomic bombs. And killed just three people, since that particular area in Russia was all but uninhabited.

These facts do not comfort Janet because she understands that Dino Killer, or DK for short, will hit the city of Melbourne. She understands this at the subatomic level, within the molecular structure of her bone marrow. She understands it inside her dreams.

She has nine months to build an underground bunker. Plenty of time. And she has plenty of ground too: her cottage sits on half an acre of bushland. However, what she lacks is plenty of money. The cost turns out to be prohibitive; about the same again as her mortgage.

Which is why she is inspecting the cellar.

She has ignored it ever since moving in.

Because it is cold down here. Damp. The scent of earth is strong through the wooden panel walls. It reminds her of a grave. The floor is a poured slab of concrete, the ceiling low. Access is via a ladder through a trap door in the yard. The previous owners had used the cellar as storage space. Janet hasn't used it at all.

She kicks at the cobwebs. Roams her torchlight across the overhead beams. The cellar is small, about the size of the lounge room and kitchen combined, but it will have to do.

Besides, the shock wave from DK won't last long. She only needs to protect her family from the short-lived blast of hurricane winds that will fling uprooted forests, pulverised houses, airborne cars, and everything else in a single, titanic gust. Once the shock wave has passed, they can climb out. Rebuild the cottage. Start over.

And she will have Archer to help her.

He was a carpenter, wasn't he? Yes, she remembers that snippet from their conversation at the party. It explains his callused hands. All tradesmen have callused hands. Archer will construct a new weatherboard home for his woman, child and dog. His message in the townhouse's laundry: *Prepare for disaster, and wait for me to come back.* She remembers. The knowledge surges to the surface from where it has lain dormant in her bone marrow.

Now to get ready. For starters, the cottage already has a rainwater tank. Good.

So, Janet's first purchase for her makeshift bunker is a food dehydrator.

The machine looks like a microwave but with six metal racks inside. To prepare food, she needs to slice the items thinly. She starts with fruit. Oranges and apples; Aurora's favourites. Who knows how long it will take Melbourne's food supply chain to resurrect itself? Janet is planning for at least three months.

"I wanna help," Aurora says.

"Not with the knife. Here, put the slices on the rack. Keep them spaced apart."

The machine is simple to operate, with two buttons for temperature and time. It works as described. She stores the dehydrated fruit in labelled freezer bags. Next, she works on vegetables. She and Aurora are having fun, enjoying themselves. Janet hasn't told her about the asteroid. Comet lies near their feet, his head on his paws, twitching both eyebrows as he watches them. Periodically, Janet's phone rings but she lets it go to voicemail.

Next, she buys boxes of tinned goods from discount outlets. Packaged foods too. Giant bags of rice and dried pasta. The shelving units in the cellar are filling up with produce. She buys a camp stove and gas bottles. Doesn't bother with a refrigerator since the power stations will be out of commission. She hoards camp lanterns. Candles. Batteries, lots of batteries, and torches. Nightlights.

A compost toilet is the biggest expense, apart from paying a plumber to route a pipe from the water tank into the cellar, and put a tap on it. Drainage for a shower is impractical and expensive. They will make do with a basin. Online, she discovers portable hand-cranked washing machines and buys one. Cot beds, board games, books, puzzles. Second-hand sofa and table. Rug.

The months go by. It starts to look like a home down there. A cluttered, crazy home.

One evening, she is bathing Aurora. Time is fleeting. DK is almost upon them. Janet raises both hands, as is their custom. "Ready to sing *Twinkle, Twinkle, Little Star*?"

Aurora shakes her head.

"What's the matter?" Janet says, dropping her hands.

"Are we really gonna live in the cellar?"

Janet hesitates. "Not for a little while yet, honey. And if so, only for a few weeks."

"I don't like it down there."

"Oh, why not? Don't you like cosy places?"

Aurora pouts her lip. The blip of DK, represented in her pupils, is larger. Has been growing steadily larger, in fact, with a longer and brighter tail every day. It is now the biggest object in Aurora's pupillary night sky. Janet is afraid but excited. Melbourne will be flattened, yes, but Archer is coming back. Some days, the tug-of-war of these contrary feelings overwhelms her, stymies her, whispers for the peace and release of sitting back in a warm bath with a sharp blade, the suggestion so intense that she has to shake herself out of its lure. Comet watches her these days. Watches her closely. As if he knows. Can read her mind.

Now, she tries to smile at Aurora, and says, "The cellar is okay. Come on, what's wrong, hon? There'll be lots of fun things to do. We'll spend all our days playing together."

"It's too dark."

That's true. It is autumn. By the time DK strikes, it will be winter. Janet imagines how cold it might be for them, buried under the house, buried deep inside the earth. And what if DK sparks bushfires? What if the cottage burns above them? Kills them with smoke? With falling, fiery debris? Her resolve falters.

But then she remembers Archer. She wishes she could tell Aurora that her father is coming back. They have never discussed him. Not once. Not ever.

"Comet doesn't want to live in the dirt either," Aurora says, pouting.

From dollar stores, Janet buys cutlery, plates, bowls, cups, glasses. Knives and serving spoons. More knives. First aid kits. She wants to buy an indoor gas heater but is scared of carbon monoxide poisoning despite the manufacturer's exhortations of safety stamped on the box. Yet the weather is cooling. The sun is withdrawing, rising later, setting sooner. In the night sky, Janet can see DK. It resembles a lit match head with its blue halo.

Blankets, blankets, blankets. Janet purchases them by the armload from op shops.

She buys a small generator and stockpiles cans of petrol. She will need, at the very least, to keep her phone charged and there is no other way. Without her phone, she will be cut off.

She receives a text, an ultimatum, from Megan: I'M FLYING TO MELBOURNE.

Janet is compelled to call. It is the first conversation they have had since Megan expressed the fear that Janet might hurt Aurora.

"Are you okay?" Megan says, sounding out of breath. "Is Aurora okay?"

"We're both fine. There's no need for you to visit."

"Listen, have you heard the latest news about the asteroid?"

Janet sucks on her top lip. Finally, she says, "Yeah. I've heard."

"Oh my God. I mean…shit. Holy fuck."

Janet doesn't reply. Feels that she doesn't have to say anything. Not anymore. Not now.

"Did you hear?" Megan says. "NASA reckons it might hit after all."

"Uh-huh."

"And you knew," Megan says, her voice reedy. "Jesus, you *knew*. Months ago. Can you send the photos now? Of Aurora's eyes. And the dog's too. Do you still have the dog?"

Comet walks into the kitchen, his claws clicking on the linoleum. He stops. His expression seems to communicate something important. Janet tightens her grip on the mobile. "Don't come here, Megan. There's no room for you. I haven't allowed for an extra person."

"What? What do you mean?"

"If you come here, I won't let you in. That's all."

There is silence on the line. Eyes closed, Janet rides the waves of static and crackle, breathing, aware of the steady beat of her heart, fluxing, strumming, singing her blood.

"We're sisters," Megan says. "Remember?"

"But I'm the crazy one. Remember? Don't come here," Janet says and hangs up, shaking.

The last few days consist of ferrying belongings into the cellar. Aurora helps when she can. She has mastered the ladder; Janet no longer needs to help her. Comet is dextrous, bolting up and down whenever the trap door is open, acting more like a sure-footed cat.

"You see?" Janet says on one of the last days. "Comet likes it in here. You should too."

Aurora says nothing. She often stonewalls instead of talking. Such behaviour makes Janet uncomfortable. But what to do about it? She can't change her daughter's personality. Maybe Aurora gets this quirk from her father. Will Archer notice when he meets Aurora for the first time? Will he love the reflection of himself? Love his mirror image?

Janet keeps a variety of radios in the cellar, including a crystal set. She has thought of everything. They will be safe down here. Safe and sound. She dreams every night of Archer. He is streaking across the Milky Way without a spaceship or suit; a ghost, an alien, perhaps even a god. In a lockbox, she has cash. A few thousand. The DK asteroid will take out not just power stations but the Internet too. Electric cash registers, the tap-and-go facilities.

And she has knives.

In apocalyptic situations, the unprepared — those who assume that governments will take care of them — are caught short and turn on the preppers like Janet, stealing their food, their water. No, no. Janet can't get a gun because of restrictions and licences, but knives are freely available. Cleavers, chef's knives, a range of paring, bread, utility and steak knives. Stashed around the cellar. Taped to the underside of drawers, hidden beneath mattresses. At any point in the cellar, she could put her hand on a hidden knife. Just in case. Because people in crisis, desperate people, can lose their humanity as well as their sanity.

Janet is a good mother. Has made sure that Aurora can't find the knives by accident.

The days count down. The world comes together, apparently, with a plan called "Defending Earth", which is devised by the signatories to something called the *Planetary Defence Conference*. Janet doesn't bother checking the Internet anymore. It doesn't matter to her what the world governments plan to do. DK burns in the night sky. It resembles a spotlight. The brightest object apart from the moon. Soon, the moon will be outshone.

Aurora and Comet are agitated. Janet often sings nursery rhymes to them including *Twinkle, Twinkle Little Star*, but her forced jollity has no effect.

"It's okay, we'll be safe in the cellar," she urges on the Final Day, carrying Aurora against her body instead of propped on her hip. She can't bear to look into her daughter's eyes. She descends the ladder and puts Aurora down. Comet follows, padding around and around the cluttered room, whimpering. The furniture, the bookcases, the shelves. Barely space to move.

"No, I don't like it here," Aurora announces, hands over her eyes.

"It won't be for long," Janet says, as she reaches up, closes and bolts the trap door.

Comet stares at her. His blighted pupils are ablaze with twin flares.

DK bears down. The light show is grand, insistent. Its brightness burns through the chinks in the boards. Curiosity gets the better of her. Janet opens the trap door.

"Stay inside," she cautions.

Meekly, Aurora and Comet cower. Janet emerges.

It is after midnight. Yet the yard is alight. For a moment, Janet wonders if she has lost her mind. She steps out, shades her eyes with her hand. In the sky is a bright burn of fire, shimmering in shades of blue, yellow and orange. Janet blinks away the after-images.

Melbourne will soon be obliterated. Buildings gone. Greenery erased. Yarra River choked with debris. Janet has never been a fan of the CBD: too noisy and busy, an assault on the senses. But how many people will die? However, it is only one city after all, and the bulk of the world's population doesn't know, doesn't care, or makes jokes and creates memes.

DK is alluring, mesmeric. Janet smiles, despite herself.

She scans the sky. *Archer, where are you?* The recollection of his scintillating touch provokes tears. Not long now. Her mobile jangles. Baffled, she takes it from her pocket. She remembers how to touch a button, put the device to her ear. She hears the crackle of distance.

"We're safe," says Megan's joyful, trilling voice.

"What?"

"The asteroid. It's going to pass us by. Oh, wow. Oh, God. Can you *believe* it?"

In the glittering firmament, DK glows as red as a hot coal. Janet understands that Megan is scoffing, cajoling, bullying, gaslighting. Megan didn't believe that Archer existed, had wanted her to abort Aurora, has never taken Janet's side against the doctors and psychiatrists. Megan is evil, trying to make Janet expose herself and her daughter to Armageddon.

"You're lying," Janet says.

"I swear, it's passing right on by. Like, missing us by a million miles or something."

"Goodbye, Megan."

"Wait a minute! There's no crisis—"

Janet hangs up.

Comet is alongside. She didn't hear him on the ladder. His eyes are luminous.

There are sudden noises beyond the trees. The breaking of branches. Is that a scuffle of footfalls? *Interloper*. An unprepared neighbour wanting to steal Janet's stash. She realises she has knives on her person already, and takes hold of them. The night sky is dazzling. The bushland glows. Where is Archer? Janet scans the heavens, murmuring in prayer to him.

"Mummy?" Aurora says, for she has emerged too.

What a naughty little girl. So wilful. So defiant all the time.

"Go back inside," Janet orders, nudging her towards the ladder. "Do as I tell you."

Aurora pouts her lip, stands her ground.

To pick her up, Janet must drop one of the knives. This is a difficult decision. Child or knife? Leaf litter crunches beneath the shoes of the unseen interloper. Janet must protect her family. On the other hand, it could be Archer out there. The footsteps cease. She waits. Nobody presents themselves. Nobody calls to her.

"Archer?" she cries.

DK has turned blood-red. Janet remembers the warm bath, the sharp blade.

Where is Archer? Is he coming or not? Or must she go to him instead?

Comet's eyes are communicating with her. Helping Janet to make a decision. The answer turns out to be simple once she realises that DK *is* the message from Archer. DK's purpose is to tell her exactly what Archer needs her to do. And Janet obeys, even though it's not what she anticipated. Not what she wanted. But the solution is neat, perfect, precise, and rises up from her molecules and bone marrow, from her dreams. Everything makes sense now.

"Come here, hon," she says. "Let's go and meet Daddy."

A Small Village in Crete

After buying tickets at the bus station, they put their backpacks on the floor and sat on them, waiting. Susie and Greg were leaving Chania for the southern coast. Chania reminded Susie in many ways of Athens—albeit a scaled down version—with its tangle of narrow streets, traffic fumes, grey concrete buildings, noise and hustle. She was looking forward to spending a few days in a quiet village by the sea.

"How long till the bus comes?" she said.

Greg checked his watch. "About half an hour."

"Real time or Greek time?"

He chuckled, took out his harmonica and started playing the Cold Chisel song, *Khe Sanh*—the unofficial national anthem for Aussie backpackers in Europe—and repeatedly lifted his eyebrows at her in encouragement. But God no, she wouldn't sing. Not with scores of other people around. Tutting, Greg shook his head and put the harmonica away.

Gazing around the dingy bus station, Susie felt a pang for the clean streets and pure white houses of Santorini, and then she stopped to marvel at herself. Why, just three weeks in Greece and already she felt seasoned, mature, worldly. It was June of 1985 and she was twenty-two years old, fresh out of university, taking a year off with her boyfriend before starting work as a primary school teacher. She would be a completely different person by the time she returned home: a woman, not a girl. Before they'd even bought their plane tickets, Greg had warned they would be *travellers*, not *tourists*, and now she understood what he'd meant.

"Want something to drink?" Greg said.

"Oh, maybe water if you're getting some."

"Mind my pack," he said, like he did whenever he left her side to negotiate or investigate.

She smiled, and made her usual show of holding one strap. He headed to the little kiosk.

Greg could speak enough Greek to get by. In fact, he could speak conversational Italian, Spanish and French since his mother was a Classics professor and had taught him Latin from a young age. Apparently, Latin is the foundation of all Romance languages. Greg had Berlitz books stashed in his backpack and studied at every opportunity. Susie couldn't get the hang of Greek, couldn't remember the strange combinations of sounds, the conjugations of verbs. Annoyed, Greg had stopped trying to educate her. Without him, Susie would be lost.

Sometimes she believed he preferred it that way.

He was twenty-nine. They had been together nearly four years. At first, she had been flattered and astonished that an older man would even be interested in her, a shy and gawky teenager, nothing special. And now… Well, now she wondered if the size and weight of his personality was making hers more compact, forcing her to take up less space.

The journey wended through mountainous terrain. Blind turns snaggled the road. Every time the bus driver approached a corner, he tapped his horn. The countryside was patchworked with blocks of wilderness next to blocks of cultivated, orderly vines.

After a couple of hours, Susie began to drowse.

"Look at that," Greg said, nudging her ribs.

Out the window was an old man astride a clip-clopping donkey. A typical sight in rural Greece. Susie closed her eyes again.

"Don't you want to see Crete? You'll probably never come back here."

Susie sat up, yawned, and stared out the window at the monotony of landscape.

After a while, they drove alongside a cluster of buildings and the bus stopped, idling. The front door creaked open on its pneumatic arm. Three young men with backpacks raced onboard. They wore singlets and boardshorts, all of them burnt brown with dots of pink, peeling skin on their shoulders and noses, unkempt hair bleached blonde by sun and surf.

The first one called, "Aussie, Aussie, Aussie!"

Greg shouted the required response, "Oi, oi, oi!"

The trio guffawed and barrelled down the aisle to take seats nearby. Susie felt ill from motion sickness. Greg chatted, laughed, shook hands. Paul, Robbo and Shunt (actual name "Shane") were drinking their way through the Greek islands. With relish, interrupting and talking over one another, they spoke mostly of their stay on Ios; of boozing around the clock, throwing up, catching colds, getting laid, punching German bystanders in the face, bashing Americans to the catch-cry of "Don't fuck with Australians, mate!" All the while, Susie closed her eyes and tried to close her ears too.

"Your girl's so fucken *quiet*," one of them whispered. "Is she okay?"

"Just very young," Greg said.

Susie feigned sleep.

The bus parked in the village plaza. Hawkers jostled. As tourists disembarked, the hawkers called out their accommodation offers, some adding enticements like free breakfasts, ocean views, private bathrooms. Susie followed Greg into the throng. He was speaking Greek. That set him apart as far as locals were concerned and always got him the best deals. Susie felt nauseated and dizzy. Robbo and Shunt both volunteered to carry her pack. Paul told them to *show respect* and *back off* because she was *taken*. She rolled her eyes but said nothing.

Greg bundled her into a minivan that stank of musky sweat and cigarettes.

"This is Teris," Greg said of the driver, a man with curly yellow-ed hair like sheep's fleece.

"And I'm Michalis," said the man in the front passenger seat. "Friends call me Mike."

Greg snorted. "G'day, Michalis."

Laughter. Susie looked about. *Shit.* Paul, Robbo and Shunt were in the back. Greg had latched onto strangers again. She would be forced to spend time with them, like it or not.

Teris put the van into gear and exited the plaza via one of the cobbled streets, and then zigzagged along one-way lanes bordered by terrace houses.

The village sat on the tip of a thin, finger-like peninsula. The Red Tomato Hotel was built into a hillside that overlooked one of the beaches. The hotel had a long central corridor with rooms off either side. The owner was Teris and Mike's mother, a shrivelled old woman, who welcomed them enthusiastically and fished keys from her skirt pocket. Greg had negotiated a room with a balcony for just 650 drachmas—about AU$3—each per night. Considering their daily budget of AU$25 each, this was a *bargain*. Perhaps now they could splurge on food. Susie's shorts were slipping about her hips. To afford accommodation on Mykonos—sleeping on the beach had turned out to be illegal—they'd had to skip meals.

The owner unlocked their door, pressed the keys into Greg's hand, and limped away.

Their room was cool, clean, tiled and painted white. Susie put down her backpack. Two single beds, bedside tables, a free-standing wardrobe, a communal bathroom across the hall. But it was the balcony that drew her. God, what a *view*. Below, whitewashed houses nestled into the hillside; beyond, a mountain furrowed with craggy, angular faces, its sandy base lapped by blue waters; the picture-perfect vista set against a backdrop of endless sky.

She sat in a chair, lit a *Hellas* cigarette, and said, "Wow! This place is gorgeous."

"Come on." Greg ducked onto the balcony while buckling his money belt. "Time to have a look around."

"Already? Can't we just rest here for a while?"

"You rested on the bus. Hurry up. The guys are waiting."

"The 'guys'?" Paul, Robbo and Shunt were staying in tents at a nearby camping ground despite Greg's exhortations that they should take a room at the Red Tomato Hotel. "You mean the bogans from Queensland who like to punch people?"

"Oh, here we go again," Greg said. "Little Miss Prim. If this trip is to do you any good, you have to try broadening your horizons once in a while. Now put your shoes on."

"But I'm still crook from the bus ride."

"We're only here for three days."

"But look at this view!"

His face darkened. "Fine, maybe I'll see you later," he said, and left the balcony.

The door to their room slammed shut. Susie contemplated going after him—when Greg got angry, he tended to sulk for hours, sometimes all day—but instead, she gazed across the sea. The mountain, cloud and sky formed a pastel reflection on the water. How soothing to look into a great distance instead of being cramped inches away from, say, a typewriter.

Greg appeared below, hurrying down the steps of a laneway that ran between houses.

"Hey, when will you be back?" Susie called, but he flapped a dismissive hand without turning his head. "Ah, get fucked," she muttered under her breath, and then wondered how she would negotiate dinner if Greg decided to stay away and teach her another lesson.

Well, one more skipped meal shouldn't matter.

She leaned back in the chair and stretched her legs. It was so quiet. The occasional calling of Greeks, trill of cicadas, the tremulous brooding of a chook in the next-door yard. At the bottom of the hill, wavelets kept washing onto the sand. It occurred to Susie that she felt calm and relaxed for the first time since arriving in Greece. She stood up and leaned against the balcony. Along a nearby laneway sat three crumpled-up old women dressed in black widows' weeds. A common sight, but Susie felt uneasy. The widows reminded her of crows or ravens.

Without warning, the swoop of three fighter jets boomed overhead. The planes flashed along the coastline and ducked behind the mountain outcrop inside a split-second. Christ, the shock of it nearly gave Susie a heart attack. The old women hadn't reacted though. Perhaps they were deaf. Or, more likely, used to the noise. Crete's nearest neighbours included Turkey, Israel, Egypt, Libya. The Cretan air force certainly didn't keep a low profile. Lightning-fast jets had often cruised overhead in Chania.

The three widows turned their faces towards Susie at the same time.

Susie baulked. Were they staring at her?

She ducked out of sight and locked the balcony door. She decided to have a lie down... Oh, what do you know, Greg had dibbed which bed was his by putting his backpack on it. Susie considered commandeering his chosen bed out of spite but opted for the other.

Greg came back after all. That night, they went Greek dancing at a restaurant, invited by the brothers Teris and Mike. The music reminded Susie of an old Anthony Quinn movie. Ceramic plates got smashed. When Susie went out to the courtyard for a cigarette, Teris followed and tried to kiss her. Shocked, she pushed him away. In the shadows lurked Mike. Greg appeared, yelling and blustering. Teris got down on his knees—theatrically, melodramatically, *sarcastically*, in Susie's opinion—to entreat Greg's forgiveness while Mike kept offering him free drinks. Paul, Robbo and Shunt spilled from the restaurant, keen to fight. Other Greek men wandered out to watch the commotion.

"We should leave," Susie whispered to Greg. "Right now."

"What for? I haven't done anything wrong."

"Look how many there are. What if somebody has a knife?"

Greg blanched. Forcing a smile, he shook Teris's outstretched hand and helped the curly-headed bastard to his feet. They reconciled in Greek, laughing together, gesturing at Susie as if to say, *Oh, what a siren she is! Who could blame a man for trying? All is forgiven!* Mike grinned. Meanwhile, Susie stood motionless in the spotlight of everyone's gaze.

Breath stinking of Retsina, Shunt put an arm about her. "Listen, I'll bust his skull for ya."

"Just say the word," added Robbo, crowding her from the other side.

"Hey, what did I tell you dickheads already?" Paul hissed, shoving them. "She's *taken*."

Susie slipped away and pulled Greg's wrist. "I want to go back to the hotel," she begged.

He clutched her hand and ran with her through the maze of narrow streets, leading the way at every turn because Susie had lost her bearings amongst the whitewashed walls and had no idea where the Red Tomato Hotel could possibly be, since every street looked the same.

The next morning as Susie exited the bathroom, towel in one hand and toilet bag in the other, Teris accosted her. Again, he knelt down and screwed up his face in a parody of weeping, but this time the performance was for her, not Greg.

"Sorry," he moaned in English. "Sorry, sorry."

"Forget it," she said, sidestepping him.

"My brother is a simpleton," Mike said, standing nearby. "He gets the wrong idea."

"It doesn't matter," she said.

Mike smiled. "So, we are friends?"

"Yes, of course," she said, and hurried into her room, closing the door.

Greg was sitting on his bed, perusing the *Let's Go Europe* book. Without looking up, he said, "I've found a cheap café for breakfast. Ready?"

"My hair's still wet."

"It'll dry on the way."

The morning was clear and bright. The cobblestones felt cool beneath her sandals. The houses were squared off, flat-roofed, the rendered walls left white or else painted yellow or pink. Doors, window shutters and trimmings were typically blue. Susie and

Greg passed various cats tucked into brickwork recesses, each sleeping feline curled as tight as a croissant.

Around a corner sat the three old women in black widows' weeds.

Susie faltered. The women turned their wrinkled raisin faces towards her. Greg said *good morning* in Greek. The women had eyes only for Susie. They were crocheting. Susie remembered an ancient legend or story which she couldn't recall in its entirety, but it was something like…one old woman spins the thread, one knits, and the last cuts the thread.

They watched Susie as she walked by. She felt unnerved, expecting them to lunge out and touch her, but of course they didn't even move. Susie was being silly again, that's all. Immature and silly. Greg had told her so last night when she'd had trouble sleeping.

The beachside café sold a cheap type of churros, perfect for breakfast. Greg bought himself coffee. Susie's tea tasted cold and soapy. They sat at an outside table with a red-checked cloth and wooden chairs painted green. A middle-aged couple approached the café window and tried to order but couldn't speak Greek. What were they speaking…Spanish?

"Italian!" Greg rejoiced, and introduced himself in their native tongue.

Relieved, they were happy to let him order on their behalf, pleased to join him at their table. Greg always relished the opportunity to speak with older Europeans who didn't know English. However, Susie didn't understand Italian. Their conversation went on and on while she ate her breakfast, smoked a cigarette. The woman smiled pityingly at her from time to time, shrugging a resigned shoulder. *Too bad*, she seemed to be saying. *Tough luck.*

"I'm going for a walk," Susie said to no one in particular, and stood up.

The sand was soft but hard-packed, easy to traverse. The air smelled clean and salty, while the sea lay flat. At this hour of the morning, the beach was largely deserted. The sudden boom of overhead jets made Susie duck in panic. Then the planes were gone. She climbed a wooden staircase to the promenade. A group of people were gathered, taking photographs and laughing. Curious, she wandered over.

A pelican!

She had never seen one in the flesh before. God Good, the bird was *huge*, at least four foot high, the wingspan perhaps twice that. It weaved and bobbed on webbed toes, flapping outstretched wings, its feathers a range of subtle shades from white to frosted pink. Magical! Giggling, worrying at and playing with the pelican was an old Greek man. Both of his arms ended at the elbow in withered stumps. Susie took a step back. Had the poor man, maybe a fisherman, suffered an accident with a shark or a propeller? Was the pelican his pet? He turned to smile at her, toothless. One eye socket was empty and black. Squawking, the pelican dropped open its beak to reveal a red, wet, crinkled tunnel into a gaping gullet.

"Susie!" came a shout. "Susie, how ya goin'?"

Robbo and Shunt were closing in on her, striding across the promenade. Where was Paul?

"Join us on the beach," she called, waving, darting to the wooden staircase.

She clattered down the steps. Heavy footfalls meant Robbo and Shunt were following close on her heels. She ran across the sand towards the café. Greg was still at the table, yammering to the Italian couple, the wife looking decidedly bored, jaw propped on one fist.

"Look who I found!" Susie gasped, throwing herself into a chair.

Greg scowled at her, then noticed Robbo and Shunt. "Hey!" he proclaimed. "Sit down!"

The old Italian couple offered their goodbyes and left, but Greg hardly noticed.

"What happened to Paul?" he said. "Too hungover?"

"Nah, on some kind of tour," Robbo said. "He'll be back tonight."

"Feel like a beer?" Greg said. "The café sells hair of the dog. My shout."

"Yeah, sweet, why not?" Robbo said.

Susie would have declined a drink except Greg didn't ask. He left the table for the café. Robbo and Shunt watched her. To keep busy, she lit a cigarette and tried to focus on the sea.

"You're really pretty," Robbo said.

"Nah," Shunt said. "She's beautiful."

Susie fidgeted, drew hard on her smoke. "Okay."

"Does he treat you right?" Robbo said. "Or…maybe not?"

"Yeah," Shunt said. "He's a bit of a prick. Wanna know what he says about you?"

She escaped towards the water's edge. When she looked around at last, Greg was seated at the table. Impatiently, he waved her over. She dropped the cigarette and returned.

"I'm off to the hotel," she said.

"But we're hiring motorbikes," Greg retorted, as Robbo and Shunt smiled and nodded.

"Have fun," she said, and turned her back.

The sand felt softer, looser, her sandals bogging in the grains.

"What about the beach party tonight?" Greg called. "A big piss-up, Aussies and Kiwis."

"No thanks," she yelled, and kept walking.

She had a paper map to consult this time. Even still, she made a few wrong turns. She knew she was close to the Red Tomato Hotel when she stumbled upon the three old widows. Hurrying past, Susie skimmed the far side of the laneway while the women called out, gesturing for her to come closer, *closer*, their faces deeply wrinkled, eyes black and sunken, mouths empty pits. She imagined crinkled gullets and raced on. The stairs to the Red Tomato Hotel were steep, steep, *steep*. Narrow treads and high risers, burning her thigh muscles. Jet fighters boomed overhead. Susie ducked, heart pounding, and flung herself inside the hotel, shutting the front door and leaning against it.

The white tiled hallway was cool and quiet.

No sign of the other travellers: the German girls who had blocked Susie from using the kitchen this morning, the Americans who had ignored her last night when she was smoking on the balcony right next to them. Tears welled. She held a breath for a moment. Took the room key from her shorts pocket. Opened the door and paused to admire the room. Today, she would write postcards, an airmail letter to Grandpa, an entry in her travel diary. How she'd longed to be *alone*. She needed the break. The peace and solitude. She went inside and began to shut the door. Something stopped the door from shutting.

Mike's hand.

"Sorry," Mike said. "For last night. For my brother Teris."

Susie blinked. "Look, we've already sorted this out. Please."

"No. My brother is upset. He needs to make friends with you."

Behind Mike stood Teris.

"It's fine," she said, trying again to close the door on them. "Excuse me, I'm tired."

Mike forced open the door. The brothers stood together on the threshold.

Susie's heart rate kicked up. "Get out," she said.

Over Teris's shoulder was the owner of the hotel, their mother, who caught Susie's eye before looking away and retreating inside a bathroom with a mop and bucket.

"Hey!" Susie shouted. "Hey, wait! *Hey!*"

Mike and Teris entered her room and shut the door. Susie couldn't believe what was happening, couldn't make sense of what was going on, her mind working and flailing.

"Don't worry," Mike said, smiling, lifting a palm as if to shush her. "We are friends."

For a moment, Susie thought she had misinterpreted the situation. She began to laugh. After all, everything was normal, wasn't it? From the balcony, she could hear the brooding chicken, the cicadas, the widows in their weeds keening from the laneway.

Teris said in English, "Me first."

Cast Down

There is shouting and panic. Through the oar-hole, I glimpse the enemy's galley ship approaching at speed. The *souscomites* lash the whips across our backs. We pull at the oars, muscles burning. I pray to God for deliverance.

Their ram hits us broadside. We are thrown from our benches as the stern explodes in a shower of splintered wood and foaming gouts of water. The enemy has no time to board us. Our galley ship lists, floods. The sea rushes over my head. The ruined craft plummets down, down, as fast as if dropping through air. All of us are underwater, sailors and slaves, trapped together. Men wrestle against their chains. I offer my soul to God.

As we fall, pressure begins to crush and crumple me, push my eyes into my head, squeeze my innards. My last breath is wrung from my lungs in a wheeze of frothing blood. I pray, waiting for death.

The colour of the water darkens from clear blue to green. One by one, the bodies of my fellow *galérien* start to wander at the end of their chains, limbs outstretched and limp. Drowned *souscomites* roll and bump against the beams.

The water turns deep blue.

At last, the ship hits bottom, splits open along her keel, and comes to rest. The dead shift about. The sound of the ocean tide beats against my ears. Soon, I hear other noises: scuttling and scratching. There is just enough light to show the crabs and shrimps, a few at first, and then in ever-increasing hordes.

Nipping and snapping, the creatures swarm the dead,

consuming, laying bare the bones. In horror, I watch them eat my own flesh, powerless to bat them away, unable to move, to breathe, to die. Fish arrive next, poking, nuzzling, sucking. My tattered skin ripples in the current like pale seaweed. An octopus gropes its tentacles through the ruptured gut of a nearby man, pulling and tearing, gnawing at intestines with its beak. I want to scream but I cannot. God has abandoned me.

Or is this death?

Is every man on this ship awake like me, dead like me?

My lower leg, finally stripped of its meat, eases out of the manacle. I drift away from the ship. Thank God, the shrimps and crabs let me be.

In time, my torso bloats, the putrefaction gases in my belly raising me up and up. As I ascend, the dark sea lightens to deep blue, to green, and then clear blue. Shafts of sunlight pierce the water. When I was a free man, I worked the land. I praise God for this small mercy, to feel again the sun and air.

The bite of a passing shark tears my body.

My gases escape. The only parts of me that will ever reach the surface are these streaming bubbles. I stare at them as I sink towards the abyss, where the shrimps and crabs are waiting, hungry, with their clicking mandibles and claws.

Hand to Mouth

April 7

James, I'm not a monster. First things first: despite reports to the contrary, I love your mother. Even now, after the terrible things she and I did to each other, my love remains unshakable. Relatives, police, lawyers, media (even those damned lab technicians) say otherwise, but I hope you'll believe me. Pray that you'll believe me. Consider this: when I've already lost everything, why would I bother lying to my own son? Especially about something so life-changing as the accident. This is my confession, written to you, the only person left who might listen.

Fair warning, you're not a child anymore so I won't keep back details in order to "protect" you. In fact, since you'll be turning eighteen this year, I'll do my best forthwith to talk only man-to-man. (For the record, I'm not sure why our relationship has never been especially close, but I suspect it's because your mother is such a robust communicator. She did the talking for me. Do you consider me a distant father? If this is the case, I'm sorry, and I hope to make up for it with these letters. Yes, plural. I aim to write to you weekly. I have access to a laptop and a librarian helps me with the printer.)

James, I'll get straight to the point.

The day of the accident.

(This will be an honest account of what actually happened.)

We were driving from your grandmother's estate, having attended her seventy-fifth birthday soiree held in what I secretly call her "back yard". Ha ha. (Something I've never told you: I despise "the terrace" with its topiaries and fountains. So vulgar.) The dress code was over the top, but the waiters in tails and the diamond-shaped ice sculpture shot the whole shindig into the upper stratosphere of ostentation. Of course, I said nothing to your mother but I knew she'd be watching me anyway for so much as a quirked eyebrow. In the end, I decided to be amused by the excesses of Matriarch's party. Well, you know your grandmother—never one to do anything by halves.

James, I had *not* been drinking. Check the police report. My blood alcohol reading was *zero*. Bottled mineral water the whole day. (And I hadn't taken drugs either, despite the insinuations from relatives on your mother's side.) Whenever we socialise outside of our own house, your mother drinks and I don't. You remember that rule, don't you? It's inviolable. I swear on your own precious head: no alcohol and no drugs.

And yet, I can't explain the accident.

That's how rumours start: when the truth doesn't satisfy, people make up stories. Prior to that day, I'd never caused a bingle. In the thirty-plus years I've held my licence, I've been involved in just *four* motor vehicle accidents, and each time the other driver was at fault.

So, we were travelling along a dual-carriage highway. Green fields on either side. The hilly nature of the Yarra Valley causes roads to often dip and climb like rollercoaster tracks. The posted speed limit was one hundred kilometres per hour, and yes, I was doing the speed limit *exactly*. I remember steering the car over an incline. The descent and subsequent rise promised a queasy, lurching sensation in the guts. The asphalt was dry. It had rained the night before, but the autumn sun had burned off the moisture. The sky shone blue with a few wispy clouds. No other traffic.

How to explain what happened next?

I drove the car over the incline. Your mother, who had been quaffing champagne, was in a spiky mood. Well, you know how she gets after a skinful. Agitated, prone to repeating herself. That's how she was that day. I didn't mind. After twenty-two years of marriage, you get used to mercurial moods. She's a passionate person, which is one of the reasons why I fell in love. Because opposites attract. She had such *zest* in her youth. Such feisty *zest*.

She said to me, "For Christ's sake, Graham, you ought to make more of an effort."

I said, "With your family? What do you mean? I thought I talked to everybody."

"No, you *greeted* everybody. There's a big difference."

According to the prosecution, that particular exchange constituted an *argument*. James, you know how it is between your mother and me, how it's always been? That "exchange" was simply a discussion. No, not even a discussion—just normal, everyday conversation. Mundane stuff. After the relatives on your mother's side threw their weight around, minor details such as that conversation took on a disproportionate significance. Legal eagles saw *nuance* and *subtext* in our words but, driving home that day from Matriarch's soiree, there *was* no nuance or subtext. As usual, your mother wished that I had been more verbose at a social event and, as usual, I expressed hurt surprise. That's it. She's an extrovert while I'm an introvert. Case closed.

So, I steered the car down the incline at exactly one hundred kilometres per hour. The car reached the road's nadir. James, there was nothing there; no animal, no obstacle, *nothing*. The front wheels caught and bit. The car slung itself into a tree. (Strictly speaking, first took out a fence and then hit an old-man eucalypt, square on the front passenger door.) Your mother's arm took the impact. I remember the exclamation she made: a soft, disappointed and querulous "ugh" sound, as if she had unexpectedly dirtied her hand.

Other sounds… The car crunching itself around the tree trunk, the smash of breaking glass, explosion of plastic shards. Then sirens. What I remember most, however, is the *ugh*.

Emergency lights. Staccato red and blue.

"My wife," I said, the strobes beating at my eyes. "Forget about me. Please help my wife."

The firemen had to cut the wreckage to get her out.

Memories of the hospital are vague. Cream walls. Smell of disinfectant. Chatter of nurses in the hallway. Beeping machine noises. Your mother and I were kept separate for days, perhaps weeks, or possibly the concussion befuddled my sense of time.

In any case, the hospital staff chose a dramatic way to reunite me with your mother. An orderly pushed my wheeled bed along corridors while a nurse kept pace, blathering about how I should *mentally prepare for God's plan* and that *things are bad, but they could have been much worse* and that I should *thank the Lord above for small mercies*. The nurse seemed upset. I stared down at my gold wedding ring and felt absolutely fine. Most likely on account of the painkilling medications; they fed pills to me every four hours whether I needed them or not. The trundling bed bumped over joins in the floor as we slogged from one wing into another. I remember thinking that the hospital must have grown in ungainly stages to keep pace with Melbourne's population. It's funny what you think about in times of great stress.

Your mother's face looked pale and flabby. When she saw me, she smiled with one side of her bruised mouth, tears streaming down her cheeks. Then she lifted her arms to me, as if for an embrace. Her bandaged left arm ended in a stump.

I have to go now. It's lights out.

April 14

James, my last letter was difficult to write. I expect this one will be too.

After I was discharged from hospital, they kept your mother for a further five weeks: one last week on the wards (in case of infection) with the balance at the Rehabilitation Centre. I visited her every day and brought chardonnay smuggled in a thermos.

However, she had to schedule my visits so they didn't coincide with those of her relatives. They blamed me for what happened. In particular, Matriarch blamed me.

(Finally, Matriarch had a reason to justify her hatred. I'm sorry to disillusion you about your grandmother, James, but that stone-cold bitch loathed me from the moment we first locked eyes: over the dinner table during Christmas week. As a young man with a full head of hair, I'd been seeing your mother for a few months when your grandfather, Pa Rupert—you still remember him, don't you?—invited me to join them at the Yarra Valley estate for their traditional Boxing Day lunch. I didn't mind the old man, God rest his soul. Rupert shook my hand, proffered expensive Vouvray, seemed interested in my upcoming teaching post at the university. Matriarch glowered at me the whole time and didn't say a goddamned word. I think it disgusted her that I acknowledged the servants. Riddled with "upstairs downstairs" prejudice, she considered me decidedly "downstairs". Ha ha. I'm not ashamed of my social standing. Intellect is considerably more valuable than wealth.)

But with regards to the accident, yes, as the driver of the vehicle at the time of the crash, technically the fault was mine. But not the *blame*. I didn't crash the car *on purpose*. That's an important distinction for you to understand. A distinction that the Court failed to make. (My lawyer wasn't competent. Too bad. I got what I was given because I didn't have the money to engage my own counsel. Your mother and I had joint bank accounts, and Matriarch made sure to freeze them all.)

On your head, James, I *swear* I didn't aim for the tree. Think about it: I'm not trained in stunt driving. I've puttered my sedan to and from work, keeping to the speed limit along back roads, ever since getting tenure in the English department, which was before you were even born. Twenty years! I don't know how to do a "burnout" or a "donut". How could I have planned your mother's traumatic amputation? And in her own car, no less: the fancy Audi with its emphasis on driverless technology.

I'm innocent, James.

Innocent.

I can only pray that you believe me.

When your mother came home from hospital, I was her willing serf. She would sit up in bed, resting against pillows I had plumped, and request camomile tea or wine or something very specific and particular for lunch, and I'd obey. She wanted *me* to tend to her; not our staff, not a hired nurse. And I would do *anything* for your mother. James, you *know* that to be true. Throughout our marriage, I've rubbed her feet and brushed her hair every night, and you're my witness to such attention, such utter devotion.

However, the *degree* of her helplessness surprised me at first. Then again, I'd never encountered such a disability before. It turns out there's not a lot you can do with only one arm. The littlest things were the most frustrating. For example, she couldn't unscrew a toothpaste tube. Pull on underwear or socks. Tie a shoelace. Open an envelope. Use a knife and fork. Do you see? Your mother felt like a newborn and frequently got upset. I assure you, I would've slaved for her tirelessly, without complaint, for the rest of her days.

The prosthetic was entirely Matriarch's idea.

James, I don't know how familiar you are with prosthetics, so here's my summary: once upon a time, an arm prosthetic was a dumb hunk of metal with a hook that had to be adjusted manually — switched to either "closed" or "open" — in order to work. Not so these days. Modern prosthetics can be wired to respond to your *nervous system*. You think "open my hand" and the metal fingers open. You think "make a fist" and the metal fingers close. Like a *real* hand. Disquieting stuff. Quite literally, the stuff of science fiction. Until a few years ago this technology was only the gleam in a fantasist's eye.

Of course, such advanced bio-robotics isn't available to just *anybody*. At least, not yet. No. It costs a toe-curling amount of money. And when it comes to toe-curling amounts of money, Matriarch has a few feet's worth. (Ha ha! There's a rather sophisticated *Dad Joke* for you.) APRI — the Advanced Prosthetic Research Institute — received a one-million-dollar donation from Matriarch and then, miraculously, found a slot for your mother in its exclusive trial.

Oh, I shouldn't be so cynical. I'm grateful to Matriarch. Truly. The prosthetic was (at first blush) a *good thing* for your mother. It gave her hope. Focus. Purpose. If surgeon Dale Friedman hadn't made contact, your mother would have boozed herself to death, no doubt.

But did I resent the surgeries?

According to the prosecution, yes, because I wanted your mother to remain in my clutches. Let me explain. The surgeries were difficult. Painful. Exhausting. They demanded more than your mother could take. Many nights, I wept by her bedside as she suffered. None of that is in the court records. And do you know why? Because no one would take my word for it. The prosecution demanded *proof* of my state of mind, but what proof could I offer? I don't keep a diary. They asked if I had ever recorded my tears and distress on my damned *phone*, as if I were some kind of angsty teenaged blogger. And no, I didn't confide in anyone, God forbid. (James, if you show your vulnerabilities, people use them against you; the urge to play little games of one-upmanship is an instinct hardwired into the human brain. Trust no one, I always say. Remember? If I taught you anything as a father, it was this basic principle.)

I'm rambling. I'm sorry. I still feel insulted, flabbergasted, blindsided by the court case.

Back to the surgeries. There were several, but the central aim was to relocate your mother's nerve endings.

How Dr Friedman explained it to me is how I'll explain it to you. Extending from the brain, three major nerves—the median, ulnar and radial—branch through the arm, down along the hand and into the fingertips. Even after amputation, these docked nerves may keep sending impulses that cause the brain to hallucinate the entire arm. That's why an amputee might feel "pain" in their missing limb. So, the surgeries took those docked nerves from your mother's stump and stitched them into the skin of her shoulder.

After healing, if you pressed a spot on her shoulder, she felt it on her "hand".

In fact, the surgeons tattooed your mother's shoulder with coloured dots to show the relocation of her hand-nerves. Here's the map as I recall it:

> Black – thumb
> Blue – pointer
> Red – middle
> Yellow – ring
> Green – pinkie

After recovery, your mother was instructed to touch these dots multiple times per day to synchronise her brain with the relocated nerve endings. Whenever she was tired, which was often, I touched the spots on her behalf.

Doesn't sound scary on paper, does it, James?

But imagine touching a wheel of coloured tattoos on someone's shoulder while she says things like, "Ouch, don't pinch me," and "Let go of my finger," and "Why are you biting my thumbnail?" Imagine triggering a set of phantom digits which don't exist, and if that doesn't raise the hairs on your neck, you're a braver man than me. I used to dream about all of that. Have nightmares. For the first week or so, I slept in the spare room. Until your mother put her foot down, and insisted I return to the marital bed. Naturally, I had to comply.

Until my next missive. Take care.

April 21

James, now that I've started unburdening to you, I can't seem to stop. Am I oversharing? I wish you would reply to my letters. At the very least, I hope you're reading them.

The prosthetic. Dear God, the first time I saw it...

An avulsion injury is also known as "degloving", which is a much more evocative term in my opinion. Have you heard of degloving? Picture a man riding a motorcycle at eighty kilometres per hour along a bitumen road. He's dressed in a t-shirt and shorts instead of the recommended leathers. Now, if that man were to fall off at speed and slide along the road, he would slide at eighty kph, and the abrasive road surface would grip and evert his bare skin—meaning, rip it inside out. (And now you understand why I was opposed to you getting a motorcycle licence.)

"Degloved" is what sprang to mind when I first saw your mother's prosthetic appliance.

To be frank, it shocked me. *Repulsed* me. It resembled the skeletal structure of the arm but was instead coloured silver and black: titanium for the "joints", carbon fibre for the "bones". Almost human but not quite. And *degloved*, for God's sake. Fleshless. Dr Ingrid Hofstadter (the APRI chief) had propped the appliance upright on her desk; the fingers splayed as if ready to catch a baseball, grip a waterglass, crush a face.

Oh, but your mother was *delighted*. She put her one remaining hand to her breast, and with eyes shining through unshed tears, gasped, "My goodness, Ingrid, it's just so *beautiful*."

Applause broke out. There were other staff members clustered in the room, all of them as happy and emotional as your mother. At least two saw my negative reaction and glared at me. (And later, testified against me in court.) But James, I wasn't upset at your mother's chance at independence. No! I was unsettled by the metal bones without muscles or skin, the fingers without fingernails, the goddamned precise and squared-off *lifelessness* of the appliance, its creepy mimicry of a living human arm. The *deglovement* of the infernal thing.

"Please, sit down," Ingrid invited your mother. "Let's see how things fit."

Above the titanium pretence of an elbow joint, the appliance ended in a socket. Ingrid fitted the socket over your mother's stump. Clicked the straps into place. Secured the "receiver"—a flat, rubberised square of material—to your mother's shoulder, covering the black, blue, red, yellow and green tattoos that marked the nerves of her missing fingers. Dizzy, I needed to sit but there was no spare chair. The two staff members kept fixing me with suspicious eyes. I tried to smile, to appear normal and joyful at the occasion, but…I had psychological trauma too. Didn't I count? For some reason, no, I didn't. Everyone ministered and fawned over your mother, but no one gave me a moment's thought. It was then, during that appointment, I first suspected Matriarch of paying for more than just the prosthetic.

"How does that feel?" Ingrid said.

Your mother smiled. "Perfect."

With the appliance fitted, she became something else: a sci-fi robot, a hybrid machine-monster. And that was even before Ingrid activated the ON switch. My skin crawled. I knew I would never want to touch your mother again. *Not ever again.*

Ingrid turned to her computer monitor, hovered over the keyboard.

My breath caught. I recalled the car accident, and wished that my body had hit the tree instead. That I had died instead.

"Here we go," Ingrid said, and pressed a sequence of keys.

The appliance made a faint and anticlimactic sound, akin to the hum of a faraway hair dryer. I almost laughed. Your mother actually *did* laugh, blurting out a shrill bray of surprise.

"Good God, I can feel it!" she said. "A vibration. Is it alive?"

Ingrid said, "Focus as practised. Shut your eyes if you prefer. Now. Close your hand."

On tenterhooks, every muscle in my body tensed for flight. I couldn't blink. I gaped at the appliance. At the flat, matt shine of its fake bones and pretend fingers.

Seconds passed. The robo-thumb moved. A single twitch.

Your mother choked and gulped. The staff whooped.

My heart spasmed. A buzzing noise knocked inside my skull.

Next, when the robo-digits clenched in concert, I broke from the room and found myself in a corridor, panting, retching. The technician who tugged at my arm was a young man with long blonde hair. *I'm not lying.* And I didn't imagine him either. The police never found him, APRI denied his existence, but he was real. He tugged at my sleeve. His eyes were wide. *Frightened.* Other things about him I recall: crooked front teeth, a long and pointed chin. I offered to describe him to a sketch artist. My offer was promptly rebuffed. They didn't want to *hear* my side of the story, James. What does that tell you?

The technician said, "They can program the appliance. To do anything they want."

Dazed, all I could reply was, "I'm sorry?"

"Listen. The remote control for making resets and adjustments is also a conduit for covert instructions. There's Trojan horses. Malware that can backdoor into the software. I helped write the programs. Watch yourself."

The young man hurried away. By the time others emerged from Ingrid's office in pursuit of me, I was alone. Contrary to court records and the sworn testimony of every single member of the APRI staff including the director Ingrid Hofstadter, the mysterious technician whom no one can identify *was* real, and I believe what he told me to be the truth: *your mother's appliance was hacked*.

Soon after the fitting, the appliance attacked me for the first time.

Your mother was in the lounge room, reclined on the couch and tucked under a blanket. I had just brought out her lunch: one sandwich and another glass of wine. I put the lunch next to her on the coffee table. The prosthetic appliance, as usual, was humming. (I had taken to whistling so that I wouldn't have to focus on its ceaseless noise.)

I said, "I'll help you with your exercises later. I need to prepare for tomorrow's lecture."

"Oh, *sure* you do," she said in her drunken, sarcastic singsong voice. "Uh-huh. Okay. No worries."

She's always been the jealous type, remember? She resented my working from home; she considered it my duty to give full attention to her whenever I was within those walls, and that was even *before* she lost her arm.

I tried to ignore her tone. "I'll be in the study."

"Ringing Amy, I suppose."

"Well, why not? She's my tutor. We have to consult—"

"*Consult?* Is that what you're calling it?" Your mother sneered. "You son of a bitch."

The appliance hit me across the face. During the trial, the technicians were adamant that the appliance can only move slowly, tediously, deliberately. I'm telling you, it hauled off and belted me in the wink of an eye, so fast I hardly saw it coming.

The blow split my lip. I staggered. Held a hand to my bleeding mouth.

Rapt, your mother stared at the appliance in awed reverence. "It read my mind. How extraordinary. I wanted to slap you and it actually *read my mind*."

"So, from now on, any physical abuse won't be your fault anymore, is that the implication?" Bristling with sudden anger, I whispered through my teeth, "Don't push me."

She regarded me for a time, as if committing my features to memory, and then she smiled. "If I ever wanted to kill you, Graham, I'd never be imprisoned for it or even arrested. You know why? Because I'd tell the police that you beat me. That you'd beaten me for years and years, and I was terrified of you; too afraid to ever tell anybody or seek help. And I would be believed. Because I'm a woman. And you're a man."

I felt cold, sick. "You're exactly like your goddamned mother."

"Do you see how it is, Graham? How it's going to be?"

I hung my head. "Yes. I see."

"Ring Amy," she said, using the robo-hand to pick up her wine, "and break things off."

And I did. (For the record, Amy was indeed my lover, but that's not the point I'm trying to make here.)

Until next time, James. All my love.

April 28

I'm sorry, James. What I told you in my last letter was a fabrication. Not all of it—just the last part, the argument with your mother. That particular argument never happened. It's the same story I told in court, under oath, a story that my lawyer and I concocted in an attempt to sway the jury. However, the story isn't so much a *lie* as a *distillation*. For example, your mother *had* threatened me using similar words, but it was many years ago and she was playing around; only teasing, I think. She didn't mean anything. Not at that stage, at least.

Hand on heart, I included the story because the prison adminstration reads my letters (hello, Governor!) and I was afraid to contradict my testimony. But God, what kind of father would I be if I cared more about an additional charge of perjury than telling the truth to my own son? Forgive me. I promise to be nothing but honest. As honest as I can possibly be.

It's true the accident changed our marriage. Not for the better, of course. How could it?

The three main reasons for the change:

I felt riddled with guilt, consumed and tortured by it. After

148

all, I'd been driving the car.

Your mother resented me, blamed me. Oh, she tried to hide it, but I could discern traces of bitterness in her voice, her manner, in the way I'd catch her looking at me. I tried to talk with her about this, but she denied every accusation. Would spend an inordinate amount of time attempting to reassure me. *The lady doth protest too much, methinks.* Yet, sometimes, she almost had me convinced I was imagining things.

Her family, headed by Matriarch, began a slur campaign. They wanted me charged with various crimes including, but not limited to, your mother's attempted murder. Their constant insinuations wore your mother down in the end. That's what I tell myself, anyway. She wasn't in her right mind. You mustn't hold any ill will towards your mother.

While she was meant to use the appliance during waking hours, your mother also had a program of daily exercises to perform. The program entailed a set list of manipulation attempts. Typically, she would sit at the kitchen table and I'd arrange the prerequisite items for her to pick up, manipulate and put down. These items ranged from the relatively easy to grasp (such as a tennis ball) to the increasingly more challenging (such as pens and even paperclips). The strain made her puff and sweat as if she were running a marathon. I'd rate her performance in the journal, which APRI staff perused at a later date.

James, doesn't my cooperation, my willingness to help, prove my love for your mother? Because watching the appliance never failed to make my flesh creep. It resembled a real hand but didn't move like one, and the joints used to *click*. In the evenings, reading in my study, I'd often hear that *click* and have to check the hallway to convince myself that I was alone and safe.

The next time your mother hurt me was during one of these exercise programs. She picked up a pencil and stabbed me with it. *Bang.* Straight into my wrist. Plunged with enough force to stick the pencil fast. (A piece of lead broke off. To this day, if you part the hairs you can see the dark grey smudge through my skin.)

Your mother shrieked. As did I. We both jumped up from the

table and regarded the pencil stuck in my arm. I pulled it out. There was a surprising amount of blood. While I rinsed the wound under the running tap, your mother swore to me—James, she *swore* to me—that she hadn't planned or intended the stabbing. That the appliance had done it. And I took her words at face value.

Naturally, we brought up the incident at our next appointment with Dr Ingrid Hofstadter.

"I know you want answers but I can't explain what happened," she said. "We've run the diagnostics. We can't find any evidence of a malfunction."

"Perhaps it wasn't a malfunction," I said, remembering my encounter with the young, frightened technician, an encounter I'd kept to myself at that stage of the game. "Perhaps the appliance was simply following its backdoor programming."

They both stared at me as if I were mad.

"You believe," Ingrid said at last, "that we programmed the appliance to *stab* you?"

"I believe," I said, "that firstly, my mother-in-law has bribed APRI—indirectly, of course—with a grotesque amount of money for this device, and secondly, that everybody has a price."

Your mother gripped my leg, *hard*, with the robo-hand. "Graham, for Christ's sake…"

"I don't understand," Ingrid said.

"Software Trojan horses," I continued, voice rising. "Covert instructions to finish me off."

"Wait a minute, you think I'm some kind of paid *assassin*?"

"I think you'll do whatever it takes to keep receiving cheques from my mother-in-law."

Ingrid was a convincing actress; I'll give her that. She looked both stunned and insulted. Then she turned to your mother and said, "Is your husband receiving psychiatric support?"

Which is how the slander got started. Bankrolled by Matriarch. Why everyone now thinks I'm unbalanced. Yet the besmirching is a smokescreen. To hide the truth: Matriarch wanted me out of the way because she decided from the get-go—from the very first Boxing Day lunch with Grandpa Rupert—that I'm with your mother solely for her inheritance.

But consider the facts. We've been together twenty-five years. *A quarter century.* If I was in it for the money, good God, then I've been playing quite the long con, haven't I? Therefore, purely from a logical point of view, Matriarch's hypothesis is *insane*. And why drag my poor tutor, Amy, into this delusion? Well, because doing so further helps to smear my reputation. Do you see?

Oh, James, how people *love* juicy gossip. And me trying to murder your mother in a car crash in order to become a rich playboy and elope with my younger lover? Ha ha! So juicy!

And untrue, I might add. Untrue and wicked. (Although, as the prosecution pointed out, it would be fair to say that, on my salary alone, I couldn't possibly maintain the lifestyle to which I was accustomed. In my opinion, it was this fact that swayed the jury into swallowing the prosecution's entire hare-brained theory about my motives.)

I'm in jail solely because the average person likes to believe salacious gossip.

Damn, the unfairness makes me gnash my teeth, rip my hair.

Everyone is against me. Everyone!

Oh God, James! God! The noise in this place after dinner is unbearable. Confined to their cages, the men are beasts, shouting and hollering and shrieking. A madhouse. I'm sitting here on my cot, weeping. James, I'm not sharing this information to curry sympathy. How could I fool you? Such a smart boy. You've *always* been a smart boy. I couldn't have asked for a better child. A better son. James, oh James, I'm sorry.

For everything, for all things.

Please. I need you to forgive me.

I promise, I never meant for *any* of this to happen.

Sometimes, I lie awake at night and mentally retrace every step that brought me here, to this cell, to this tiny cell with its flat, lumpy mattress, vandalised walls, metal toilet. The answer is the same: *the prosthetic.* But your mother accused me of paranoia. She said that the appliance, being experimental, still had bugs to iron out; that the odd occasion when it would turn on me without warning to pinch or twist or punch were nothing but glitches.

That's why we keep going back to the lab for updates, she would tell me, *to fix these glitches and fine-tune its programming.*

And at times, lying here in the dark, I believe her. It could be that my revulsion for the appliance, and my suspicion of Matriarch, skewed my interpretation of what was actually going on. Perhaps I connected the dots when a few of the dots weren't really there.

Tell me, James. Which version of the truth do you find more plausible?

The version put forward by the prosecution? Or mine?

May 5

James, we never had *The Talk*, did we? About the birds and the bees. Another failing of mine as a parent. I could never seem to find the right time or opportunity to bring up such an embarrassing topic. (To be honest, I thought your mother would've had that conversation with you, or that you would learn about the mechanics of sex during Health Education at school. Did either of those things happen? I'm sorry to say I have no idea.)

So now, without having ever broached the topic, I'm about to tell you about Amy.

Contrary to what was stated in the trial, our affair wasn't "sordid". As you know, she was the tutor for my classes. Therefore, we shared a lot in common: a love of language, poetry, literature and etymology, just for starters. Amy was almost my intellectual equal. (And yes, while your mother has her endearing traits, intelligence isn't one of them. Opposites attract, is how I would explain it. Your mother has passion. *Zest.* And a temper, let's not forget. A temper that was very fetching in her youth; less so in middle age, particularly when booze would give it that hard, sniping edge. She liked to go for the jugular. Never show anyone your weak spots, James, or you'll see them used against you. Mark my words.)

Amy was intelligent, yes. And attractive in a strait-laced "librarian" kind of way. (Not that she wore glasses or her hair in a bun.) Picture a slim, demure woman with minimal makeup, unpainted nails, sensible clothing, flat shoes. The kind of cool understatement that suggests a possibility of sexual heat simmering beneath—if coaxed to the surface in the right way. A clichéd fantasy? Yes, there's probably a category for that kind of thing on pornography websites. (I apologise for my frankness, and hope I'm not making you too uncomfortable.)

But James, her cool façade is what first piqued my interest, because I speculated about her repressed, hidden, *carnal* possibilities. And yes, oh God, she was *young*. Twenty years my junior. The vanity of a man well past his prime can't be overestimated. I've lost most of my hair, my belly has grown soft, limbs thinner, chest saggier—and yet I was desired! By an intelligent, attractive, youthful woman! She sought out my company. Laughed at my jokes. Held my gaze for a few seconds too long. It got so that I couldn't stop thinking about her. I fantasised about touching her, kissing her. And more, of course. Much more…

Naturally, I felt guilty. Breaking the marital vows that one makes in church, before God and family, is a terrible thing. But I felt alive for the first time in years! Sharing any details would be grossly inappropriate (and sickening for a son to hear), so I'll give you this brief summary: when it came to sexual congress, your mother was reticent; Amy was enthusiastic. There. That's all you need to know to understand my extended period of weakness.

Did your mother know? She suspected. Did she share those suspicions with Matriarch? Yes, I believe she did. And Matriarch wanted me out of the picture, to keep the Old Money safe from my clutches in case of divorce. James, can you see how the threads are tying together?

They put Amy on the stand. Initially, I thought she would be a witness for the defence, but no, no. The prosecution asked her questions, and her answers put me in a bad light.

Q: Did the defendant ever suggest the possibility of you running away together?

A: Yes.

Q: How many times? Once? Twice?

A: Many times. Dozens of times.

James, it was agony to see Amy up there, testifying against me, never meeting my eye. I remember shaking, feeling dizzy. My lawyer asked for a recess, but the judge wouldn't allow it. Once, I'm sure that damned judge looked behind me, to where Matriarch was sitting, and actually *smiled*. Collusion once again. *Money talks.*

Q: Did the defendant offer any plan as to how the two of you would run away?

A: (loaded silence and fidgeting; oh, Amy put on quite a show for the prosecution)

Q: Please answer the question. How did the defendant plan to leave his wife for you?

A: Um, he mentioned the possibility of her maybe...dying.

Q: His wife? *Dying?* (approaching the jurors with open arms) And was his wife *ill* at this point? Was anything *wrong* with her medically? Had she been diagnosed with terminal cancer? Dementia? Anything of that nature, to your knowledge?

A: No.

Q: And let's be clear; this is *before* the defendant caused the car accident, which didn't take her life but took her limb.

My lawyer: Objection!

Judge: Overruled! The witness may answer the question.

A: Yes, this was before the car accident.

Q: When you heard about the accident, what was your conclusion?

A: I don't understand the question.

Q: Okay, let me put it another way: did you believe the car crash was actually an accident?

My lawyer: Objection!

Judge: Overruled!

A: I wasn't sure if it was an accident. All I knew was that Graham often wished his wife dead, so I guess...I wasn't surprised to hear about the crash.

God, and on and on the smear campaign went. James, can't you see the obvious truth? *Matriarch paid Amy to lie.* There's no other explanation. Well, either paid her off or threatened her life. I'm not being paranoid here. Pay careful attention: Amy was *in love* with me. She had said so, often, and not just while lying in my arms, giddy with post-coital hormones. She had whispered it at work too. In the corridors as we passed, she liked to brush her fingers against my hand. She loved me wholeheartedly, unreservedly, wildly.

But did I love her back?

Well, in retrospect, it's hard to say. With twenty years between us in age, there's a generation gap that can't be bridged. Her taste in music was dubious. She was a fan of "memes", which I never found amusing. Social media platforms didn't interest me in the same way they interested her. And James, to be honest, I still loved your mother. We shared history. We shared *you*. We understood each other in ways that Amy and I never could.

However, I *did* talk with Amy about leaving your mother. That part is true. You see, Amy liked to pipe dream. In particular, she enjoyed picturing our future home: a middling two-bedroom apartment somewhere in the dreary outer-eastern suburbs of Melbourne.

Yes, that's the meagre size of mortgage we could have afforded. A lecturer and a tutor at a third-rate university hardly enjoy stellar wages, and real estate is expensive. So, James, my admission is that your private school education, our live-in staff, the twice-yearly holidays at our various European properties—in fact, every privilege you've enjoyed since birth—have all been paid for by your mother's side of the family. But I suppose you knew that already.

(However, I don't feel *sorry* for myself. God, do you think I'm upset because your mother's side of the family is filthy rich? Not in the slightest. Money is cheap, available everywhere in any society that maintains a reasonable economy. Consider this: what use is a university without lecturers? No use at all. Therefore, the rich fee-paying families are the minions that serve the king, ergo, the lecturer. It is the *lecturer* with his skillset that holds the power. Not Matriarch with her money. Do you understand? *Skill* is what counts.)

Talking about our mythical two-bedroom apartment in a blue-collar suburb enthralled Amy, but had the exact opposite effect on me: it took the shine off our affair. The more Amy wittered on about me leaving your mother, the more reluctant I became about doing so.

Jealousy. Perhaps *that's* why Amy testified against me. Not because of money or fear.

Let me explain further.

One day, Amy gave me an ultimatum. In my office. She said she wanted a baby. *My* baby. She wasn't getting any younger, our affair wasn't just "mucking around", etc. I demurred, pointing out that I was married already, had a near-grown son, couldn't imagine at my age the rigmarole of nappies, late nights, swimming lessons, or life in a small apartment with one car between us and no European holidays. Amy's response to my reasonable refusal?

Threats.

That she would report me to the police, to the Dean, to your mother. In short, destroy me in every way she could think of unless I freed myself to marry her and sire her child. Oh, it's a mistake to trust people, James. As a general rule, people only look out for themselves. Remember that.

Stalling, I told Amy I needed time to think.

Upon reflection, perhaps she didn't lie on the stand because of Matriarch's influence. Perhaps Amy lied solely because she wanted to make good on her threat: to destroy my life. And destroy it she did. I could actually *see* the impact her testimony had on the jury. The men and women scowled at me with open hostility. Amy, light of my life, besmirched me for her own selfish ends. Or because Matriarch had paid her or intimidated her—look, I can't decide which scenario is more likely.

You're a smart boy, James. I can't fob you off. The central question remains and I know you're wondering about it: had I ever discussed with Amy the possibility of running away with her *if your mother happened to die?*

The answer is…yes.

But I hasten to add, it was nothing but idle speculation, *not* an admission that I would try to kill her in a car accident. Look, your mother drinks too much, is grossly overweight, never exercises, has a penchant for foie gras and other such fatty, artery-clogging foods. And she's menopausal. A heart attack is not beyond the realms of possibility. And *that* was how I framed your mother's death. I swear it. As a pie-in-the-sky dream. Like winning the lottery. It was *not* a promise. Whatever Amy surmised, I never promised that your mother would die.

I have to stop here. The guards want to search our cells.

May 12

James, it's taken me a long time to tell you exactly what happened on that fateful night. I've tried to provide crucial background information first so that you can grasp the *actualities*. Please, set aside everything you may have read in the newspapers. Forget the sensationalist details of the trial. The podcasts, the theories, the fascination.

Please *listen to me*.

First things first: I appreciate that the revelations about my relationships with your mother and Amy may have come as a shock. Before I wrote these letters, I'm sure you would have described your mother and me as a *happy couple*. This was how we had decided to present our marriage to you. It was our tacit agreement. Unless you've had a child yourself, James, you can't appreciate the degree of pretence that an outwardly-successful marriage requires. Who wants to damage their son (or daughter) with the truth? Not us! Your mother and I weren't especially happy but we *weren't* especially unhappy either. Most marriages are like that. Unfulfilling. Try to understand. Once the honeymoon period is over (and it lasts about, oh, I would guess about five years), it's a long and anaesthetising grind to the bitter end.

Surprise! My marriage wasn't ideal. So what?

Okay, James, I'm being honest now.

And keep in mind that your mother's prosthetic arm kept *hurting* me. Tried to *kill* me on more than one occasion. Quite often, I think it was simply doing your mother's bidding, whether she was conscious of it or not. Other times, I've no doubt that at least one technician at APRI, having been paid off by Matriarch, was programming the arm. (Probably that bitch Dr Ingrid Hofstadter.) The truth must lie in one theory or the other.

157

Or both? It's hard to say.

I can't prove either theory beyond a reasonable doubt—which is why I'm languishing in prison—but I swear to you that everything I've told you in my letters so far is true, or as near to the truth as I can make it.

So, the fateful night in question…

Look, as you know, your mother has various sleep difficulties. Insomnia, for one. And she is occasionally afflicted by dreams about being attacked. By dogs, usually. Or lions, sharks, spiders—any creature that's frightening. Strictly speaking, these dreams are more than just nightmares. They are episodes of *night terrors* and the dreams feel *real* to her. She thrashes to defend herself. Many times, I've shaken her arm or called out to her, and copped more than a few kicks to my legs over the years. Usually, she wakes up confused and distressed for the first few seconds until she realises that the danger was only a dream. Then she apologises. It's not an issue. I've never held these episodes against her.

James, do you remember the incident when you were about twelve?

Your mother was attacking me. I was yelping in pain. You ran into our bedroom, turned on the overhead light, and yelled, "What the hell is going on?" Your voice woke up your mother. She cried when she saw the blood on my face. Remember? Do you remember, James? Yes, of course you do. How could you forget? It affected your sleep for weeks afterwards. You kept worrying that your mother would attack me again. One time, you actually said to me, "Dad, what if she tries to kill you?" Out of the mouths of babes…

Soon after the prosthetic arm was fitted, your mother took to wearing it overnight. That seemed crazy to me. Like wearing dentures, contact lenses or corrective shoes in bed; why on earth would you? But the staff at APRI—and in particular, Dr Ingrid Hofstadter—kept suggesting that your mother *never* remove the prosthetic. That she should consider it *as her own arm*. Ostensibly, to faster train the software. (Ultimately, they planned to permanently affix the prosthetic—or more precisely, its next generation model—into the bone of her upper arm. Meaning, drill and bolt the damned thing. Christ, just the thought of that makes me ill.) But asking her to wear the prosthetic at all times, apart from when showering, smacked to me of another, more sinister agenda.

The prosthetic hummed at night.

Kept me awake.

The robo-arm would often rise into the air, fingers working and flexing, even while your mother snored, drunk and dead to the world. Was she dreaming and moving her arm in her sleep? Or was the robo-arm responding to commands from a corrupted APRI technician?

This one terrible night I'm talking about, somewhere around 2:00am, the violent flapping of bedclothes startled me awake. I looked over. Your mother was sitting up, dimly lit by our electric clock, wrenching frantically at the bedlinen and kicking, as if reacting to the scratch of huntsman spiders or cockroaches swarming in their hordes over her bare legs.

"What is it?" I said, and pulled out an earplug. (I'd taken to wearing earplugs at night; otherwise, I couldn't sleep for the humming.)

Your mother didn't answer me. Instead, her thrashing became more frenzied. Something was in the bed with her, scaring her, and my heart rate kicked up.

Panicked, I yelled, "What's going on?" and reached out.

Remember, James, I was lying prone and your mother was sitting upright. At the sound of my voice, she turned to me, wrenched the bedclothes away in both hands—one real, one monstrous—and then began to beat me. Silently, without a word. I screamed. Her flesh-and-bone fist was nothing more than a tap, but the prosthetic fell on me as weighty as a hammer.

"Wake up!" I yelled. "You're attacking me, wake up!"

No good. Your mother redoubled her efforts. The prosthetic pummelled me. A rib bone broke. The agony was terrible, and took my breath. I lifted my hands in an attempt to defend myself against the onslaught, until the smash of the prosthetic crumpled my fingers. I rolled out of bed. Leapt to my feet, panting, frightened.

Your mother leapt out of bed too.

"Wake up!" I shrieked, as she came for me, robo-fingers clacking.

And now, after all is said and done, I believe that your mother knew what she was doing. She was trying to murder me. Whether she hated me because of the car accident or because of Amy or a combination of both, the end result was the same: *your mother tried to murder me.*

Check the police reports. No one disputes that your mother had experienced night terrors in the past. No one disputes that the prosthetic had glitches. But here's where the narrative becomes blurred: how your mother died. According to the police and prosecution, I took the lamp from my bedside table and staved in her head, but that's not what happened.

What happened was that the prosthetic closed its degloved fingers around my throat and squeezed. I felt pain. A terrible pressure within my cranium, behind my eyes. Blackness encroached on my vision. It occurred to me that I was dying.

I was prone on the floor. Your mother was sitting on top of me. I grabbed something—as it turned out, the metal door-stopper, the one shaped like a rooster—and hit her with it. One strike. Not to kill her, you understand, but simply to get her off me, to stop her prosthetic arm from choking me to death.

But as it turned out, the door-stopper knocked her unconscious. That damned rooster door-stopper I'd always despised (but your mother insisted was her absolute favourite out of all the ornaments crowding every surface in the bedroom) had cracked her skull. She fell onto her side and lay still. I thought it was over, that I was safe.

The prosthetic, clacking and whirring, rose up and again clamped its cold metal fingers on my windpipe. Yes, I wrestled with the damned thing. Yes, I got to my feet and, using all my strength, wrenched it from your mother's stump. And as it fought me with superhuman power, this degloved and amputated monstrosity, I believed in my panic that your mother's thoughts still directed it. And *that's* why I brought it down on her head. Terrified, I thought she was playing possum, only feigning unconsciousness, and that I had to knock her out *for real* in order to save myself.

LIMINAL SPACES: HORROR STORIES

Yes, James, I bludgeoned her to death. May God forgive me, I kept whipping her with the full weight of the prosthetic, over and over, while it hummed and whirred and clenched its fingers, twisting, attempting to grab me. When the infernal thing finally switched off, becoming locked and rigid, I stopped too. Threw the disgusting thing away from me. It clattered across the floorboards and I stared at it in horror, expecting it to right itself and begin crawling and scrabbling towards me. After long minutes, when it didn't move, I finally looked down at your mother.

And saw her brain tissue.

James, I'm crying right now. Bawling like a newborn. This letter has taken me the best part of a day to write. I'm not sure if I've adequately captured my shock, my confusion, on that awful night. I never intended to kill her. I swear to you. I swear on your precious head. I love you, James. Oh, my son, my only son. My only child. I'm so sorry. Can you forgive me? Can you ever find it in your heart to forgive me? All I can do is pray. Cry and pray for your forgiveness, tonight and every night, for the rest of my miserable life.

May 19

I've been talking in circles these past weeks. Round and round and round...

You know it, and I know it.

James, do you remember when you were little and questioned me about Santa Claus? That particular evening, we had put up the Christmas tree. You, me and your mother. We'd festooned that stinking pine with lights and tinsel, with your mother's expensive trinkets, and the lovely paper ornaments you'd made at kindergarten. Afterwards, I'd tucked you into bed. And you'd blindsided me by asking, "Daddy, is Santa real?"

Now, keep in mind, you were only four. (You were a smart boy right from birth; verbal at such an early age. So curious about the world. Intellectually, a veritable *sponge*.) And children are supposed to believe in Santa Claus, the Easter Bunny and the Tooth Fairy etc. until they are at least six years old, apparently, or perhaps even seven. For God's sake, I didn't know what to *say*. Your mother was busy in the kitchen pouring herself another slug, and the staff were retired for the night. James, I was at a loss. With nowhere to turn, I tried to stall with generic blather.

"As long as there are children," I began, "and as long as there is Christmas, there will always be Santa Claus because he embodies the spirit of the season." I still think it's a good answer, and one that should have satisfied you. (But then, I shouldn't have underestimated you. James, my smart little boy, ever sharp as a tack.)

"But is Santa *actually* real?" you insisted.

"Yes."

"As real as I am? I mean, could I see him? Touch him? Could he pick up this teddy bear?"

"Well," I said at last, trying to chuckle. "I'm not sure. After all, he's a magical being."

"You told me magic isn't real."

Because of that blasted pantomime with the wicked witch getting crushed to death. God, it gave you such nightmares. I had to explain—over and over—that "magic" was nothing but lies, deception, sleight of hand, smoke and mirrors. Via the Internet, I even showed you how a few tricks were done. Your mother accused me of stealing your *Childhood Innocence*, but I saw it as offering you reassurance in an uncertain world. And that scene from the pantomime no longer gave you nightmares, which means I did the right thing. Didn't I?

Regarding Santa, I tried to fudge the issue, replying, "Some types of magic might be real."

Oh, James, you fixed me with your sideways stare. The stare I came to know very well over the years; the look that means you're sniffing what you term as *bullshit*. "Magic is real or it's not," you declared.

"Yes," I sighed. "Very true."

"Is Santa real?"

"I can't tell."

"How does Santa get the presents to every house in the world in one night?"

"I don't know," I said.

"There's no chimney. How does he get inside *our* house?"

"I don't know."

"Does he break in? Is he a bad guy?"

"No. Stop. Please."

That side-eye again. You said, "Is he real? Like me? *Alive* like me? Don't lie, Daddy."

I sat on the edge of the bed and took your hand. It was so small and warm. I can still recall the wriggle of your fingers against my palm. I said, "What I'm about to tell you, you can't tell your mother. Or any of your friends at kindergarten."

Your eyes widened and you sucked in your breath. "All right."

"This has to be our secret."

You nodded.

And I told you the truth. You were pleased, actually. Happy that you had already figured it out. And I was so proud of you. My smart little boy. And you never told your mother or, as far as I'm aware, your friends either. The farce of Santa Claus remained our secret.

Often, this memory wakes me up.

Like everybody else, I keep secrets from myself. We all do. Reality is *painful*. We couch ourselves as the "good guy". That instinct is hardwired into the Ego. Does a criminal ever define himself as evil? Does he ever see himself as justified in his actions, as some kind of hero righting a wrong, as a rebel sticking it to The Man? Possibly. In all likelihood, I'm as blind to my own actions as the dumbest of dumb criminals. I don't know, *I don't know*.

But here's a bit of insight.

There's another reason why your mother may have wanted to kill me.

And to be honest, I can't really blame her. I've thought about killing myself, many times. If I had the guts, the wherewithal, I probably would have done it by now.

Oh God…drawing breath is difficult. My hands are shaking, eyes filling with tears. Nevertheless, I have to go on. Do I have the strength to tell you? We'll see. No more games.

Let's return all the way back to the first letter I wrote: about Matriarch's soiree at her Yarra Valley estate. We were there to celebrate her seventy-fifth birthday. Us and about two hundred other people. (That bitch collects hangers-on like stamps.) Once again for the record, I didn't have anything to drink and I hadn't consumed any drugs. Naturally, your mother was soused and angry by the time we were driving home. Along that rollercoaster road in the Yarra Valley. With nothing to hit.

Green fields. Me behind the wheel. A speed of one hundred kilometres per hour.

I still don't know what happened.

The buck of your mother's Audi, the punch through the fence and that sideways slew into the old-man eucalypt, the disappointed *ugh* sound your mother groaned as her door crumpled itself around the tree and the twisting metal pulped her forearm.

Emergency lights. Staccato red and blue.

"My wife," I said, the strobes beating at my eyes. "Forget about me. Please help my wife."

James, I only said that because when I looked into the back seat, you weren't there. I wasn't thinking straight. I had concussion. For some reason, I thought you were at home, playing one of your online games with your mates. I forgot—for a quite a while, actually—that you had been with us at Matriarch's soiree, grinning sarcastically with that slight roll of your eyes at everyone's gasping exclamation about how much you'd *grown* since the last soiree, the one celebrating Matriarch's seventy-fourth birthday.

And when I remembered, red and blue lights flashing, that you had been in the back seat, I thought your absence meant that you were strolling around outside the wreck, hands in your pockets, slouching, huffing with impatience. You wanted to get home, of course. You had a *game* scheduled, of course. No wonder you'd be annoyed. Pissed off with me. I was forever thwarting your online plans for various reasons that weren't my fault, such as social events requiring the whole family. But I couldn't have cared *less* about all that rubbing-shoulders stuff and nonsense. Honestly, I didn't care! Like you, James, I preferred to stay home and keep my own counsel.

Bleeding, I said to one of the firemen, "Tell James to let his mates know he'll be late. Maybe they can reschedule the game."

"James?" the fireman said, and his eyes were very blue. "Who's that? Your son?"

164

"Why, yes. He's a keen gamer. Very keen."

The fireman gripped my shoulder. I didn't understand why. I gazed out through the shattered windscreen and wondered why the fireman was gripping my shoulder so tightly.

"Can you tell him?" I said. "Tell him to let his mates know."

The fireman left my side of the car. Everything went black. I woke up in the hospital. The painkilling drugs made life a soft, gentle dream. I remember seeing your mother's stump, and being told by somebody—a priest, a police officer, a doctor?—about your death. Apparently, without a seatbelt, you were shot through the windscreen. Broken, you landed in a roadside ditch. None of these details about you sank in at first. Over the subsequent weeks and months, life moved in a sideways, otherworldly blur that didn't make much sense. You were gone from the house, the staff never spoke of you, and I didn't understand why. Then I killed your mother. No, *defended* myself against your mother.

I'm so tired. I try to eat. Food turns to ashes in my mouth. I'm losing weight. My trousers are baggy; I hold the waist of them in my fist. I have no friends here.

So, James, I write you these letters. I post them to our home address and they get returned to me in the prison. The envelopes are opened and resealed. By the Governor, no doubt. (Hi, Governor!) But James, I know in my heart that you read these pages too. I'm sure of it. Because you're a smart boy. My precious, smart little boy.

Lights out already. I'll write again next week.

This is your father, signing off with much love.

Shift

He hid in the basement while she checked outside. Quiet. Deserted. Backlit by the moon, clouds whipped across the night sky.

"Hurry," she whispered, taking his hand.

He had his eyes squeezed shut, trusting her to lead him. She laughed. They ran from the yard into the woods. Already naked, they tumbled to the grass and kissed, limbs entwining. She arched her hips, gasping as he entered her.

"Now look at me," she said.

"What if I hurt you?"

"Open your eyes," she demanded.

He obeyed her. The moon came out. With a grunt, he began to change and grow.

The Stairwell

Penelope opens her eyes, as if she has just finished praying, and sees her clasped hands resting in her lap. She is wearing a black pants-suit. Before her is a wooden pew, exactly like the one she is sitting on. It's made from a rich red timber like mahogany and polished to a high and shining lustre, so glossy it looks wet. Penelope looks around the church at the other mourners. They seem aged in their late fifties, like her. And then she looks at the priest.

He is a handsome man, devastatingly so. Dark hair, square jaw, full lips. Blue and penetrating eyes. Penelope knows she has been staring at him throughout the entire service, fantasising, wondering if he belongs to a religious order that demands celibacy. Her cheeks flush with shame. To think of such things at a funeral, in a church, is indecent.

With a flourish of red robes, the priest opens both arms and raises his palms. As one, the congregation stands. The funeral is over. The mourners shuffle from the pews into the central aisle. Everyone is smartly dressed, well-groomed. The priest nods while people murmur their gratitude and file past. Penelope approaches him, touches her hair. She is wearing it in some kind of bun or French braid. The priest watches her, intently and without blinking, a grin curving his mouth. Penelope imagines kissing him.

To draw him away from the others, Penelope strolls towards the front of the church while making small talk. He follows her, still grinning, still unblinking, as if curious or amused.

"Thank you for such a lovely service," she says, then stops.

She has nothing more to add because she can't recall any particular detail. This perturbs her for just a moment. The priest's blue eyes are bewitching. Penelope keeps backing away and he keeps following her. Shouldn't there be a casket somewhere near the altar? A casket with the remains of her friend, possibly, or a loved one. A colleague? It occurs that this may not have been a funeral after all. Perhaps some other kind of religious ceremony.

Penelope resorts to a coquettish smile, chin lowered so that her coy glance at this handsome man comes up through her lashes. She used to flirt like this, very successfully, as a young woman. A wave of embarrassment freezes her. At fifty-eight, she is far too old to behave in such a girlish manner. And where is her walking stick? She has arthritis, a constant pain in her feet, ankles, knees. Now she has no idea where her stick could be, and feels afraid.

The priest stops, coughs and chokes, holds both hands to his throat, staggers back.

Alarmed, Penelope reaches out to touch him but doesn't. "Are you all right?" she says.

He recovers quickly, chuckling, wiping the spring of perspiration from his forehead, and says, "Yes. I've just never been so close to an altar before."

This remark strikes Penelope as odd. Unsettling. She gazes about the church. At its high rib-vaulted ceilings, the columns of interlocking blocks that resemble spines, and the rounded walls, at all the ruby-red quartz that glitters and glimmers under a soft crimson light that emanates from nowhere as there are no lamps. Anxiety tightens Penelope's chest. Everything looks red and moist. As if she were inside something. The priest no longer strikes her as handsome. She mutters goodbye and hurries down the aisle to catch up with the congregation.

The people are milling about, appearing concerned, agitated, confused. Dead ahead should be exit doors. There is only the start of a stairwell.

A stocky balding man with rosacea turns to ask the crowd, "Are we in a basement?"

People look around at each other for answers with the same puzzled expression.

"Hey," says a woman who is wearing too much makeup. "There aren't any windows."

Everyone, including Penelope, gazes about at the smooth, wet, windowless and shining walls, which seem for a moment to pulse and shiver like the peristalsis of a giant stomach. Penelope decides that she has imagined it until others react in panic.

"Whoa, did you see that?"

"The goddamned walls are moving."

"Is this some kind of church or what?"

"Let's go."

"Where's the door?"

"God almighty."

"Can someone tell me how we got here? I can't remember how I got here."

"I woke up sitting in a pew, that's how."

"Same."

"I hope I'm dreaming."

"We're all strangers, aren't we?"

"I think so. Does anybody know each other?"

"No, I don't recognise a single soul."

"Me neither."

"What in heaven's name is going on?"

"It was a funeral, wasn't it?"

"Yeah, but for who?"

"We've been drugged. Kidnapped and drugged."

"How are we supposed to get out?"

Penelope doesn't say anything. The congregation tightens up, huddling, fear spreading. Penelope turns to check down the aisle for the priest, but he has disappeared. It occurs to her that she is scared of him. Has always been scared of him. How she had felt a sexual attraction is as mysterious as it is revolting, and she dry heaves once or twice, abdomen clenching.

The stocky balding man with rosacea says, "We've no choice. All right, come on."

He leads the way. The others follow. Penelope, caught up in the mix, finds herself ascending the first flight. It's an industrial stairwell. Grey bricks. Grey metal stairs. Grey metal railing. Fluorescent lights.

"Are we inside a factory?" somebody says.

The railing feels cold and bumpy, the enamel paint chipped, a stark contrast to the warm and voluptuous décor of the previous room, the details of which Penelope can't now recall. It's as if she has emerged from a long sleep. The metal stairwell rings with many footfalls.

After thirteen steps, Penelope reaches a landing. It turns hard right. She keeps going, following those in front and pushed on by those behind. The soles of her pumps scuff the steps. Penelope counts each lift of her legs, drowsing. She bumps into the woman in front, a slender thing with red hair. Then Penelope's right foot drops into empty space and she starts awake, stunned, tightening her grip on the railing in fright. The line ahead of her has stopped.

"Careful!" shouts back the stocky balding man with rosacea. "These steps are broken."

Penelope looks down. The metal steps with their cross-hatching of tread are half-melted. The line of mourners begins moving again, cautiously. At the next landing, instead of steps the stairwell has metal wheels, rusting and jutting from the wall. The wheels are slippery. Penelope has to keep a vice-like hold on the railing with one hand, and grope for purchase with the other against the wall, which is corrugated, knobbly, coruscated.

Short of breath, Penelope wonders how no one has fallen yet. The railing is intermittent and the stairwell has a central maw leading straight down. These overweight, underweight, hunched and hobbling middle-aged people are somehow energetic, agile, reaching and stretching and hauling themselves from one obstacle to another, negotiating wheels that are transmogrifying into bits of broken rubble. Yet no one slips. How has Penelope herself not fallen? She recalls her walking stick and quails, heart fluttering.

"Stop!" someone ahead yells. "The steps are gone!"

"We'll have to cling to the wall," shouts someone else.

Murmurs of shock and dissent ripple down the line.

"Forget it."

"Are you kidding me?"

"Screw that."

"Let's go back," pleads another voice. "There must be another exit. A door we missed."

And then they hear it. The distant growling of some beast from far below. Penelope realises that it's the priest, who has reverted to his true self. People scream.

"Go up, go up!" comes the cry from lower levels.

"Get moving!"

"Hurry!"

The press from behind surges the panicking congregation onwards. Penelope glances down into the stairwell. Despite being only five or six floors away, the ground has disappeared into foggy blackness. The growling echoes and becomes much louder.

The beast must be at the bottom of the stairwell.

Must be coming after them.

Panic and sweat. With strenuous leaping, hoisting and grappling, everyone climbs higher and higher, flight after flight after flight. The stairwell tapers as if nearing a point, walls closing in. Soon, there won't be any room left. Penelope looks ahead, notes the frail members of the congregation managing the ascent like goat-footed aficionados of a bouldering gym, and understands she has left the temporal world for another dimension. No wonder she doesn't need her walking stick. Penelope wants to cry but is too frightened, too focused on the next rocky outcropping, too alarmed by the snarling of the beast coming up fast.

The landing twists again. Penelope faces a dead end.

There are no more stairs.

In the ceiling is a rectangular slot that resembles the entrance of an old-fashioned brick chimney. Tentatively, Penelope approaches, peers inside. Pitch black. There are steps built into the wall ahead, protuberances of melted slag. But do the steps go all the way up the chimney? And if this is the way out, why isn't there light at the end? Penelope's heart kicks and gallops, becomes a messy, sloppy knocking of alarm.

"Get going!" yells the person behind her, a woman with jowls and an underbite.

"Come on, for Christ's sake!" shrieks the scrawny man behind the jowled woman.

Yet Penelope can't move. She is petrified. The chimney's rectangular entrance is narrow, barely wide enough to fit her shoulders. If she pushes herself up there by her feet, one melted step at a time, her arms would be pinned by her sides. And what if, halfway, she runs out of steps? Is unable to thrust herself any higher? With arms wedged, she would be stuck—

So, how did all the other people get up the chimney?

Many ahead of her were taller, wider, fatter. How did the stocky balding man with rosacea lead the charge? The slimness of the chimney must be an optical illusion, a trick borne from Penelope's anxiety, her phobia about confined spaces. She doesn't remember much about herself, but she remembers this. A dread of suffocation. Of being trapped without air—

The woman with the underbite nudges her. "Quickly!"

Penelope stands beneath the throat of the brick chimney and gazes into it.

Maybe the chimney is dark because it's full of stuck people. But if people are stuck, why aren't they calling for help? Unless the chimney is so tight it compresses their ribcages, stopping them from taking sufficient breath. Or maybe she can't hear calls of distress because the people are free, blinking in the sunshine, running to safety. Or maybe they're dead, plucked away by whatever malevolence is fuelling this place, crushed by teeth into paste.

Those behind her shriek, push and beat at her. Threaten that if she doesn't go inside the chimney now, right now, they'll throw her down the stairwell. Panting, hyperventilating, claustrophobic, sweating, Penelope yells, "Wait a minute, just wait a minute! Let me think!"

But there is no time to think.

Hands force her against the dead-end wall, shove at her haunches. She enters the chimney. Begins to climb. Her feet find protuberances. The air smells mouldy and damp. Blindly, wedging further and further into the deepening dark, Penelope flails her toes against the wall, keeps chancing upon bulges, again and again, forcing herself inside the chimney.

A memory washes over her: both arms squashed. She's wrapped and trapped, tight inside a caul. Helpless. The end of it all, the end of everything she has known or would ever know.

In the crushing confines of the chimney, Penelope lifts her foot once more. Scrabbling and searching for some kind of grip, she finds none. Oh no, no, no. She tries to wriggle back down. She is stuck. *Help me*, she wants to scream. Her ribcage is constricted. She can't make a sound. Thrashing her legs, she barks the skin off her knees through the light material of her trousers. Terror tastes like copper.

Miraculously, Penelope's foot stumbles against an outcropping. She digs her toes against it and levers herself upwards through the chimney, scraping away both jacket sleeves. Her other foot finds another bump. As she straightens that leg, shunting herself higher, the raw brick and mortar begin sloughing the skin from her bare arms. The thin air smells like smoke. Penelope feels faint and hot, breathless, close to passing out.

The chimney ends in a metal shaft.

Grey, like an air-conditioning duct. Seamed and rivetted.

Grey, because Penelope can now see a tiny bit of light.

The duct arcs like an upside-down U, and Penelope, sobbing and laughing, realises this is why no light shone down the chimney. She clambers over the hump. Cool and smooth, wide, soothing, a gentle slippery dip. Below are glossy mahogany floorboards.

Penelope slithers out, drops. Crawls, wet with sweat and blood as if freshly born, cracked from an egg. Exhausted, panting, she stands.

Looks around.

Pews. She's inside a church. People are already seated at the front near the altar. And there is the priest. He is devastatingly handsome. The funeral is about to start. Penelope must be late. She hurries down the central aisle to the second pew on the right. The priest smiles, blue eyes shining. She wonders if he belongs to a religion that demands his celibacy.

Taking a seat, Penelope clasps her hands, rests them on her lap, and closes her eyes.

A Multitude of One

Richard entered the bedroom, this time dressed as their daughter. The disguise looked farcical. Ratty blonde wig, pink lipstick, his blouse padded to mimic the swell of breasts. Kathleen snorted on a laugh. This was despite the heavy medication… Which meant Richard must have forgotten to give Kathleen her last dose. How lucky! She would feign weakness or else he would realise his mistake and come charging back with a solicitous glass of milk, the drink gritty with crushed tablets, and stand over her until she drank every last skerrick.

"Mum, it's me," Richard said. "Brooke."

"Oh, when will you drop this charade?" Kathleen sighed.

"You still think I'm Dad?"

"For Christ's sake, Richard. What makes you think you could pass for a thirty-year old woman? Quite frankly, you appear ridiculous."

Richard sat on the chair next to the bed and wiped at his lashes as if brushing away tears. Kathleen rolled her eyes and looked the other way, towards the French doors that opened onto the balcony. A stab of longing tightened her fists against the bed linen.

Her birch forest must be in full autumn bloom with leaves turning yellow, orange and brown. At the base of each pale and satin-sheened trunk, the winter bulbs would be pushing their lush green spears through the mulch. Soon, there would be daffodils, jonquils, bluebells, freesias, irises. Ordinarily, Kathleen would be awaiting morning tea on the balcony right about now, admiring the view of her estate. Isaac would be carrying in the silver tray with its pot of English breakfast tea, a selection of biscuits, a single flower in a thin vase—

Wait, where was Isaac?

She hadn't seen him for a long time.

Richard must have fired him. If Isaac were here, she'd have an ally, someone to help her, to smuggle her out in the dead of night to safety. But Isaac was gone. So was Kathleen's landline that normally sat on her bedside table. Richard had her mobile phone too. Her laptop.

"Mum, listen," Richard said. "I've arranged for a neurologist to come visit today."

"Another one of your 'characters', I presume."

"You can't recognise my face but surely you know what my voice sounds like?"

"Our daughter's voice isn't a fucking *baritone*."

"Mum, I swear, it's really me—"

"Oh, please! Brooke is in Perth, pregnant, too far gone now to travel. Give me *some* credit. No airline would allow her to fly all the way to Melbourne."

"I had the baby in December. You don't remember your own grandson? Little William—"

"That's a lie!" Kathleen snapped, glaring, her eyes suddenly wet and stinging. "God, is nothing sacred? You're a despicable person, Richard. Fucking *despicable*."

He leapt out of the chair and lumbered from the room, high heels clumping on the hardwood floor, his broad, flat arse quaking through the skirt fabric. What a joke! Their daughter Brooke was tall, elegant, aristocratic. Richard's mimicry was ludicrous…

Kathleen worried at the sheets with nervous fingers. Where were her employees? Her board members, solicitors, accountants? Her personal assistant? Richard must be keeping them at bay. What was he telling her friends who called? Helpless, drugged, unable to leave this fucking bed, denied access to a phone, what could Kathleen do? *What could she do?* The urge to weep ached her throat but she lifted her chin, clenched her jaw.

Kathleen King was a powerhouse, not a quitter. She would find a way out of this predicament. Because she was *whip-smart*. A businesswoman with experience and acumen who could figure a solution to any problem. Why, her shrewdness was *legendary* amongst competitors —

Richard entered the bedroom, this time dressed as a female nurse. Red wig, same pink lipstick, same breast padding filling out a green zip-up uniform, same blue eyes.

"Get the fuck out of here, Richard."

"Morning, Mrs King. How are we feeling today?"

"You're going to a lot of effort for nothing. I'm not signing that paper. Not now, not ever."

"Once again, my name is Martina," Richard said, flipping back the linen. "Have you used the bedpan? Yes? Good girl. Okay, time for your sponge bath, Mrs King."

"I'd rather have a shower, if you don't mind."

"A sick old lady like you can't have showers," Richard giggled. "One side of your body don't work."

"Bullshit. Look at this." Kathleen held out both arms. The hands shook a little, but still…

"Look at what?" Richard said. "One arm lying there dead?"

"No. You can't gaslight me."

Laughing, Richard unbuttoned Kathleen's gown. "Nobody wants to gas you, Mrs King."

"You'll never convince me I'm crazy. Never."

"I don't want to convince you of anything. Except maybe to roll over. Shall I sing to you?"

"Fuck off."

He began to sing anyway, making up the lilting, lyrical, trilling words to sound foreign since Richard didn't speak any language other than English. However, neither did Kathleen. The words sounded vaguely Italian. If only she knew Italian, she could call him out on his pretence. As it was, she had to lie there and endure the singing, the sponge bath, the red wig and lipstick. Distraught, she closed her eyes.

Kathleen woke up some time later.

She couldn't recall Richard-as-nurse leaving the room, couldn't remember getting changed into a fresh nightgown. The light through the French doors had brightened, yellowed, become more intense, throwing a glow across the sitting area at the foot of the bed, across the dual wing chairs and table. She and Isaac sometimes played chess there. She had taught him the game from scratch. What kind of upbringing doesn't include chess? At first, he had constantly mixed up the value of pawns and rooks, but with her quiet instruction—

Wait, where was Isaac?

Richard entered the room, this time as himself. Balding, wearing a sensible yet expensive cardigan, a greasy smile. He held a manila folder and shook it, wobbling the lightweight card.

"Forget it," Kathleen said. "I'm not signing."

"But listen, sweetheart. Listen to me. The world's best rehab centre is in *Israel*. How many times do I have to tell you? Our medical insurance won't cover the expenses. Sign over your power of attorney so I can make the arrangements and book the next flight."

"You're a fucking *dentist*, Richard. How much do you charge per quarter-hour? Three hundred bucks? Pay it yourself. Pay it out of our joint bank account if you must."

"There's not enough money and you know it."

"For your make-believe Israeli hospital? To treat my make-believe stroke?" She chuckled, dropped her head back on the pillow. "Ah, Christ, spare me. I still want a divorce."

"We'll talk about that when you're better."

"No. Let's talk about it now. Stop drugging me with Tramadol. Then we can have a proper discussion and behave like civilised human beings. I'll even pay for your lawyer."

He shrugged. "There's no Tramadol. No drugs. Sweetheart, you had a stroke."

"Right after telling you I wanted a divorce. How convenient."

Richard's face blanched and hardened. "Bitch."

"Gold digger."

Eyes glittering, he flapped the manila folder. "I'm trying to help you. You'd better sign."

"Or what? Go fuck yourself," she snarled. As he stomped from the room, she shouted, "Who's visiting me next? Brooke again? The nurse?"

Sweating, she tossed her head back and forth on the pillow, gasping, panting, hot and feverish. When was the last time she'd had anything to drink, anything to eat?

The French doors... If she could get to them, she could...*leap* from the balcony? She was on the third floor. The fall might not kill her. But then she would have to crawl across the grounds which were many acres, and somehow climb the stone fence... Unless Richard, desperate for her signature, called an ambulance. Of course. It made sense. If he wanted the money, he would *need* to save her life. She could speak of his treachery to the attending paramedics, emergency staff, who would surely contact the police...

Coming awake, mouth cotton-woolled, lips chapped, she opened her eyes. It was late evening. Twin lamps and downlights illuminated the bedroom. Richard sat in the chair beside her. He wore an expensive suit, pocket square, tie, gold tie-clip. And a groomed black wig.

Exhausted, she turned away, close to weeping. "Give it a rest," she murmured. "I'm so sick of your bullshit. Please stop. If you ever loved me at all, please stop."

"Delighted to make your acquaintance, Mrs King. You think I'm your husband. Correct?"

"For God's sake," she wailed.

"I'm Dr Colin Tan. Your daughter engaged me as your personal neurologist."

"So personal that you'd make a house call after hours?"

He smiled gently. "If the case is urgent, yes."

She tried to scoff, to mock, but her throat felt too dry. "I'm dying of thirst. Give me something to drink."

Richard feigned surprise. "Why, you had a drink with dinner not twenty minutes ago. A large bottle of sparkling mineral water. You ate pea and ham soup. Strawberry mousse for dessert. Hot chocolate. Your nurse, Martina, helped you with every mouthful."

Kathleen closed her eyes against tears. They slid down her cheeks anyway, one after the other, fast and warm. "All right, let's get this over with. You're a neurologist this time?"

"One of the best in Australia."

"Hah, it's always 'the best', isn't it? You know, this ruse might be a tad more credible if you brought things down a notch or two."

"Look at these pictures if you wouldn't mind."

Kathleen sniffed, glanced around.

Richard held what appeared to be playing cards. "This is a picture of a world-famous person," he said, selecting a card. "In your opinion, Mrs King, who is it?"

She peered at the photograph. At the ruddy cheeks, jowls, blue eyes, receding hairline. She groaned. "You're kidding me, right? It's you, Richard."

"That's fine. And what about this picture?"

"You again."

"Very good. And this one?"

"You, you, fucking *you*," she howled. "They're all *you*. Stop it, Richard. Stop it."

He grinned, eyes twinkling. The black wig sat askew on his scalp. "Actually, Mrs King, the photos were of Elvis Presley, Albert Einstein and Ingrid Bergman. In that order."

"I don't believe you."

Richard scooted the chair closer to the bed. "Five weeks ago, you had a stroke. It's not unusual for stroke patients to experience impairments in facial recognition. In your case, Mrs King, you're misidentifying different people as one person—namely, your husband—despite the obvious physical differences. This condition is called the Fregoli delusion."

She glared at him. At the cheap black wig, tie-clip, that fucking *pocket square*.

"Oh, no," she said. "I'm not delusional. He wants my money. Wants me to sign it over." She stared at the shining, greedy face. "*You* want me to sign it over, you son of a bitch."

"Me? But my name is Dr Tan and I'm your private neurologist. Now, Mrs King, can you remember any details from the day of the stroke?" He took a notepad from an inner pocket, flipped a few pages. "According to Richard and Brooke, you were on the patio by the pool, hosting a dinner party. A seafood buffet for Christmas Eve. There were approximately fifty people in attendance, including Brooke with her newborn, little William. Remember? The hired band played Rachmaninoff; naturally, they had to perform simplified, adapted versions to suit a mere ten-piece. You specifically requested Prelude No. 24 in D major. Is any of this ringing a bell? Your butler, Isaac, supervised the wait staff plus the cooks who prepared the feast in the outdoor kitchen. I've seen your Tandoor oven, by the way. Very impressive."

Kathleen's eyes fluttered. *Frutti di mare. Garlic prawns. Grilled lobster.*

Oh, Christ. Did she remember the dinner party? Did she? Perhaps. Ghostly echoes in the recesses of her mind, fleeting images... Brooke cradling little William, making a toast with orange juice because she was breastfeeding. The stars above, a meteor shower, a blinding flash, an agonising crackle of light... Kathleen opened her eyes. The white, taupe, grey and lavender bedroom furnishings stared mutely back at her from the shadows. Darkness pressed against the glass of the French doors. Could Richard be planting a false memory? Isaac would know, would tell her the truth... Wait, where was Isaac? She almost cried out for him.

But her breath wouldn't come, lodged in the dried-out tissues of her throat.

And her throat was dried out because she hadn't been given anything to drink for hours, perhaps days. That bottle of sparkling mineral water with "dinner"? The hot chocolate? *Bullshit*. For decades, she'd had to steel herself against sycophants, opportunists, liars, cheats; people who tried to climb on her professional shoulders while kicking her in the face because, *yes*, life was a fucking *rat race*, and everyone in it was a *rat*. Including her husband, Richard, that *motherfucker*. Her instincts were right. This was Richard's scam. Unless Dr Colin Tan was telling the truth. Which seemed far-fetched. Didn't it? Yes.

She rallied, found her inner strength. "There was no stroke," she said. "How the hell could I talk? One side of my mouth wouldn't work."

"One side *doesn't* work. You're slurring your words and drooling."

"What? I don't believe you."

"Yes, I know. That's part of the Fregoli delusion. Part of your brain-damaged, organically generated paranoia-persecution complex. Here. Let me show you how fucked you are."

With a flourish, he took the pocket square and held it to her chin. After half a minute, he presented it to her. The lilac material was wet. Presumably with her saliva. She gasped.

"That can't be right," she said. "You must have already put water on it."

"No, Mrs King, I did not."

Exhausted, frightened, Kathleen searched his blank, mild face. Richard must have adjusted the wig while she wasn't looking. It sat askew on the *other* side of his head. Didn't it? Yes.

He continued, "Your only chance is the Israeli rehabilitation hospital. But your insurance won't pay. The joint bank account doesn't have enough funds. You need to sign over power of attorney so your husband can access the best medical help that money can buy."

"Oh, the best, always the *best*." Kathleen grabbed his wrist. "He's drugging me. He's a dentist with access to all sorts of medications. Please help. Get me out of here and help me."

Richard patted at her, smiling. "You're imagining things, my dear. Sign the paper."

"If I do, he'll take my money and stick me in a nursing home."

"Sign the form." He produced a pen from his jacket pocket. "Save yourself."

Kathleen cried. Not the meagre dribble of tears she'd occasionally allowed herself over the course of her high-pressure life, no, but an unfettered flood with great, wracking sobs. *Was she crazy?* If only Isaac was here. Such a kind-hearted boy...the only kind-hearted—

"Sign it," Richard demanded, looming over her.

Kathleen shrank back into the pillow and shielded her face with both hands. But she felt just a *single* hand against her cheek. Impossible. Unless she was strung out and hallucinating. Gaslit and dreaming? She woke up again. A lamp burned in the dark room. Her dry mouth made a cracking sound as she unstuck her swollen tongue from her palate. What the hell was going on? What the actual—?

"Sweetheart," said Richard's voice.

She turned her head.

Richard sat in the bedside chair, brandishing papers and a pen. "Are you ready?"

"No," she whispered.

"I'm trying to help you," he continued. "Let me help you."

She closed her eyes momentarily. Licked her scabbed lips. "Well, all right," she muttered.

He extended the pen. "Quickly. On the dotted line."

"I have one condition."

He paused. "Being…?"

"Everyone in here at once."

"What?"

"You, Brooke, Martina, Dr Tan. If everyone comes into my room at once and stands next to each other, side by side, I'll sign the power of attorney."

"But sweetheart, it's night-time. They've gone home. It's just you and me."

"Take it or leave it."

"Yes, but—"

"Take it or fucking leave it, Richard. If I die, all the money goes to Brooke."

He fled the room. Kathleen fidgeted, worked her head against the pillow, wriggled her toes, fluttered both sets of fingers against the sheets to reassure herself that she was whole and functional. Fear pummelled her pulpy, wet heart against her sternum. She thought about touching her face again, to see if she could feel both hands this time or only one, but decided she didn't have the mettle for it. And then she dropped away, fell away, dozed and drowsed.

Lost again in a dark place.

"Wake up!" Richard shouted. "We're here. Every single one of us is here!"

Kathleen jolted awake. She had been dreaming about Isaac. About jonquils and freesias, about lying on the warmth of mulch and gazing up through the branches at a cloudless sky, free and easy, relaxed and cherished, with the softness of Isaac's lips on her cheek—

"Kathleen, can you hear me?" Richard said.

She nodded, but kept her eyes closed.

Shoes scuffed and shuffled across the hardwood floor. Various people seemed to be arraying themselves at the foot of her bed. In the next moment, she would know the truth. All she had to do was look. Open her eyes and look at the people lined up in front of her.

And if they were multiple iterations of Richard?

Christ. Then she had actually suffered a stroke and was no longer tethered to reality.

A fate worse than death. A fate much, much worse than a gold-digging husband who had never loved anything about her.

Maybe Kathleen didn't want to open her eyes. Maybe she wanted nothing but the memory of the balcony beyond the French doors, to imagine the birch forest with the winter bulbs pushing their green leaves through the mulch, remember the gentle deference of Isaac offering the tray at morning tea-time with its biscuits and the single flower in a thin vase. She'd never asked him for a flower. It was something he had done of his own volition.

"Sweetheart?" Richard said. "You wanted it, you got it. Well? Ready to face the truth?"

"Hold on, for God's sake," Kathleen said, breathless.

"No. Open your eyes," Richard demanded. "Right now."

And, trembling, she did.

The Coach from Castlemaine

In Castlemaine, the coaches lined the station at its heart
And the air smelled rank with dust and horses' sweat.
Minnie Sutton looked for porters, had a hold of luggage
    cart
While her little son named Edward seemed to fret.
"Can you see the coach we want?" cried Minnie, gazing
    down the row
As the noise and voices clamoured all about.
"It should stop at many towns but it will state that
    Bendigo
Is the final destination on the route."

They found the Cobb & Co., the driver dropped down
    from his seat,
He was a thin and older man with scowling air,
And silently, he stowed their bags and didn't fuss to
    greet,
Minnie lifted Edward in, tried not to care.
A portly man of middle-age who held a fancy staff
Came aboard and dropped himself upon the bench.
"Good morning," Minnie said, the man let loose a
    hearty laugh
Replied, "The name is Pollard! Horseshit—what a
    stench!"

The driver, Blyth, secured the door and cracked the
    window pane,
Which helped to block the dust yet grant a breeze.
The carriage rocked, the horses neighed, the coach went
    down the lane
And the dandy showed his teeth and spread his knees.
"In Bendigo, I own a pub, I hope you'll not compete.
I can't afford to fight another foe."
But Minnie said, "We're selling clothes, a shop along the
    street,
And my husband hopes we'll have a win to show.

"We came from London," she explained, "in eighteen-
    sixty-one,
Yet our poultry farm just failed to thrive and died.
The foxes and the dingos took our stock despite the gun
And the fences, all the tricks and traps we tried."
The coach advanced, the buildings thinned, and
    Edward stared about
At the paddocks holding cattle, goats and sheep,
Then at eucalypts and mallee scrub, the stony land in
    drought
Until he yawned and laid on Minnie's lap to sleep.

They rode for miles through ironbark—a bugle
    sounding loud
Broke the quiet and started all of them awake.
"The changing station's coming up," the driver Blyth
    avowed,
"And, my fingers crossed, the missus offers cake."
At the home of logs and shingles, while the husband
    swapped the team,
His wife served up the stew and floury bun.
Then pulling Blyth aside, she gave her guests the cake
    and cream
Millie overheard her say, "Have you a gun?"

"I store a rifle at my seat," he whispered, gave a curse,
"What's the news? Are thieves and robbers on the
　　prowl?"
"A Yahoo-Devil-Devil," said the woman, "maybe worse,
Every farmer all around has heard its howl."
The driver scoffed and strode away. "That's
　　superstitious lore."
Then he slapped the kitchen table with his hand.
"We have to leave at once if we're to reach the town by
　　four."
And for not the first time, Minnie cursed the land.

Back on the coach while Edward drowsed, she crooked
　　for Pollard's ear,
To ask, "What's 'Yahoo-Devil-Devil', pray?"
She figured it a dingo, but his answer gave her fear—
"Like the giant orang-utan from dark Malay.
Yet larger, more ferocious, hairy arms that reach the
　　ground
And its instinct is to dash your brains from skull.
Some people call it *yowie*, 'round these parts it's quite
　　renowned,
But I'm sure the truth in legend must be null."

In time, the rhythmic clopping of the horses' hooves did
　　quell
All the passengers aboard into a doze.
Then the coach slammed to a halt and every horse
　　began to yell,
And a wretched stink made Millie hold her nose.
"What the deuce?" said Pollard, angry, tapping cane
　　upon the door
While Blyth exhorted *giddy-up* unto his team.
"If we're getting robbed by rangers," Pollard said, "I'll
　　sue, for sure,
And I'll put this Cobb & Co. in low esteem."

Clinging hard to Minnie, Edward asked, "Are we to
    die?"
And the dread upon his face gave her some grit.
"It's nothing but a snake," she said, "that makes the
    horses shy."
Pollard spat, "A snake? My dear, you're full of shit."
She could see the huddled horses bunched on her side
    of the coach,
Rearing up with bulging eyes that showed the white,
There was something in the bushland, smelling rank, on
    the approach
And she gripped her little son who shook with fright.

A yard or two along the trail, the monster left the trees,
And Minnie's heart compressed at such a sight.
It was something of a giant, like the hairy chimpanzees
That they had viewed at London Zoo with such delight.
From underneath the bench she hauled out mailbag and
    a case
Urging, "Hide!" to Edward as she pushed him down.
"Stay there until I tell you," she said, packing in the
    space
While the horses shrieked in terror, pawed the ground.

The yowie ran and launched itself, the coach rocked on
    its bed,
And with Blyth in arms, the monster dropped to land.
Its yellowed fangs closed fast about the crown of his
    poor head
And the blood and gore of Blyth sprayed on the sand.
The monster slurped the brain up like an oyster from a
    spoon
Gently sucked at what remained as if at fruit.
Gagging, Minnie cried, "We need the rifle, quick, before
    I swoon,
It's at the driver's seat—and Pollard! I can shoot."

His face the hue of lard, he screamed and bolted from
    the coach
But instead of heading straight to get the gun,
Pollard, whimpering and sobbing at the yowie's quick
    approach,
Faced the wide and open bush, began to run.
The monster dropped the last of Blyth and jogged in hot
    pursuit
Like an ape employing knuckles, swinging arms.
Minnie whispered to her son, "Stay there, I'm off to kill
    the brute
Then we'll ride the coach pell-mell and flee to farms."

She exited on shaking legs and groped towards the seat
Wrenching up her bustled skirt to climb aboard,
Her gut reaction—*take the reins!*—resulted in defeat
Since the frightened horses weren't of one accord.
The gun was one she knew, Martini-Henry, single shot
So, she packed the breech with cartridge, sighted in,
And here came Mister Pollard, purple suit a vivid blot
Against the bush—the yowie must have failed to win.

Minnie cried, "Did you escape?", but Pollard failed to
    shout,
So, she put her eye to rifle-sight and aimed.
And sure enough, his skull was gone, his face a
    bloodied gout
The yowie held him like a doll, one badly maimed.
She pulled the trigger—BANG—which stopped the
    yowie in its tracks
But the bullet hit the white of Pollard's shirt.
And cursing, Minnie fumbled with the bullets, spilled
    the packs,
While the yowie snarled, threw Pollard to the dirt.

"Mother, here!" came timid voice, and it was Edward
    by her side,
With a cartridge in his hand, face wet with tears.
Yet she had no time to scold him, for the yowie took to
    stride
And she loaded up the gun, heart choked by fears.
She shot again and hit its arm, which didn't slow its
    pace
Yet it bellowed, loud and deep, such like a bear.
The bullet next punched hard into the dark hide of its
    face
And the yowie staggered, blood dripped down its hair.

She turned to Edward. "Take the gun!" she yelped, and
    took the rein
As the monster found its feet and tried to run.
But this time "Giddy up!" provoked the horses, and the
    train
Took off fast along the track—she cried, "Hold on!"
The messy gallop tossed the coach, which nearly took a
    spill
And the horses screeched and screamed in mortal fear,
For the yowie bounded fast upon their wake, was
    gaining still
Minnie said to Edward, "Do your best to steer."

The little boy took hold the straps, his mother took the
    gun
Resting barrel on the coach and taking aim,
And she thought of husband waiting for them, standing
    in the sun
Waiting for a coach that somehow never came.
The tremble in her fingers went away, she took a breath
Staring at the monster square within her sight,
And she pulled the trigger, sent the yowie straight unto
    its death.
As it dropped onto its face, she felt delight.

"Did you get it?" Edward said, as Minnie sat and took
    the reins.
He was rigid in his seat and couldn't scout.
"I got it and we're safe," she said, "I'm sure I'll find the
    lanes,
And we'll reach the town of Bendigo, no doubt."
Edward sobbed and sagged against her; they were all
    atremble still
But after time the rattled horses settled down,
And the coach from Castlemaine at last descended final
    hill
Spread before them, Bendigo, the promised town.

Shedding

My foot calluses have fallen off. They're floating around me like rinds of parmesan cheese. Disgusting. But fascinating at the same time. Twirling in slow motion. When I signed up, nobody warned me about this. I was a big guy—over six feet, more than 300 pounds—and foot calluses have been part of my life ever since puberty hit.

And now?

Well, the calluses fled like proverbial rats abandoning the sinking ship. I expect you're mulling over my choice of analogy. Does it mean I believe the ship is my body? Or my mind? I'm not sure myself. If only you would answer. Making sense of what's happening is getting trickier by the day, Dr Sharipov, let me tell you.

For starters, it's too quiet in the station. Deathly silent. Nobody warned me about this either. Prior to blast-off, I figured the equipment might buzz or tick or whirr, but the hush makes my eardrums ache. I gaze out the porthole and try to imagine the whisk and whipping *zip* of planets circling and asteroids streaking, the creaking *crack* of space. But there's no air or water, meaning sound waves can't travel, so I can't fool myself.

In some ways, the training gave me too much information. In other ways, not enough.

A few of my calluses look honeycombed. Ugh. That my shed skin resembles food—either cheese rinds or honey—makes my stomach turn over. I miss real food. Dream about it. Can a stomach turn over in zero gravity? The station rotates so fast. One full orbit every ninety minutes. From the porthole, sixteen times a day, I can watch Australia whizz past. I do this month after month after month. And Earth just looks like a blue-green beachball.

Such a disappointment.

Ever since the moon landing, astronauts have crapped on about how special and magnificent it feels to look upon Earth; for the whole human race to be down there and the astronaut up here, mimicking God. Well, it doesn't feel that way at all. That transcendental holier-than-thou blather is bullshit. Want to know how it feels? Exactly like staring out a window at a blue-green beachball.

I sleep lashed to the side of the privacy pod, cocooned within a million-dollar bedroll, which keeps me from bumping around. Apparently, bumping around is dangerous. Not every switch is foolproof. Apparently, I could accidentally touch a switch and trigger a catastrophe. A single knock could wrench this space station from its orbit and send it hurtling through the atmosphere at 17,500 miles per hour, aflame with a white-hot tail, to crater its wreckage on some point on Earth. A city somewhere in South America, I imagine. Or Europe, maybe. I lie awake, swaddled in my bedroll that slides and heaves on weightless waves, and think about the apocalypse. I like to contemplate the world's terrible, awful end.

Because this wasn't my ambition: I never gave a shit about space travel. I wanted to play football. Hah. Too slow, too heavy. But you knew that already, didn't you, Dr Sharipov? All my stats on file. I needed the money. Lately, I've got to wondering why you people okayed me for this test flight. Was it to see what would happen to a big guy's body? Well, you've learned that foot calluses peel off. What else were you hoping to find out? What else do you hope for me to shed?

Ground Control's radio channel is dead. But you're my psychiatrist and I'm obviously your lab rat, so there must be hidden microphones. I know you're listening. As this space station twirls and spins, I know you're listening to me. There must be hidden cameras in here too. Can you see my foot calluses, Dr Sharipov? Floating, yellowed strips of parmesan rind. Can you see the rest of me? All of me? I shucked my spacesuit a long time ago. My cock and balls bobble about, pale and goose-fleshed, so pathetic I can't help but laugh. At blast-off, I had a crewcut but now my hair waves its overgrown curls like seaweed caught in the tide, and my beard is long and knotted. I'm so thin I can see my bones. Knobbly knees, swollen elbows. My hands and feet look too big.

And whenever the sunlight hits the porthole just right, the air inside this station reveals itself to be full of dust. On Earth, household dust is seventy percent skin cells. But what else is there to comprise the dust inside this station but skin cells? Perhaps spit. Phlegm. Snot. Every time I cough, sneeze, talk, sing, beg, shout, scream, I must release globules. They're floating around me, thick as soup. I'm choking on the detritus of my own unravelling body. There's more of me outside than inside by now. I piss down the vacuum pipe but since I ran out of plastic bags, my shit bobs around me too. These days, I don't shit that often. After careful rationing, the food supply finally ran out today. My last meal was a tablespoon of rehydrated peanut butter.

Please, I'd like to come home. I've had enough.

What bothers me most is the teeth. Not my own teeth. The other volunteer and I couldn't share this tiny space together without eventually going mad. But you knew that would happen, didn't you? One of us *had* to go mad. I think it was him. I tore him to shreds and stuffed most of him in his bedroll. But his teeth keep drifting past my eyes, as well as little chunks of him that resemble foods like prosciutto and blobs of fig jam, making me both salivate and want to puke, so won't you let me come home? Please? Or maybe I should flip a few switches. Try to crash this thing. But I don't know what any of the switches do.

Dr Sharipov. Let me come home.

The Tea and Sugar Train

The railway tracks outside Cecelia's door began to vibrate and hum, signalling the approach of the Tea and Sugar Train. She put her darning aside and took up her shopping list.

The door of their four-room shack opened onto the Nullarbor Plain, a flat and endless expanse of Australian desert in the middle of a godforsaken nowhere. The red soil, red-hot as a fever, sprawled level and unbroken from horizon to horizon while the cloudless blue sky glared above it. Blue over red in every direction, resembling a flag. Sometimes, especially if Cecelia felt tired—as she often did at this stage of her pregnancy—the lack of trees, shrubs or grass played tricks on her vision: the sky and earth appeared to press up close against her nose. She had to blink and focus on the railway tracks before she could regain a proper perspective across this wide, dead, barren world.

Cecelia shut the door against the dust and eased herself into one of the veranda chairs to wait. The other chair, next to the pile of old railway sleepers they used for firewood, was empty. As usual, Henry had left early this morning on his handcar, trundling west to join his team of gangers and fettlers. The Commonwealth Transcontinental Railway spanned 1100 miles from Port Augusta to Kalgoorlie, and some 300 men strung along those miles took care of the tracks. Warped or rotten sleepers had to be replaced, recalcitrant lines kept to the required elevation and gauge, lineside equipment maintained. Henry's job prevented derailment. Too bad the pay didn't reflect the importance of his work. Some weeks, Cecelia's shopping list for the Tea and Sugar

Train took most of Henry's wages. Last week, dear Lord, he had *owed* money to the company.

She must be even thriftier. Count every shilling, every sixpence. Every ha'penny.

From the east, the train appeared as a black dot, growing larger. Cecelia referred to her shopping list and licked the tip of her pencil. *Half pound lamb chops.* She crossed out the item. Two bags of flour instead of one, she decided. Wilting fruits and vegetables were cheap. She would bake sweet and savoury pies, and pasties; rely on damper and scones to bulk out their meals...

She placed a hand on her belly. Soon, another mouth to feed. And when the child was old enough for learning? Why, they would have to leave this dirt-raddled shack and move to a railway stop with a school. The company's rental fee would be high. Textbooks, pencils, stationery, proper clothes. And shoes! Lord, a child is always outgrowing its shoes. Cecelia recalled last night's argument, a fight they had played over and over since her monthlies had ceased. *How are we going to live?* Henry had shouted. *I don't know,* she had replied, as always. Weeping, as always. *I don't know.*

The plume of steam from the locomotive was visible now. Perhaps ten more minutes and the train would be here with its hotchpotch of carriages. From habit, Cecelia glanced at the dead-end siding. Yes, the switch was in the correct position. The Tea and Sugar Train would not derail.

On the siding sat her own little handcar that Henry had scavenged from the scrap heap. Its seesaw pump-lever, platform and battered iron wheels meant the world to her. It was supposed to be for emergencies only. Some mornings after Henry left for work, she would double-check the train schedule—even though she knew it by heart—switch the tracks and take the little handcar, squeaking and rattling, onto the main line. She would work the pump-lever up and down, up and down, the wind in her hair, eyes closed to imagine the hubbub of Melbourne, Adelaide, or even the dusty streets of Kalgoorlie. She always saw herself on a promenade. In her mind's eye, she wore a dress with shoulder pads, a homburg hat topped with an ostrich feather.

But her arms would soon tire. When she opened her eyes, there was nothing but the blue and red flag of this blasted Nullarbor. Puffed from her exertions, she would swap sides and trundle back home again.

Home...

When Henry had returned from the war, morose and aloof, empty as a cored apple, he had wanted to live in isolation. As his wife, Cecelia had followed him out here. Out here into this wide, dead, barren world. No neighbours for two hours by handcar in either direction. No telephone. No radio—

The baby thrashed its limbs, breaking into Cecelia's thoughts.

"Hush," she murmured, patting her belly. "Hush, now."

It would be a relief to visit Dulcie, the nurse on the Tea and Sugar Train. At six months, should the baby be so restless, so agitated? This morning, the child seemed to be fighting against the walls of Cecelia's womb. This was her first pregnancy. No one had told her what to expect, not even Mother, who had kept a dignified silence on such matters despite undergoing seven births herself.

The train puffed and wheezed, brakes grinding.

Cecelia stood up with one hand on her aching back. She waved. Ollie the engine driver, a giant Irishman, waggled his arm out the window in return. Cecelia's heart lifted.

People!

For a few minutes, she would chat with Ollie, and Nick the greengrocer, Wilfred the livestock handler, Albert the butcher, George the dry goods man, Reggie the water man, and share a laugh with them, hear the latest news from towns and cities. Dulcie was good for a yarn... *I'm so lonely*, Cecelia sometimes whispered to Henry over dinner. *Please talk to me.* He would only bend his head over his plate and attend to his meal.

The train, growling and heaving like a beast, came to a stop.

"Hello there!" she called, waving and smiling. "Good morning! Good morning to you all!"

"Are you grand today, Mrs Young?" Ollie shouted out the window. "I'll be down in a sec. How's your sweet tooth?"

"As sweet as ever!"

Most weeks, Ollie the driver gave her a box of chocolates. She didn't know why. It frightened her but she always took the gift, hiding it in the pantry, scoffing the treats while Henry was gone, burning the box in the fireplace. What did Ollie want in return? He hadn't told her yet. She hoped her smile was enough. Occasionally, though, she wondered what might happen if, one day, she packed her suitcase and climbed into the locomotive's cabin and went with him all the way to Kalgoorlie. The Indian Ocean must be as green as jade.

The frantic bawling of ewes spun her around.

From the livestock carriage some yards distant, two sheep fell onto the ground. The screeching animals couldn't get up. Instead, they rolled and bucked in the dirt. Cecelia saw the blood. It squirted out of each sheep from where their four legs should have been, and yet were not. Cecelia's stomach turned over.

Where were their legs?

She called for the livestock man—"Wilfred! Wilfred!"—and the ramp emerged, teetered, and touched down on the dirt. About a dozen sheep, bleating and jumping, fled from the carriage and ran in panicked circles around each other. Close behind them hurried a few shrieking pigs. Out tumbled the flapping chickens. The birds scattered and ran into the emptiness of the desert without hesitation, as if the Devil himself were on their heels. The sheep and pigs rushed after them. There was no water in the Nullarbor Plain. The animals would die. How had they escaped their cages? And why hadn't Wilfred left the carriage yet?

What was taking him so long?

Cecelia held a palm to her throat, the keening of the mutilated sheep raking her nerves. She was about to call for Ollie when Wilfred's arms finally appeared, hands groping at the ramp, followed by his head and the rest of him.

But how in the world...?

He was descending the ramp on his hands and feet, arched over backwards, spine bent at an impossibly sharp angle. His head dangled loose on his neck, grey hair sweeping the boards. Shock and dread fired through Cecelia, freezing her to the spot. Wilfred shuffled like a broken spider down the ramp. Blood smeared his cheeks.

When he reached ground, he worked his jaws and turned his face to gaze at her.

They locked eyes.

Cecelia couldn't breathe.

What kind of hellish vision was this? Could she be dreaming?

Like a rusty flywheel, Wilfred's head began to rotate, slowly, jerkily, notch by notch, until it was the right way up. Even from this distance, Cecelia could hear the bones in his neck cracking and splintering. His mouth opened, releasing a glut of blood and raw meat. From the sheep's missing legs, she knew.

This couldn't be happening.

Had she lost her mind?

Wilfred scuttled towards her at great speed. Cecelia drew a lungful of air and screamed.

"Saints preserve us!" Ollie bellowed.

She glanced around. Ollie dropped the box of chocolates and launched himself back up the ladder and into the engine's cabin. *Dear Lord,* Cecelia thought, heart pounding. *He's going to leave me here with this monster.* But the next second, Ollie leapt out with a coal shovel.

"Stand clear, Mrs Young!" he cried.

The monster that had once been Wilfred yawned open its maw and picked up its scrabbling pace as if to attack. Ollie swung the shovel two-handed like a cricket bat. The blow against Wilfred's head made a loud, slapping, wet sound as it caved in the bones. Cecelia squeezed her eyes shut. The blows went on and on and on.

Thud. Thud. Thud.

Ollie meant to smash the monster's skull into pulp. Her racing heart fluttered and skipped. The maimed sheep kept bawling.

Thud. Thud.

And then, one final time.

Thud.

She opened her eyes. The monster that had once been Wilfred lay in the dirt, limbs twitching spasmodically, blood and mush spattered around him in a curdling puddle. Ollie strode towards the sheep. Before Cecelia could look away, he had dispatched both animals with the shovel, bringing the blade straight down, first upon one neck and then the other.

Now, all was silent apart from the soft, billowing breaths of the train.

She tried to gather her fractured thoughts.

A demon.

Wilfred must have been possessed by a demon.

Oh Jesus, she thought. *My Lord, Jesus Christ, remember that I am a sinner. Most Holy Virgin pray for me. You shall always be praised and blessed. Pray for this sinner —*

"Mrs Young?"

Ollie had turned to her. His chest heaved. Blood covered his bib-and-brace overalls. He took off his billed cap, wiped his forehead with the back of his hand and walked over, unsteady, trailing the gory shovel through the soil behind him.

"Mrs Young, are you unharmed?"

"Yes. And you?"

"Sure." He gestured at his overalls. "Ain't none of this blood's mine."

She locked her knees to stay upright. "What in God's name happened to Wilfred?"

Ollie's face was blanched, eyes glazed. "Damned if I know. He was fine at our last stop. Taking the piss as usual, playing the fool." He whistled a reedy note. "Damned if I know."

They stood together for a time, panting, trembling.

"We'll have to send for the constables," Cecelia said at last.

"I suppose you're right."

"I'll be your witness."

"If anyone believes us." He groaned, seemed to droop. "Oh, shite. I killed a man."

"No, not a man. A monster."

Ollie blew out a breath. "How do you suppose he...*twisted* himself in that way?"

"I've no idea. I've never seen anything like it."

Ollie put his cap back on his head. "Well, I'm not leaving you here. You can't stay with him looking...like *that*. Hop in the cabin. You can ride with me, sure enough."

"Oh, thank you, Ollie. Thank you so much."

"Right. Let's crack on."

He started for the engine. And then it occurred to her, in a sick and panicky rush, that the other train workers had yet to appear. Surely, they had heard the commotion: the shouting, bleating, smashing and slaughtering... Why hadn't they shown themselves? The possibility felt too ghastly to contemplate. Her teeth started to chatter.

Carriage doors rattled open. Simultaneously, Nick the green-grocer and Albert the butcher showed themselves, alighting from the train wrenched over backwards.

"Ollie!" she wailed. "Ollie!"

In unison, the heads of Nick and Albert turned right way up, bones snapping.

Brandishing the shovel, Ollie ran past her at the abominations. "Get in your house and lock the door!"

Cecelia staggered on rubber legs towards the shack but took in the danger of it within a moment: one way in and out, a flimsy wooden door; thin panes of glass in each of the four windows and no shutters. If a monster got inside, she'd be finished. A monster would do to her what Wilfred had done to those poor sheep.

Gnaw at her limbs.

Eat her alive.

With a sob, she veered towards the woodpile. Images of Henry flashed through her mind. Henry's shoulders rolling as he chopped the sleepers. His affectionate smile, rare as it was. The calm, unhurried way he packed and smoked his pipe after dinner. His sombre hazel eyes gazing across the Nullarbor Plain as if he could see for a thousand miles or more. Sometimes, he would take her hand and kiss her fingertips. Henry. *Oh God, Henry.*

Cecelia grabbed the axe.

The blasted thing was so *heavy.*

Her baby jolted and kicked. Could it sense Cecelia's fear? She had to be strong. Had to fight like a man if she hoped to save the child and herself. She wrapped an arm about her belly and, breathless, faced the melee.

Nick the greengrocer was down, a broken and bloodied heap in the dirt.

Ollie, swinging the shovel, was defending himself against Albert the butcher.

Albert darted around Ollie's legs with the speed and agility of a huntsman spider, gnashing his teeth. In life—for surely, he must be dead and somehow reanimated?—Albert had been a stout and strapping lad, unlike Wilfred and Nick, who had both been thin, elderly, frail. Cecelia *must* help before the monster overwhelmed him.

Except her legs gave way.

Dizzy, she stumbled against the pile of wooden sleepers. Good Lord, she almost dropped the blade of the axe straight into her own thigh. The scare of it cleared her head. She struggled to get up again.

Ollie's shovel broke in two.

Cecelia stumbled towards them, axe held out from her body in one hand, the other cradling the weight of her belly as the baby struggled and flailed. Ollie dodged the champing teeth and sprang into the butcher's carriage. Albert went to follow.

Unseen from behind, Cecelia swung the axe sideways into his knee.

To her surprise and horror, the heavy blade went straight through his leg. Unbalanced, Albert toppled like a three-legged table. She lifted the axe to chop again. Ollie bounded from the carriage armed with meat cleavers. His flurry of blows on Albert's head and neck released fountains of blood. Hot droplets spattered her face. She turned away and gagged.

"Mrs Young," he yelled, "want a bollocking? Get yourself in-doors."

She shook her head. "They've all changed. All of them. Look."

Out came Reggie the water man, George the dry goods man. On the landing of the Health Centre Coach, grotesquely arched and distorted like the others, face upside-down, was Dulcie the nurse in her starched uniform, the triangle of her veil hanging loose.

Their three heads rotated. Three necks cracked and broke.

Three mouths stretched open.

"*Nách mór an diabhal thú*," Ollie murmured, but Cecelia didn't know what that meant.

He stepped back. Cecelia moved closer to him.

"Let's go," she whispered. "Can you uncouple the engine from the carriages?"

"I can, but not before these devils attack us."

She swallowed. "Are we to die?"

"More than likely." Ollie reached out and squeezed her hand, briefly. "I'll do my best."

The monsters rushed them.

Ollie lunged forward to intercept Reggie. George, stocky as a hog, lumbered at Cecelia with his teeth bared. Terror shot through her arms and gave her strength to swing the axe two-handed in a sweeping arc. She brought the blade down on the monster's skull. The blade cleaved the head in two and lodged itself in the jawbone. Cecelia gasped. She had expected the skull to be tough, as hardened as a length of sleeper, but it had offered no more resistance than an eggshell. George collapsed in an untidy heap, bleeding, fitting and spasming.

Dulcie was still picking her way down the steep ladder of the Health Centre Coach. Cecelia tried to free the axe. Impossible. Stuck fast. Her efforts only managed to tug and shift George's twitching corpse in the dirt.

Behind her, Ollie and Reggie struggled, tussling like wrestlers. Ollie had lost one of his meat cleavers. She had to defend against Dulcie and then help Ollie. But how? She couldn't pull this blasted axe from George's head.

Dulcie reached ground and came at her in a spritely, loping gallop.

"Come on, goddamn it!" Cecelia shrieked at the axe, yanking with all her might.

The axe wouldn't budge.

She turned and fled towards the house, Dulcie's teeth catching at the hem of her dress. Could she stove in the monster's head with a sleeper? No, no, Henry had not yet cut these ones to length. How could she lift a sleeper the size a of a tree trunk?

Henry had taken his pick, shovel, ballast fork and lining bars with him. Vaulting across the veranda, Cecelia bolted inside and went to slam the door.

Too late.

Dulcie's head was already over the threshold.

Grunting with effort, Cecelia leaned against the door and shoved, shoved, shoved. No good. Her shoes lost purchase, began to slip and slide as Dulcie shouldered further and further inside. The toe of Cecelia's shoe found a knothole in the floorboards. Now she could push back. A stalemate for a few moments; equal force against equal force. Praise God, was the door closing? Yes, it was. It *was* closing.

The monster's tongue unfurled and whipped about.

Cecelia yelped.

The tongue elongated. Soon it would be long enough to wrap itself around Cecelia's ankle and pull her into those teeth that were growing, sharpening, extending.

"In the name of Christ, get away from me!" she screamed.

Dulcie burst open the door, throwing Cecelia against the table.

They faced each other, motionless, for what seemed like an age. The hideous mouth opened wider. Its throat convulsed. The tongue roped onto the floor, its tip switching back and forth like a snake's tail.

A weapon. Cecelia must find some kind of weapon.

The cast-iron pan?

She took a single step towards the woodstove. Hesitated when Dulcie shifted on four limbs. The distorted body started to tighten and pull itself together as if preparing to jump.

Cecelia lunged for the pan. Dulcie sprang. The flat of the pan caught the monster across the face. The nose broke away cleanly and drooped alongside one cheek. The monster didn't appear to notice. The tongue intercepted the second swing. Prehensile, it lashed itself around the handle and ripped the pan from Cecelia's grasp. The tongue had touched her for a split-second, the texture of it dry and scaled, and Cecelia howled in revulsion and terror.

The pan clattered to the floorboards.

The tongue retracted.

The advancing jaws snap, snap, *snapped.*

Cecelia grabbed the skinny little poker from the fireplace and held it out just as Dulcie leaped, all limbs in the air at once like a spider. The poker entered the gaping mouth and Dulcie's impetus drove it straight down the gullet. Cecelia felt it punch and lodge somewhere deep inside. The monster dropped, short-winded and retching, tongue lolling.

Cecelia wrenched out the poker and brought it down on the grotesque head over and over, crunching the bones, staining the gauzy white veil first with blood and then with brains. At last, Dulcie teetered and fell.

Strength ebbed from Cecelia. She leaned against the table and wept. The baby, oh dear Lord, the baby started to thrash in what felt like a wild, animal panic.

"Shush, my darling," she whispered through quivering lips, patting at her belly with one bloodied palm. "Hush, now—"

Was that a contraction?

Shocked, Cecelia stopped weeping.

That quick, vice-like sensation in the cradle of her pelvis? *There it was again.* She knew what that meant. No, she was only six months along. She had to get to a hospital.

"Ollie?" she called. "Can you hear me?"

No answer.

She cocked her head to listen.

Nothing but the huff and respiration of the Tea and Sugar Train.

Her heart started knocking again. Lifting the bent and crumpled poker, holding it out like a sword, she stepped around Dulcie's corpse and approached the open door. The fight with Reggie the water man, the monster that Reggie had become... Had Ollie won?

"Ollie, please say something," she cried.

No reply.

She peeked around the jamb.

And there was the Irishman, standing over the remains of Reggie. She sagged and shook with relief. Every monster was dead. She made her way outside haltingly, painfully, groping for support against the doorframe, the chair next to the woodpile, the nearest veranda post.

"I killed Dulcie," she said.

Ollie turned. The sight made her flinch. He was covered in gore from head to toe as if dipped in a vat. Eyes shining white in his bloodied face, he stared at the meat cleaver in his hand and dropped it, raising a puff of red soil.

"Can we leave right away?" she said. "I think the baby is coming."

He didn't reply.

She hugged the veranda post, watching him. Her womb clenched and released again.

"I need a hospital," she said. "Will you drive me?"

The closest hospital was four hours away. And if she got there in time, could the doctors stop her labour? Save the baby? She had names picked out already: Douglas Ross for a boy; Maureen Joy for a girl.

"Ollie?" Tears rose. "For God's sake, answer me."

He coughed. Brought a hand to his throat and coughed again. It was an alarming sound, a choking sound. Cecelia pushed off from the post, stepped from the veranda and managed a few paces on unsteady legs. Woozy, she had to pause. Ollie started wheezing. It worsened into a strident, whooping sound.

"What's the matter?" she said, frightened. "Where are you hurt?"

Ollie hacked and barked, clawing at his throat. Dear God, how could she help? No medical training, no medical supplies... Then, as if punched by an invisible fist, his head flung back with a loud pop and stayed there.

Cecelia froze.

The coughing and wheezing ceased. Ollie's knees started to bend.

"Dear Lord," she whispered. "No. Please no."

Ollie swung his arms overhead so violently that both shoulders cracked. Methodically, steadily, he bent over backwards, lowering himself inch by inch until his palms lay flat on the ground. He shook himself with the vigour of a wet dog. Shuffling, he faced her with his upside-down head.

Cecelia lifted the crooked poker. "Stay away. Can you still

understand me? Stay. Away."

Neck bones cracked and broke as his head swivelled the right way up. He bared his teeth.

The fight left her with a sob. How could she defend herself against this giant of a man? Ollie must be three times her size. She had nothing but a flimsy poker. What now? What?

She would kneel and pray.

There was no other recourse. And while this monster that had once been Ollie murdered and defiled her, she would hold the love of God our Father in her heart. Lifted into Heaven with her unborn child, she would wait there for Henry until his time on earth came to an end, until they would be a family once more, together again for all of eternity.

And then she remembered the handcar.

With a spurt of fresh energy, she dropped the poker and sprinted.

Ollie shuffled noisily through the soil behind her in pursuit. Her lead was only a few yards. She hauled the switch to move the tracks, checked over her shoulder.

Ollie was too close.

Jumping aboard the platform, she grabbed the pump-lever and worked it. Shuddering, creaking, the handcar began to inch along the tracks.

Faster, faster, she had to go *faster*.

She looked back. Saw the open mouth. Instinctively kicked out, once, twice. The sturdy heel of her shoe broke his front teeth. Panting with exertion, grunting, she wrenched on that damned pump-lever as quickly as she could. The handcar gained speed. It bumped onto the main track, began to zip along. Negotiating the wooden sleepers would slow Ollie down.

Unless he retained enough human sense to run alongside on the dirt.

She looked back again. He was stumbling over the tracks, almost upon her. She kicked out again. Yet she couldn't kick and work the lever both.

"God help me," Cecelia yelled to the heavens.

Shutting her eyes, she focused on the lever. *Up down up down up down up...*

Her muscles burned. The flesh on her legs crept as she awaited Ollie's bite.

A flurry of contractions buckled her. Stars danced in her vision. She lost the pump-lever's rhythm. Was Ollie close? No time to check. Near, too near, she heard him clattering over the tracks. Panic would be her undoing. She brought to mind the padded shoulders of a new dress, the ostrich feather in a homburg hat. The promenade, the promenade. She would be strolling the promenade with Henry while he pushed the perambulator with their child sitting inside, a chubby little girl, Maureen Joy, with her waving arms and strawberry blonde hair…

Cecelia glanced around.

Ollie, some yards back along the tracks, had stopped. Had given up the pursuit.

Thank you, God. Oh, thank you.

Shaking, Cecelia slowed the pace, arms on fire. How far was Henry and his gang? Surely, no more than an hour. If she spared her strength, she could make the distance in good time.

Up down. *Breathe.*

Up down. *Breathe.*

The wind dried the tears on her cheeks. Willpower stopped her legs from folding. All she wanted now was to feel Henry's arms about her, his kisses on her mouth. How to explain the horrors from the Tea and Sugar Train? The events defied description. She glanced back. The locomotive lay far in the distance. She was safe.

But what had changed everyone? What had changed Ollie?

Something from the sky, perhaps, something out of the air…

A cold fist closed around her heart.

What if she, too, were doomed to turn into a monster?

Unnerved, she took one hand off the lever to knead at her neck. Did she feel all right? Any different? It was hard to tell, her body wracked with pain, cramps, fatigue… Yet she didn't need to cough. No choking sensations. That meant she was okay.

Didn't it?

She put both hands on the pump-lever. Focus. Up down, up down. Her mind raced.

What about Henry? She might come upon him and the other fettlers and gangers, only to find them contorted upside-down. Could the whole Nullarbor Plain be infected? Or even the whole of Australia?

Another contraction took Cecelia's breath.

A contraction…or was it a *bite*?

The baby stretched as if trying to arch itself.

Arch itself backwards?

Cecelia screamed into the empty blue sky. Her screams rolled out without answer or echo across the wide, dead, barren Nullarbor Plain.

Last Dance

I concealed the stake inside my dinner jacket. Sat by the dance floor, tensed and ready.

The music swelled. I spotted him moving an elegant woman through the waltz, his hand low on her hip. They swept around the room, her silver gown swirling, her enraptured face smiling up at him. The orchestral climax urged their steps faster. Transfixed, I watched him pull her tighter, closer. Too late, I gained my feet. He bent her backwards for the dip.

And bit her throat.

The crowd gasped at the blood, but I am haunted by her reddened lips opening in ecstasy.

Hair and Teeth

Blood. So much blood. It runs out of Elaine's body for weeks at a time, soaking through sanitary pads at a rate she has never experienced before in her life. Some days—on bad days—she can sit on the toilet and listen to her menstrual blood hit the water in a steady drizzle, *plip-plip-plip*. She is constantly light-headed, woozy, ready to drop. This is menopause, isn't it? Protracted and heavy periods? A normal, natural event? Yet the medical term *menorrhagia* is too clinical, far too sterile, to describe this carnage. And pain. So much pain. A nest of starving mice is gnawing through her insides. A crazy notion, but in the dead of night, when the world is smothered and unable to make a single sound, Elaine lies awake, worrying about the possibility of mice.

For the past year, maybe longer, her husband Malcolm has urged Elaine to tell their doctor. She sees the doctor every three months anyway for her prescription refills, so why not mention the heavy periods? Elaine has refused. The bleeding will soon stop of its own accord. After all, she is fifty-one. How much longer can her exhausted ovaries keep going? But when the blackened clots begin slipping out of her, raw and slick, plump, as engorged as chicken livers, Elaine panics and makes an appointment. Tests follow. Invasive tests.

And now, here she sits in her doctor's office, waiting for the results.

The autumn sun beats weakly through the windowpane. The desk holds a jar of lollipops. A cardboard box of showbags for expectant mothers sits beneath the examination table. Familiar sights. Elaine has come here for some twenty-six years, ever since her one and only pregnancy. Her daughter is grown-up now. Married and gone. Long gone.

The doctor stares at his computer monitor. One fat hand clasps the mouse, clicking, scrolling. The other hand cups his double chin. He was slim once. Back in the day. A chubby finger, preoccupied, taps at his teeth. *Tock, tock, tock.* Elaine shifts in the chair, waiting, perspiring, bleeding. The doctor steals glances at her as he reads the test reports. Time crawls by. Elaine bites her lips, clenches her toes inside her shoes.

The doctor's eyes squint, widen as if in shock, squint again. Clearly, he can't believe the information on the screen. Elaine's stomach lurches. It's mice. A nest of mice, chewing, hollowing her out. If only Malcolm were here. But he's at work. He's always at work. Malcolm fears it may be cancer, which is a much more sensible fear in Elaine's opinion.

The doctor sits back in his chair. "You have fibroids," he proclaims.

She has heard of the condition but is not sure what it means. "Cancerous?" she says.

"No. Benign tumours inside the uterus. Inside your womb."

She says, "But they're loose. The tumours move around."

The doctor taps at his teeth again. He will not meet her gaze. Elaine's heart flitters and flops against her ribs. If Malcolm were here, he would tell her to *calm down*. I am safe, she tells herself, recalling the practised mantra. Not everything is a conspiracy. All is well.

"Doctor?" she says. "Do the fibroids move around? Like mice trapped in a bag?"

He stares at her, intently, without blinking, in a way that makes her afraid. Then he arranges his lips into a grin and emits a chuckle—*heh-heh-heh*—his belly jouncing. "Move? Absolutely not. Fibroids are anchored. They grow out of the womb's endometrium like mushrooms out of dirt." He flicks a runnel of sweat from his hairline. "The uterus is very swollen, about the size of a five-month pregnancy. It'll be a hysterectomy, I'm afraid."

Hysterectomy? Elaine stiffens in the chair. Her womb taken out? That special place where she grew her only child to be excised, thrown without care into a medical waste bin? Elaine clenches her jaw to stop the tears from rising. Yet the pain prowls around, nipping and munching. A clot slithers out. No, Elaine cannot keep living like this. Bleeding like this. Her mice-filled womb is trying to kill her. She knows this to be true.

"All right," she says, smiling, smiling, smiling. "Yes. A hysterectomy."

The doctor pecks, two-fingered, at the computer keyboard. "I'm referring you to a gynaecologist named Smith."

Elaine's smile dies. "Why can't I see my regular gyno?"

The printer sounds. The doctor withdraws the page and hands it over. She takes it, blindly.

"No, I'm sorry," Elaine says, voice rising. "I want my regular gyno."

The doctor regards her from the corner of his eye. "How are your meds?" he says. "Still keeping all those strange thoughts under control?"

She nods, scrunches up the referral, stuffs it into her handbag.

"I can always increase the dosages," he says, hanging his forefingers over the keyboard again. "Double doses might help."

"No. I'm fine. Thank you."

Elaine stands, releasing a hot flood. If she doesn't change her sanitary pad now, right now, it will overflow. Dizzy, she crosses the room and scrabbles for the doorknob.

In a rush, the doctor says, "Your fibroids aren't mobile. What you're experiencing is referred pain. The tumours can't move. It's impossible. Do you understand?"

She glances around. The doctor's sweating face is set. A vein pulses in his temple. Both meaty hands are clenched. Liar. *She is on to him.* But she must not let him know that she knows.

"Yes, thank you." Elaine backs out of the room. "I understand completely."

As soon as Elaine gets home, she studies the referral letter. DR JOHN SMITH. Obviously, a pseudonym. The letters after his name are meaningless: MBBS, FRCOG, FRANZCOG, DDU. Yet what can Elaine do? Keep bleeding to death? She has a sherry. It is 10:39am. She drinks another. Her pills have the same red-rimmed sticker on each box: *This medicine may cause DROWSINESS and may increase the effects of alcohol.* She only drinks when Malcolm is at work. In the evening, she has black tea, mint tea, rooibos. A little sherry won't hurt, doesn't hurt. A glass here and there helps her to *calm down*. That's what Malcolm wants, isn't it? A normal, stable, pleasant wife. A calm wife.

She calls the number on Dr John Smith's referral letter. A man answers, "Hello?"

This is not what she expects. No one in a professional setting answers the phone in such a casual manner. Perhaps she has the wrong number.

"Hello?" the man says again. "This is Dr Smith. Is anybody there?"

"Yes," she whispers. "Mrs Elaine Grey."

"Excellent. Let's make the appointment for tomorrow morning at nine o'clock."

Elaine agrees and hangs up, breathless. Over dinner, she tries to explain what has happened but Malcolm reaches across the kitchen table and pats her hand.

"Don't worry," he says. "Specialists usually have long waiting times, sure, but this bloke must have had a cancellation. Stop reading too much into it, okay?"

"Okay," she says. "Of course."

Dr Smith's clinic is located in the midst of a tacky strip of shops. Wedged between a tattoo parlour and a FOR LEASE sign is a door bearing the weathered inscription DR JOHN SMITH, WOMEN'S HEALTH, BY APPOINTMENT ONLY.

Elaine hesitates. Perhaps she should leave. But the tearing pains in her womb change her mind. As it turns out, these pains are not caused by hungry mice. Last night in bed, kept awake by the chomping and chawing, she had a vision of the actual culprits. Limbless and eyeless little monsters, round as meatballs, purplish-black and tufted with random crops of hair, equipped with teeth. How they got inside her womb, she has no idea.

Elaine pushes against DR JOHN SMITH's door. It opens onto

a dusty, musty smell and a single flight of carpeted stairs. She climbs. Atop the landing, there is no waiting room, no receptionist. Nothing but a plain wooden door. She clutches her handbag to her swollen abdomen, clenching her toes inside her shoes. Blood and clots run, run, run from her in an endless fall, soaking the sanitary pad. Spots dance in her vision. This ordeal must end. It has to end. She will rid herself of the multitudes, of the hair and teeth. Otherwise, the monsters will chew right through her womb and escape. Kidneys, liver, pancreas: no organ would be safe. Her doctor must have foreseen this possibility in her test results. That would explain his nervous tics—the tapping of incisors, the side-eye, the sweating—and his referral to the mysterious Dr John Smith. Medical treatment for monsters requires a special doctor, an outlier, a surgeon with his office crammed between a tattoo parlour and a FOR LEASE sign, a gynaecologist without clientele or receptionist. Elaine knocks. Seconds pass.

"Hello?" she says, her voice a faint croak.

The plain wooden door opens. A man peeks his head out. It is a sleek head, with greased black hair combed into perfectly straight and even rows like an empty, tilled field. His dark eyes shine. He smiles with his lips closed. Elaine is small, barely five feet tall, but this man is smaller. Much smaller. He wears a charcoal suit, white shirt, red tie.

"Dr Smith?" she says.

He opens the door and ushers her inside with the wave of a child-sized hand. As he retreats, Elaine takes in the room. An examination table, two chairs, a desk. There is nothing on the desk. No computer, no jotting pad, no pen. Elaine's shoulders tighten even more. The start of a headache squeezes her scalp. She sits opposite Dr John Smith. He is smiling. His face is narrow and pointed as if swept back from the nose.

"Fibroids," he says. Then he wags a tiny forefinger. "Ah, but you don't agree."

This takes her by surprise. She doesn't know how to respond.

"Tell me what you think they are," he says. "Be frank, please."

"What for? You'll assume I'm crazy."

Sombre, Dr John Smith shakes his pinched little head, and

gestures for her to speak.

"All right." She lifts her chin. "At first, I thought my womb held a nest of mice."

"Mice." He nods, mulling it over. "And now?"

"Now I know it holds monsters. Dozens of them. Monsters with hair and teeth."

Dr Smith steeples his fingers, leans back in the chair and contemplates the ceiling. He says, "You believe you're harbouring teratomas?"

"Teratomas? I'm sorry. I don't know what they are."

"A type of germ cell tumour that grows in the reproductive organs. Quite rare," he says, and presses one tiny set of knuckles against his mouth, just for a moment, as if stifling a grin. "Misbegotten tumours. Often presenting with hair and teeth."

"Yes," Elaine says. "That sounds about right."

"Mrs Grey, have you told anyone else of your suspicions?"

"No. Absolutely not."

He takes a business card from his jacket pocket and offers it with just the tips of his manicured fingernails. "Tomorrow 9:00am at this hospital. No food or drink after midnight."

"Tomorrow?" She takes the card. "You're scheduling my surgery for tomorrow?"

"Pack a bag sufficient for a two-night stay. Keep taking your medications as prescribed. It's very important that you keep taking your medications. Very important."

"Don't you have any other patients?"

He interlaces his fingers and rests his hands on the empty desk. "You're quite ill, Mrs Grey. Your womb is grossly enlarged and deformed. Some of the tumours have grown so fast, they've outstripped their own blood supply and become necrotic. That means the tumours are rotting, Mrs Grey. Decaying like corpses. You are pregnant with death itself, as it were." He smiles and stands up. "Remember, nothing to eat or drink after midnight."

Elaine stands up too, breathless, faint, nauseated, bleeding, hot clots sliding out.

Over dinner, Malcolm pats the back of her hand. "Well, Dr Smith must have had a cancellation," he says. "You're really poorly. Dr

Smith said so himself. Count your blessings you don't have to wait."

The hospital turns out to be a suburban brick veneer. Instead of gardens there is asphalt for parking. The morning is bright and cloudless, glaring. Elaine clutches the handles of her valise, biting her lip, as Malcolm steers their car into one of the many vacant spots and cuts the engine. Ordinary houses where people live are on either side of the hospital. In fact, the whole street is full of ordinary houses.

"It's a private clinic," Malcolm says. "This is how they tend to look out here in the suburbs. Calm down, would you please? Stop chewing the inside of your cheek."

In the pre-surgery waiting room, behind a drawn curtain, Malcolm folds her clothes for her, ties the straps of her hospital gown, helps pull the compression stockings over her feet and up to her knees. He is whistling through his front teeth all the while.

"Aren't you scared?" Elaine says. "People can die during surgery."

"Don't be silly," he says. "You're in good hands."

Elaine stares at her husband very carefully. It was Malcolm who encouraged her to see their GP in the first place. Malcolm who reassured her about Dr Smith's deserted consulting room and unfilled surgery schedule. Malcolm who is sitting next to her, whistling a jaunty tune, now searching through a stack of magazines for something to read.

No, she must be logical.

Soon, she will bleed no more, not ever again. Her womb will be gone, thrown away. That is a good thing. *I am safe,* she tells herself. Not everything is a conspiracy. All is well. She stops staring at her husband. Instead, she looks around the room. It must have been a lounge room originally, back when the hospital was a family home. There are three other booths, each one with its curtain drawn back, each booth empty. Elaine clenches her toes against the linoleum floor, over and over and over again.

The nurse comes in. It is the same woman from the reception desk. "Ready?" she says.

No. Elaine has changed her mind. She doesn't want to do this anymore. She wants to see her regular gynaecologist instead. She must insist on a second opinion.

Malcolm takes hold of Elaine's hand. Together, they follow the nurse to the corridor.

The nurse stops and says, "Here's where you part ways. Mrs Grey, you come with me. Hubby, you go to the exit and we'll see you in a couple of hours, okay?"

Malcolm leans down to kiss Elaine. A sob chokes off Elaine's throat. She flings her arms about his neck and clings on, until he laughs, taking hold of her wrists to push her away. The nurse is laughing too.

"I'm frightened," Elaine says.

"You'll be fine," Malcolm says, and leaves.

Elaine watches him go, her fists pressed to her swollen abdomen, against her belly pregnant with monsters both dying and dead, against her womb filled with hair and teeth.

"Come along," the nurse says.

Elaine trails behind, crying, hiccupping on sobs. She turns a corner and stops.

There is a gurney with metal side-rails, a half-dozen people in green or blue scrubs. As one, they all look at her and smile with closed lips. None of them seems to mind or even notice that Elaine is weeping. A child steps forward. No, not a child, but Dr John Smith. She didn't recognise him at first in his scrubs with the cap covering the greased ruts of his hair. He is rubbing his palms together, the skin making a dry whisking sound, his dark eyes shining with anticipation and delight. Everyone else stands very still. Motionless.

"Sorry, I'm just a bit scared," Elaine whispers, embarrassed, thumbing away tears.

No one says anything. Their cold, perfunctory manner allows her to regain control. She is helped onto the gurney. The anaesthetist puts a cannula into the back of her hand. The monsters gnaw and rend and gnash. Elaine feels weak. Not long now. Not long.

A couple of women push the gurney into another room. This is the theatre. It has an enormous light fixture with many bulbs hanging from the ceiling, trolleys covered in stainless steel equipment, machines on carts, a central table. The window looks out onto a clothesline.

The women help Elaine to lie on the table. Someone puts a mask over her nose and mouth. Compressed air hisses out of it. The air smells like rubber and medicine. Someone else puts a syringe into the cannula in her hand and depresses the plunger. A sickly dropping sensation, like the downward swoop of a rollercoaster, surges through Elaine and momentarily stops the monsters from biting. Catching them, like her, by surprise.

"Well, that feels weird," Elaine says, and closes her eyes for a moment.

She opens them.

The pain is excruciating. Agonising. It claws and mauls and flails wildly throughout her body, violent and wrenching, taking her breath. She tries to bring her knees to her chest but is too feeble. A wail breaks from her throat.

"Relax," says a voice. "Calm down."

Elaine gasps, blinks. She is in a different room. The operation must be over. Her rotting uterus should be in a medical waste bin. Writhing, she cries, "Help me. Please help me."

"Calm down," intones the voice again. This time, she recognises Dr Smith.

She forces her eyes open. The entire surgical staff is arranged around her bed, watching her. Dr Smith stands at the foot of the bed, grinning. Elaine tries to lift her head.

"Why didn't you take out the monsters?" she says. "Why did you let them loose?"

The teeth are roaming, unchecked, chewing rabidly at her bowels, biting her diaphragm in frantic search of heart and lungs, gnawing through muscle to burrow down into each thigh.

"The operation was a success," Dr Smith says. "Congratulations."

He looks around at his team. They look back at him and at each other.

Elaine clutches her abdomen. "The pain," she says. "I can't stand it."

"Relax," Dr Smith says. "You're in good hands."

His hands are clasped to his chest as if in joy. The team members grip the metal side-rails of the bed. Their hands are white-knuckled. No one touches her. Smiling with closed lips, silently, they watch her as she winces, thrashes, struggles. Elaine understands now, too late, as the unleashed monsters tear and rip through her guts, that she is not safe. Everything is a conspiracy. All is not well.

Angel Wings

I t had kicked off this afternoon. David, together with about seven billion other people, recognised it as the beginning of the end. The literal end of the world. This cataclysm didn't involve the top three predictions of nuclear war, asteroid strike or pandemic. It was something unexpected by all apart from, say, a few kooky fringe-dwelling cults.

An invasion of angels.

Millions upon millions of angels.

Not the serene, beauteous, human-with-celestial-wings type but the biblically correct type. Monstrous abominations. A few hours ago, which in Melbourne had been a mild and sunny Saturday, they had descended from the heavens in hordes, a vast legion of screeching, furious and bloodthirsty avengers, hellbent on butchering every single person in every single country across the entirety of the planet.

And nobody knew why.

Maybe humanity would never know. That's what David surmised. He stared out the car window at the chaos, tears on his cheeks, and figured the human race would be slaughtered quickly, efficiently, wiped out by tomorrow night at the latest without explanation. Maybe these mutant birdlike things were aliens instead of angels— the Internet's opinion seemed divided. So what? A moot point. Extinction was imminent either way.

David scrolled through the newsfeed on his phone: more annihilation and destruction from across the globe. Next, he checked for but didn't find any messages from Grandma. Or his cousins, aunts, uncles. No replies from the friends he'd texted en masse from the camping store. He put the phone in his pocket and surreptitiously wiped at his nose.

"Are you right, kid?" the driver said, an older woman who reminded him of Mum.

"Oh, sure," he said. "Yeah, I'm just fucking great." Then he swallowed and shook his head. "I'm sorry. Look, I'm… Thanks for picking me up, okay? I really appreciate it. Sorry."

"No worries. What's your name, kid?"

"David."

"I'm Milly. The guy in back is Yiannis, my neighbour."

Yiannis sat forward and offered his hand. David glanced around to shake. Yiannis had dark eyes, dark eyebrows, a mop of dark hair thinning at the front, a sallow complexion.

"Your mouth is still bleeding," Yiannis said. "Did you lose a tooth?"

A tooth? With an anxious jolt, David felt around his gums. Blood from his lacerated cheek and lips pulsed over his probing fingertips. Although an incisor wobbled, his upper and lower teeth were intact. He felt a wave of relief. Considering how much Mum and Dad had spent on braces, they would be devastated if… Then David remembered Mum and Dad were dead and wouldn't be feeling anything ever again. He turned away.

Milly and Yiannis said nothing as he cried.

Finally, hiccupping, David wiped his face on his t-shirt and looked about. Milly was steering around a motorcycle lying on its side. No sign of the rider. Probably carried away by talons to be shredded, like a hot roast chicken, on a rooftop somewhere. *Oh fuck. Oh God.*

In the quarter-hour David had been a passenger in Milly's Subaru, they'd passed wrecks and abandoned cars, vehicles on fire, litters of ruined corpses. Road-raging brawlers. People running. The occasional swoop of angels, shrieking like a discordant orchestra of untuned violins. Horns sounding constantly from the traffic. Milly had to be cautious at intersections because drivers, panicking, tended to ignore red lights.

The carnage continued up Burwood Highway as far as the

eye could see. On the hill's crest sat a gridlock. What would Milly do then? Try for the side streets? David watched the pedestrians thronging the footpaths and the road lanes, watched them dodging corpses, traffic, smashed vehicles. Where did they think they were going? How far did they believe they could get on foot? Some were armed: golf clubs, baseball bats, cricket bats, knives. Most carried suitcases, boxes, backpacks, children, pets. Like characters from a war film. A middle-aged woman struggled with a birdcage, the budgerigar within clinging to its wildly swinging perch. Houses weren't safe; angels could tear up roof tiles. Cars weren't safe either but every now and again a pedestrian would storm Milly's Subaru, pound at the windows, plead or demand to be let in. Milly always drove on, gaze forward, blind and deaf.

David rubbed his eyes.

In the distance a giant flock of angels swarmed the sky, pulsing, forming shapes in the air like starlings or schooling fish. A mesmeric sight if you didn't realise the danger. The angels hovered over Melbourne city because that's where people were congregating; specifically, at the Sports and Entertainment Precinct with its many venues including the Rod Laver Arena and the Margaret Court Arena, both with their retractable roofs now closed according to news reports. The precinct's buildings were being repurposed into evacuation centres, getting kitted out with first aid stations, cot beds, soup kitchens—and already protected by the military. The city skyline shone with tracers, explosions, flamethrowers. David found himself smiling, jaws clenched. Well, you had to hand it to the Australian federal and state governments. Primed by yearly bushfires, they'd leapt into action pretty damn quick. But other places around the world? Eh, not so much. The bulk of seven billion people were apparently fending for themselves and coming off second-best.

Milly's destination was the Sports and Entertainment Precinct. Failing that, the other main evacuation site—the Melbourne Exhibition Centre, that triplet of vast warehouse-sized buildings standing side by side, colloquially known as "Jeff's Shed" after the former Victorian premier Jeff Kennett. Perhaps David would find relatives or friends there. Maybe... He checked his phone again for texts. Sent a few more of his own. Stared at the blank screen.

Milly hunched over the steering wheel to squint at the swarm. "Do you reckon some of the pricks are getting closer?"

"I don't know," David said, voice quiet and flat. "I guess we'll see."

He reached into the footwell to touch the handles of his machetes. He imagined killing an angel, its half-dozen feathered wings falling apart as he hacked through its central nub, the spark of its multiple eyes clouding and snuffing out—

"Looks like you got attacked back in that car park, David," Yiannis said. "Did you?"

"Yeah, kid, what happened?" Milly said. "Do you think you can tell us now?"

David again pressed his t-shirt to his bleeding mouth. Wiped away tears. Cleared his throat. "Nothing happened, really," he said. "I went to the camping store to buy a couple of machetes for protection. When I came back out, some guy punched me and stole my keys..."

Oi, cockhead. Gimme ya car.

Huh?

Gimme ya fucken car, cockhead! Now! Right now!

David had frozen. He was twenty years old, dux of his high school, recipient of a tertiary scholarship, lived at home with his parents, spent most of his time studying or playing computer games, didn't smoke or drink, had never been in an encounter even *remotely* like this in his entire life and couldn't comprehend fast enough what was going on.

Stunned, he stared at the man.

Perhaps in his forties, the man was sweaty and red-faced as if he'd been running. David wanted to explain that Mum and Dad had just been killed. Gardening, they'd sent him to the hardware store for liquid fertiliser. On his return, David had witnessed a dozen hell-spawn monsters, in a frenzied and vulturine pack, threshing at bloodied lumps on the lawn. *What the fuck?* The monsters were identical: brown-feathered, two-legged, multi-eyed, six-winged; flat and round with a two-metre diameter like a giant dinner plate; reminiscent of an owl but only if you looked at a slice of it through the mirrors of a kaleidoscope.

And Jesus, their ear-splitting shrieks…

The sky was dark, dotted, chock-full of blowflies or wasps or bees, some kind of insect. Then the shapes got closer, larger, and David recognised them as *more* monsters, dropping from the heavens, dropping in their thousands upon thousands—

And those mutilated, bloodied lumps on the lawn were Mum and Dad.

David let out a long, plaintive, guttural wail.

Two monsters stopped rending his parents and flew talons-first at his car. David, still screaming, punched the remote for the garage door. The door shuddered open. Three more monsters flew out, scraping and slashing at the car, claws tearing the metal.

They had got inside the house.

Via the roof? Yes. Tiles were smashed as if boulders had hit.

Paralysed, overwhelmed, David froze even as claws pierced the cabin. He could smell the monsters now. A sharp, caustic stink like hot electronics.

In the next second, gasping, he reversed, executed a frantic U-turn and sped away, sobbing. The angels lost either their grip or their interest. David tried to ring Grandma, other relatives, friends. Switched on the radio as he drove aimlessly and fast, listened in shaking and shivering shock to the news of the *angel* invasion, of *biblically correct* angels, happening simultaneously all around the world. Drove to the strip shopping centre to buy weapons from the camping store, the floor packed with people freaking out. Managed to grab a couple of machetes. Standing at the checkout, waiting and waiting, staff hopelessly outnumbered, he tried again to contact relatives, friends, then decided to just *steal* the fucking machetes for Christ's sake, become a thief for the first time in his life, and raced outside to his car—

Right, cockhead. Fuck ya! That's it!

David had never been punched before. The pain exploded in his head like a grenade. He didn't remember falling yet there he was, sprawled on the asphalt, looking up, incredulous.

Because the sweaty, red-faced man was opening the driver's door of David's car.

David tried to yell, *no!* That was *his* VW Golf. A birthday present from his parents that was meant to span his eighteenth to his twenty-fifth. Mum and Dad had helped him choose it from the dealership. This *arsehole* could not, should not, *must not* take David's car.

But the arsehole did.

David sat up, howling, as the Golf backed out of the parking space and tore away, bumping and jumping over concrete wheel stops and dividers, skidding onto the road.

"That's my car!" David shouted to no one in particular, to no one who gave a damn.

Because people at the strip shopping centre were running and yelping and fighting. David remembered the two machetes and picked them up. Staggering to his feet, he wondered what to do. A swarm of angels landed on the roof of the camping store. They made a hissing noise like cats. Each one had dozens of eyes along its six wings staring greedily at the stampeding humans below. One angel fixed its gaze on David and narrowed its multitude of eyes, pinned its multitude of pupils. David lifted both machetes, screaming though clenched jaws, ready for whatever was to come next.

And what came next was a white Subaru.

It had pulled up next to him, the front passenger door flinging open. The driver had yelled, *"Kid!* Get in!" and David obeyed without thinking. There had been a man in the back seat.

Milly and Yiannis. Two strangers. Stepping in to save his life.

"Ah, forget about your car," Milly said now after David fell silent. "At least you're alive."

"What made you stop for me?"

She glanced over, both eyes smudged with ruined mascara. "You look like my son."

David hesitated. "So, is he…?"

"Dead?" She hunched a shoulder, tightened her grip on the wheel. "Yeah."

"I'm sorry."

Yiannis said, "Ah, we'll all be dead soon. This whole planet is one gigantic sinking ship."

David turned to Yiannis and said, "How come you weren't sitting up here in front?"

"Why? Because of *this*." Yiannis pointed at his legs extended along the bench seat. One thigh appeared held together with a knotted, blood-soaked jumper. He shrugged at David's alarm. "It is what it is. I'll probably bleed out before we get to an evacuation centre."

"Oh, come on, we'll be there in no time," Milly said. "Try to think positive for once."

"Positive thinking leads to inaction and failure to perform. No, I'd rather be a realist."

"You mean a pessimist."

David said, "Press your hands against the wound. That'll work better than a tourniquet."

The car appeared as a red streak in the corner of David's vision, travelling fast, shooting into the intersection before he could utter a warning. The red car hit the Subaru broadside on its boot, sending both vehicles airborne, twirling them in a *pas de deux* towards the other side of the road. David felt momentarily weightless. Separating, the red car punched against the post of a traffic light. The Subaru touched down and rolled, windscreens shattering, then landed upright, joggled on its tyres, the deployed airbags farting a little as they deflated, white powder dusting the air of the cabin.

A few seconds passed.

Ears ringing, David got his bearings.

One machete was still in the footwell. The other had pierced the seat alongside him, buried to the hilt. Fuck, those blades must be *sharp*. He pulled out the machete.

"Is everybody okay?" Milly said.

"Yeah," David said, and turned. "Yiannis?"

But Yiannis was crumpled into a messy ball of tangled limbs, his back to them.

"Oh shit," David said. "He wasn't wearing a seatbelt, was he?"

Milly stamped the accelerator, wrenched at the steering wheel.

The Subaru revved but didn't move. A clacking, whirring noise sounded from somewhere beneath. Traffic crowded them, horns honking in a cacophonous blare. Across the intersection, the bonnet of the smashed red car showed a few licks of fire. No one had yet got out.

"We're fucked!" Milly yelled. "Can't move, can't go, we're *fucked*."

The engine revved and revved hard as she stomped the accelerator over and over and over. Black dots in the sky—angels—flew closer. There wasn't much time.

"Look!" David shouted, pointing through the remains of the windscreen.

Up ahead, in the middle of the highway at the Vermont South terminus, sat a tram. A yellow tram with some kind of artwork smeared on its side, all doors open as a few people climbed aboard. The LED destination sign read MELBOURNE CITY.

"Good boy," Milly gasped. "We can make it."

David unclipped his seat belt, grabbed the machetes in one hand. Milly jumped out and opened a back door. Yiannis lifted his head, looking dazed and bloodied.

"What the hell?" he muttered, slurring. "My face hurts."

Milly shouted, "Let's go, come on, *let's go*."

David and Milly each took an arm and dragged Yiannis towards the tram while his feet stumbled and his legs kept trailing behind as if boneless. Horns sounded in a discordant symphony. The Subaru's engine revved. David glanced back. A few people had jumped into the Subaru and were trying to drive away. Flames engulfed the red car. Panting, puffing, David focused on the tram, willing the machine to wait.

"The tram's gonna take off before we get there," he gasped.

"No, it isn't," Milly said.

"Yes, it is."

"No, it fucking *isn't*."

God, Yiannis was heavy. The accordion doors began to close. Lunging, David reached out. The rubber seals compressed his wrist and then the doors sprang open. He and Milly hauled Yiannis onboard and found seats. The doors closed. The tram hummed, shimmied, and with an electric whine began to slip along the rails. They propped Yiannis between them.

"Is he okay?" David said.

"I'm not sure," Milly said.

The jumper knotted about his leg was soaked in fresh blood. One of his cheeks looked concave. David turned away, ill and faint. The tram picked up speed. Suburban houses on big blocks lined this section of Burwood Highway. He knew it well; this was the route he took daily to Deakin University. Staring at the fences, flowers, lawns, at the ordinary background to this apocalypse, David tried not to vomit. He felt dizzy. Maybe he had concussion.

Someone moved into his line of vision. A bald man wearing glasses and a sneer. "Get him off this tram," he was saying, pointing at Yiannis. "All that blood will attract the angels."

"Aw Jeez, you think they're like *sharks*?" snickered a teenage girl with a nose piercing.

"Dumb bastard," said the tattooed guy next to her, clasping her hand. "How'd ya get so old and stay so fucken dumb? Ya senile dumb-arse."

"Watch your language," said a sharp-faced woman in a supermarket uniform.

The tattooed guy stabbed his middle finger at her.

"Angels attack *everybody*," said a voice at the front of the tram. "No blood required."

The bald man said, "Get him off this tram. We don't want to attract their attention."

"Nope. He's not going anywhere," Milly said.

"Let's take a vote." The bald man looked about at the couple of dozen exhausted, frightened passengers. A baby was crying, grizzling into its mother's chest.

"Mate, you'd better pull your head in," Milly said, "because I swear to Christ, I'm just about ready to lose my *shit*."

"I want him off this tram! He's a bucket of berley!"

A pregnant woman stood up and shouted, "If you don't like it, *you* can leave!"

"All of youse chill," the teenage girl said. "He's pissing blood.

He'll die soon anyway."

The supermarket worker gasped. "Ugh, so callous. Such a *failed* generation. Shameful."

"Oh yeah? Shut your dick holster, bitch."

"Right, that's it!" grunted the bald man decisively, charging at Yiannis as if to grab him.

David leapt up and shoved. *Hard.* The bald man staggered, caught a pole to steady himself, then goggled at David's left hand, which happened to be wielding both machetes upright as if ready to strike. Funny… David didn't recall brandishing them. Stifled shrieks and exclamations sounded.

"Leave him alone," David said. "Go and sit down. Go on. Take your fucking seat."

Flushing pink, staring about for backup and finding none, the bald man obeyed.

David sat, trembling. Blood slicked the length of Yiannis's trouser leg. His shoe was wet. A red puddle had formed about his shoe.

"Can we tie the jumper a bit tighter around his thigh?" David whispered.

Milly gazed at him with a sad, gentle smile. "I don't think it'd make much difference."

A bell sounded. From overhead speakers, the tram driver shouted, "Brace! Brace!"

"What's happening?" someone wailed.

The impact threw everyone from their seats. The tram stalled, whined, struggled on amidst graunching, wrenching noises. People got up. Some ran to the front to crowd the windows. David and Milly manhandled Yiannis, a dead weight, back into his seat. The cushions were saturated with his blood. Metal continued to screech as the tram crept forward.

"Smashed cars on the line," someone yelled. "The driver's trying to push through."

A babble of hysterical voices rose.

"We're doomed—"

"If we get stuck, we'll die—"

"We won't get stuck. Do you know how heavy a tram is?"

"I can't stand this. No, I can't stand it—"

"Holy Mary, Mother of God, help us sinners—"

"Who are you praying to?"

"God's angels are the ones attacking us, you fucking idiot—"

Milly gripped David's hand. "I'll make sure we're okay, kid. I promise."

David nodded and stared into her blue eyes, reminded again of Mum, of her no-nonsense grit and cool head in a crisis. Oh shit, how could Mum be *dead*?

The metal-on-metal sounds ceased. The tram picked up speed. Passengers cheered.

"We're through the blockage," the tram driver announced.

Out the windows, David glimpsed a mangled ute, an upside-down station wagon. "After Springvale Road," he said, "the lanes on each side narrow from three to two."

Milly sighed. "I know."

"Or just one if there's parked cars. There'll be so many prangs up ahead—"

"Then we'll ride this thing as far as we can, and figure shit out when we need to."

Between them, Yiannis was slumped with his eyes closed, face as white as raw dough. David didn't want to look at him anymore—

Then David's phone beeped with an incoming text. Fumbling, relieved and joyous, he took the phone from his pocket. It was Kelly, a friend from high school. *At rod laver with gaby kyle taylor U OK?* Heart thrumming, fingers trembling, David replied, *Yep C U soon.*

"A relative?" Milly said.

"No, a mate. A bunch are at the Rod Laver Arena. Let's head there." David hesitated. "What about *your* family and friends? Did you lose your phone? Go on, use mine."

She tightened her mouth. "The only person I cared about was my son."

David didn't know what to say, so he looked out the window. The tram was approaching Springvale Road. How far would they get before they hit an insurmountable block?

As it turned out—another 17 kilometres.

At the T-intersection of Punt Road on the eastern fringe of the city. The journey had taken nearly two hours. The tram had shoved through every obstacle and the driver kept stopping to pick up more passengers. (If someone deserved an Australian of the Year Award, it was this bloke. How many lives had he saved? Seventy? Eighty?) It was summer and the air inside the tram became increasingly dank, hot, moist. Despite lively debate, nobody knew why angels hadn't attacked the tram. One theory was the overhead lines. Perhaps angels were scared of entangling themselves or getting electrocuted. Whatever the case, the passengers could finally *relax*.

The tram's insurmountable block, occurring at Punt Road, happened to be a crush of cars mashed into a jack-knifed six-axle semitrailer. The truck must have shot the red light.

"End of the line," said the driver's voice over the speakers. "This is the end of the line."

The accordion doors opened. A few people began disembarking. David looked out the windows and his guts shrivelled at the sight of circling, swooping angels.

"Wait, don't leave, stop!" he ordered Milly. "We're safer inside the tram."

"Safe from angels, yeah, but not from thirst and starvation."

"Let's just wait for the authorities to come get us—"

"What authorities?" Milly said. "When? The entire world is under siege. You think the military is going to single out *this* particular tram for rescue? What makes *us* so special?"

Outside, people began screaming. Like touchpaper, fright lit the remaining passengers. Many stampeded, scrumming each other to disembark into the grip of angels. The angels were *everywhere*. Ripping, tearing, thronging. One appeared at an open door.

"Kid, get down!" Milly shouted. "Hide under the seats!"

Too late. The angel pulled in its wings, clawed up the steps. Once inside the tram, David could see the sharp, cruel beak protruding from its central nub and smell its hot electrical stink. The screaming of passengers intensified. The angel spread its six wings, opened its beak, pecked at the nearest somebody; a man in a suit who erupted into a fountain of blood.

Mum and Dad...

As David remembered his parents lying mutilated on the lawn, a kind of red mist descended and he was already slashing and stabbing with both machetes at the hellish multitude of eyes. Feathers flew. The central nub sliced as easily as rare steak. Wings fell away, the exposed meat stringy, dry, bloodless. What was left of the angel staggered and fell back through the open doorway. David leaned over the prone man in a suit.

"Mister?" David cried. "Mister? Can you hear me?"

Intestines convulsed in a messy, steaming pile next to the man's body.

"Come on!" Milly yelled, pushing at the small of David's back. "Go! Let's go!"

He came to his senses. More angels had boarded the tram. Milly shoved David outside.

Chaos.

He blinked at the beating of countless wings, at the inhuman shrieking, the human wails, blatting of horns, boom of artillery. Gasping, he threw back his head. High in the sky... *What were those things?* Zigzagging above the clouds were round, golden, glittering shapes. At such a height, those shapes must be massive, a hundred metres in circumference, each one a ring within a ring... David remembered from Sunday School: *Ezekiel's Wheel.* So, out of all the religious texts written through history, the Old Testament had turned out to be the winner. Or would that be the Torah? Both had mentioned Ezekiel's Wheel, hadn't they?

"Kid, snap out of it!" Milly said, dragging at him. "Run!"

But to where? *Where?* David followed her, past the blocked tram, through the intersection with its muddled crush of twisted semitrailer and cars. Around them, people sprinted, fought, brawled, lay dead and dying. Ammunition fired. Angels dove, mobbed and ripped.

Nearby, an abandoned car sat on the road, all doors open.

Milly jumped in the driver's side and shouted, *"Kid!"*

As he dashed over, he impulsively grabbed at a woman carrying two children and bundled her into the back seat. He took the front passenger side, dropping the machetes in the footwell as Milly stamped the accelerator. The Rod Laver Arena was just three kilometres north along Punt Road. In the back seat the mother panted, the little girl whimpered and the boy, aged about five, gazed blankly at nothing with a slack and drooling jaw.

"It's all right," David said to them. "We're nearly at an evacuation centre."

Milly gave him a proud smile. "Well done."

David felt good. Until he realised that he had stolen a car like the sweaty, red-faced man who had stolen David's Golf. *Swings and roundabouts.* Hopefully, the sweaty, red-faced man had found safety. Next, David thought of poor Yiannis left behind on the tram, remembered his words—*This whole planet is one gigantic sinking ship*—and felt hopeless, bleak. He pressed both hands to his ears against the noise and wondered if he was about to go mad...

Milly, teeth bared, drove fast.

Too fast.

An angel dropped down in front of them. Milly accelerated and ran it over, pulverising it in a slew of broken wings, crunching the monster beneath the wheels—*bump, bump, bump*—the tyres momentarily losing traction.

"Oh shit," David said, gripping the dashboard. "Hey, don't wreck the car."

"I know what I'm doing."

They approached a line of tanks, trucks, a road block, armed soldiers. A barricade was moved aside and a soldier waved them through.

Milly drove to the northern entrance of the Rod Laver Arena via Olympic Boulevard and unerringly to the entrance reserved for disabled visitors, which made David wonder about her son. She parked right up against the doors. They got out and pulled the mother with her two children from the back seat. Young military guys—Army Reserve by the looks of the uniforms—kitted out with rifles and looking scared half to death, admitted them into the building. David expected his machetes would be confiscated, but they weren't.

David and Milly were each given a bottle of water, an aluminium bowl, roll of toilet paper, a toothbrush kit like the kind you get on aeroplanes. People were dotted around the stands. Below, cot beds filled the tennis court. From outside came the constant *boom* of artillery.

An old white-haired woman with a clipboard approached and said, "Aw, you look all done in. Feel like having a kip?" She led them down a set of stairs and onto the court, through an aisle, along a row, and pointed at two cot beds side by side. "Dinner at seven," she said, writing on her clipboard. "I'll be back soon to take your details." Then she walked away.

David looked around. "Hey, where did the mother and her kids go?"

"They're here somewhere," Milly said. "Safe. Because of you."

The place held numb, listless, hushed people. No noises apart from artillery.

Tired beyond measure, David lay on his cot bed. He had never been inside the Rod Laver Arena before. Metal strips comprised the closed, retractable roof. Milly patted his shoulder.

"We'll be okay now," she said. "Didn't I promise?"

Tears pricked David's eyes and he smiled. "Yeah."

Overcome by fatigue, terror and grief, he managed to doze off despite the constant sound of explosions. Sometime later, Milly shook his leg. Sitting up, groggy, he saw a man pushing what resembled a hotdog cart. For a moment, David thought he was still dreaming.

"Dinner," the man intoned. "Two ladles of soup. Dinner."

"Yes, please," Milly said. "You're very kind."

"Present your bowls. No spoons. Sip from the bowl. Minestrone or chicken noodle?"

"Chicken noodle, thanks," Milly said.

"Same," David said.

They held out their bowls and the man doled out the food. He pushed the cart.

"Dinner. Two ladles of soup. Dinner…"

"When will you look for your friends?" Milly said.

David glanced around the arena and felt a deep, shivering exhaustion. "I don't know."

A raucous banging started overhead. They jumped, startled.

The roof.

People began to scream. Run around. Scramble. Yet there was nowhere to go.

David and Milly dropped their bowls. The banging on the roof intensified. They gaped at the rippling metal, at the steel-girder ribs that started to buckle and cave.

The angels were breaking through.

Not the six-winged angels, no, but the huge and heavy wheel-inside-wheel type.

David gave Milly a machete and said, "I think we're fucked this time."

"Yeah, me too."

"Well...guess I'll see you on the other side."

The banging went on. The metal dented, ballooned, split. The screaming of people reached a fever pitch. David and Milly brandished their machetes. Together, they stared at the holes driven into the roof by the wheel angels, watched as the holes opened up, as the six-winged angels fought and clawed their way inside. David closed his eyes for a moment, psyching himself, getting ready to fight or die, getting ready for whatever was to come next.

And what came next happened to be the literal end of the world.

Story Publishing History

All stories are copyright Deborah Sheldon. Stories are original to this collection, unless listed below (first publishing instance).

'All the Stars in Her Eyes' *Andromeda Spaceways* 2020
'Angel Wings' *The Dark Heart: Night's End Podcast* 2021
'Barralang, Pop. 63' *Dimension6* 2020
'Carbon Copy Consumables' *Midnight Echo* 2020
'Cast Down' *Anemone Enemy* 2017
'Entombed' *AntipodeanSF* 2018
'For Weirdless Days and Weary Nights' *Breach* 2018
'Hair and Teeth' *Aurealis* 2018
'Hand to Mouth' *Short! Sharp! Shocks!* 2020
'Last Dance' *Guilty Pleasures and Other Dark Delights* 2019
'Mourning Coffee' *Trembling with Fear* 2020
'Shedding' *AntipodeanSF* 2020
'Shift' *Guilty Pleasures and Other Dark Delights* 2019
'Talisman' *Guilty Pleasures and Other Dark Delights* 2019
'The Littlest Avian' *Breach* 2019
'The Sand' *Beside the Seaside: Tales from the Daytripper* 2019
'The Sea Will Have' *AntipodeanSF* 2020
'The Stairwell' *Midnight Echo* 2021
'The Tea and Sugar Train' *Dimension6* 2019